Readers on *Spider Silk, Stone Fly,* and *Mariah's Song:*

*This quick read novel [***Spider Silk***] has such incredible details and character development...it just swallows you up.*
                                        -Pat from Massachusetts

*Just had to let you know those [***Spider Silk*** and ***Stone Fly***] were the two best books I've read in awhile.... When is the third one coming out? Can't wait.*   -Beverly from Oregon

Stone Fly *is a really, really good novel! And a fun read!*
                                        -Peter from Vermont

Just finished ***Stone Fly****. What a great action-packed read. Looking forward to the next. Can I expect BB back as Bud's deputy next time?*   -Doug from Virginia

Spider Silk *and* ***Stone Fly*** *just knocked our socks off! We really like your style and story line. Can't wait for your next offering. Hope it comes soon.*   -Jerry and Pat from Oregon

I just finished ***Spider Silk****.... Gripping story meant I had to read it this afternoon. I will spend the evening reading* ***Stone Fly****. I need more!*
                                        -Marty from Oregon

Finished ***Bloodstone****: a page turner. Thanks!*
                                        - Ralph from Oregon

Stone Fly *is outstanding, perfect. Early on many characters, like being a stranger at a party and meeting everyone, but they soon stand as individuals. There's something for everyone here—plenty of action, police procedural, suspense, romance (suggestion but no explicit sex), vivid and relevant descriptions humor—all tasteful and original. A pleasure to read.*
                                        -Gloria Wolk, author
                                        The Accidental Felon

For *Mariah's Song:*

Full of wry chuckles and lush descriptions, setting the stark Southeast Oregon winter against the lazy, warm days in the Sea of Cortez, this novel is both vacation and Mission Accomplished.
~Jennifer from Oregon

Other books by Rod Collins

FICTION

THE BUD BLAIR NOVELS

Spider Silk
Stone Fly
Bloodstone
Not Before Midnight

THE JOHN BITTER NOVELS

Bitter's Run
Abiqua

NON-FICTION

What Do I Do When I Get There?: A New Manager's Guidebook

Mariah's Song

Rod Collins

BRIGHTWORKSPRESS

MARIAH'S SONG

Bright Works Press
Redmond, OR 97478
www.brightworkspress.com

© 2013, 2018 Rodney D. Collins
All rights reserved

This is a work of fiction. Names, characters, places, and incidents are the product
of the author's imagination
and are used fictitiously. Any resemblance to actual
persons, living or dead, or events is entirely coincidental.

Epigraph on page 8 is from "They Called The Wind Mariah"
lyrics by Alan J. Lerner, music by Frederic Loewe, 1951

Book & cover design & production by Long On Books
longonbooks.com

Print ISBN: 979-8-9895768-0-7
eBook ISBN: 979-8-9895768-8-3
Library of Congress Control Number: 2010911807

Printed in the United States of America

*For John and Wanda Collins,
who spent a lifetime helping other people*

Prologue

Dog Lake, West/Southwest of Lakeview, Oregon

THREE MEN CASUALLY WATCHED ROD TIPS for signs of fish nibbles as a soft evening breeze gently rocked a fourteen-foot aluminum boat anchored next to a weed bed in Dog Lake. A small black Labrador was curled in sleep on a piece of carpet in the bow of the boat.

Gino Maretti, left arm in a cast, pointed across the lake to the A-frame cabin. "Somebody is pulling in your driveway, Bud."

Bud watched through binoculars as a woman stepped out of a new Toyota SUV and walked to the door of the cabin. "I'll be damned. It looks like Amanda Spears. I wonder what she wants."

Dell BeBe smiled. "Maybe she wants your body."

"Shut up, BB." Discussions of Bud's love life were verboten. Two weeks earlier, he said goodbye to Nancy. Bud had then helped his undersheriff, Sonny Sixkiller, who was also Nancy's brother, and Roger Hildebrand, one of Bud's Deputies, load Nancy's household goods into a U-Haul truck.

The one private conversation between Bud and his fiancée, sadly convinced him that she would never be back. Not as an emergency dispatcher. Not as his wife.

She had tears in her eyes when she said, "I can't do it, Bud. I love you, but the thought of not knowing every day if you'll come home alive...well, I don't think I can live with that. And my mother needs me." She accentuated her determination by handing him the engagement ring he bought earlier in the year.

"Well," Bud said to BB and Gino, "what do you think? Shall we go see what Amanda wants?"

"Nah," Gino said, sipping the last suds from a bottle of Heffy, "Let her swim out."

BB laughed and Bud asked, "Don't you like her, Gino?"

"Oh, hell yes. That's a foxy lady. I just don't want to talk shop with her. Hey…before I forget…for good news, Agent Warren resigned. I heard that before I decided to run down and kill some fish with my buddy, Sheriff Blair."

Bud's cell phone rang as he unbuttoned his shirt pocket. "Forgot to turn it off," he apologized. "Yeah?"

"Bud, this is Amanda. Is that you across the lake?"

"Yeah. What do you want?"

"Well, that's friendly. Look, I resigned from NCIS. I'm just taking a slow trip through the West. Thought I'd stop and say hello."

"You what? You resigned?"

He could hear a giggle in her voice. "Yep. I'm a free woman."

"I'll be damned." He put his rod away and started pulling the anchor. "Let's go in," he said.

Hugs and hand shakes taken care of, with Amanda's whispered "I'm sorry about Grandfield" in Gino's ear, they just mainly stood and stared out at the lake for several long seconds until Molly barked and tried to jump up on Amanda.

"Get down, Molly," Bud said without any heat. "Sit."

Molly sat, and Amanda knelt down to pet her. Molly held out a paw for Amanda to shake. "Nice dog, Bud," she said. "And a nice cabin. You build it?"

"Yes," and without knowing why added, "I built it to stay sane a year after my divorce."

She studied the sage green A-Frame fronting the lake. "Nice," she said again. "And did it?"

"Did it what?"

"Keep you sane," she smiled.

"I'm not sure I've ever been sane."

That brought the expected chuckles, and Bud moved Amanda up a notch on his scale of approved characteristics.

"You guys catch any fish?"

BB laughed and said, "What…with bare hooks? Bud doesn't use bait. He just uses beer."

"Well, in that case, I brought some steaks. I see a barbecue in your future."

BB caught Bud's eye and nodded at Amanda. "She brought steaks?" he mouthed with raised eyebrows.

Bud gave him a surreptitious single digit salute and shook his head in disgust. Two weeks dumped, and already BB was trying to fix him up.

While Gino fired up the barbecue with his one good hand, and while Amanda worked on a salad, BB and Bud opened a big Cabela's carton hiding in Bud's garage. Bud stripped the plastic wrap and tried to lift a big steel fire pit free of the box, grunting from the effort.

"Here, let me help," BB offered.

They wrestled the fire pit to the gravel between the garage and the cabin. "That's pretty nice," BB said, admiring the cutout silhouettes of deer, fish and elk running around the circle of polished steel. "Your arm still sore, Bud?"

"Yeah. I can use it, but it seems like I'm always bumping it."

"Gun shot wounds are slow to heal."

Bud just grumped and said, "Let's get a fire going."

Evening shadows turned the lake a shiny slate color, and the high desert temperature dropped steadily, hinting that winter was lurking around the corner, waiting to bite them with cold days and wind-blown snow. Stomachs full to aching, they sat around Bud's new fire pit and stared into the embers of the dying fire.

Bud said, "Good steaks, Gino. Maybe you can start a career as a chef."

"And what about the salad?" Amanda demanded, a grin tugging at the corner of her mouth.

BB raised his whiskey glass. "Here's to the salad."

"Here, here," Gino said.

"A toast," Bud offered. "To dear friends, old and new."

They sat beside the fire until the whiskey and wine were gone and the night's chill had seeped into their bones. It had been a nice quiet party, fellow police officers swapping stories, catching up, and decompressing.

Amanda entertained with descriptions of former Congressman Kevin Ross, aka "Bloodstone," bolting from his office and leaping off his balcony into the sea. "Only thing is, he forgot the tide was out. He wound up taking a three-story jump into about three feet of water. Broke both legs. We had to haul him out before he drowned. Special Agent Dudley thought we should just wait for high tide. We think Bloodstone was trying to get to a big Zodiac pulled up on the shore. So now he's busy ratting out his criminal buddies and trying to beat a murder rap."

"Isn't he the one who was feeding cocaine to his young female aides?" BB asked?

"One and the same," she said.

"And," Bud said, "you shot Ortega."

"That," she said emphatically, "put a definite speed bump in my career path. I know in my mind it was a good shoot. He lunged at me, so I shot him. But in my heart I wonder if I didn't want to kill the son-of-a-bitch and just waited for an excuse."

And then she found herself talking about losing her enthusiasm for chasing terrorist and drug dealers, "One and same these days," she ended gloomily.

"What about you, Gino? What are you going to do?" she asked changing the subject.

"I'm going to run," Gino said. "There's this nice lady in Bremerton, a nice rich widow lady who wants to partner with me. She wants to start a detective agency."

"And what's wrong with that," Amanda challenged.

Bud and BB nearly rolled out of their chairs in laughter.

"Nothing, but she keeps telling me she loves me…keeps hinting we should get married. Hell, I tried that twice, and I don't want to try it again. At least, not with her."

"Ruby Goldstein, right? The one you saved?"

"Yep. I'm almost sorry I did."

There were appreciative chuckles and BB said, "I know what you mean. I've been married once and divorced twice. And that's once too many."

"Divorced twice?" Amanda asked.

"Yeah. First you divorce the husband from his wife. That's once. Then you divorce him from his house and half his retirement. That's twice."

"Men," she said disgustedly.

"No, young miss, it's just reality. You know what I'm going to do about it? Nothing. I'm just going to retire and move to Lake County. It's dangerous down here, and the city has gotten dull. Need something to spice up my life."

"You're not serious?" Bud asked.

"Serious as sin. Do you know, my old friend, I turn fifty in two months. I'm gonna hang it up. That's why I bought a piece of ground next door to you."

"In town?"

"No. Right there," BB pointed to some trees just beyond Bud's cabin.

"I'll be damned." The thought of BB not doing cop work just didn't compute, but he'd known BB long enough to hear the finality of his words. And having him as a neighbor was appealing.

Gino shook his head. He lifted his left arm out to his side. "I'm being forced out. Well...that's not exactly accurate. I've been given a choice...a desk or disability retirement. I'm no good as a desk jockey, so I guess I'll just retire. Maybe I'll move to Lakeview along with you," he said to BB.

Bud groaned. "I don't think I could take it." But privately he was glad BB and Gino had decided to like each other.

It got quiet, and then Amanda asked, "What about you, Bud? What are you going to do?"

His sipped his drink, only his second, and a weak one at that. He looked up at the sky, spotted Orion coming up in the east, and looked back into the embers. He said, "I really don't know. I've had a half dozen job offers from NCIS on through the alphabet, good paying jobs. But when I'm reinstated as sheriff, I'll probably stay right here in sleepy little old Lake County."

"Honky, *if* they offer you your job back, you take it," BB growled. "Now where are we going to sleep?"

Amanda chose to roll out her sleeping bag on a pad in the back of her Toyota 4-Runner. BB pulled a big piece of foam and a sleeping bag from the back of his Red Corvette. He announced his intention of sleeping on Bud's small dock. "I sleep best on the water," he explained.

With a wave of his hand he intoned, "Sufficient unto the day," and walked down to the lake, Molly padding quietly behind him.

Gino chose the recliner and Bud, stifling minor guilt pains yawned his way to the loft and was asleep before his head hit the pillow.

A man watched until the four law-enforcement officers went to bed. He keyed his cell phone and hit 'send.' A sleepy voice said, "Yes?"

"I found her, *Jefe.*"

DAY ONE

*...But when you're lost and all alone
There ain't no word but lonely...*

Day One

Midnight ~ Klamath Falls

THIRTEEN-YEAR-OLD MARIAH DODGED THROUGH an obstacle course of old tires, soggy beer cartons, a crib mattress chewed into rags by the black and brown Rottweiler chained to the front porch, an old lawn chair without a seat, and a rusty pink bicycle dying on a cracked concrete walk. All were left to the mercies of the seasons, including the dog. It was midnight. There was no bulb in the porch light.

Mariah fumbled her key into the door lock, twisted the key and pushed into a cluttered living room. She wrinkled her nose at the odor of stale cigarette smoke. The only light came from the flicker and glare of a muted TV.

She walked to the couch, sighed, shook her head, and then pulled a worn fleece blanket over the sleeping figure of her mother. "Babs," she whispered, "you gonna get high once too often."

She listened to the silence, trying to decide if Manfred was in the house. She shook her head and snorted. *Probably gone out for some meth.*

She tapped a cigarette from her mom's pack, and walked through the sour smelling kitchen and out to the back porch. Not really a porch…just a small square of concrete and two steps down to the snowy slush of the back yard. She thumbed a butane lighter, lit the cigarette, and took a deep drag. A muted argument floated through the quiet of the sleeping neighborhood.

She slipped as softly as she could between Manfred's Mazda and the closed, bumper-dented overhead door of the detached, paint peeling one-car garage. Before she could see the enclosed parking area on the far side of the garage, she heard the solid whack of wood hitting something hard. Through the slats in the tall, weathered gate that closed the short parking area beside the garage, she watched in horrified fascination as her mother's live-in boyfriend Manfred, Manny to his clients, swung a four foot piece of two-by-four again and again on the unprotected head of a prone, inert man.

The dim glow of a street light wasn't enough for her to identify the man he was beating, but she could clearly see the blood on the two-by-four. When Manfred raised the club to hit the man again, she involuntarily cried out, "Stop!"

Manfred spun around, startled by her cry. "You little bitch!" he growled. "You mind your own business and get back in the house. I'll tend to you later."

She drew back in horror and panic. "Tend to me later? Kill me you mean!" She threw the cigarette away and ran down the slippery, snow covered driveway. Her tennis shoes slid sideways on the slushy surface of the street.

Arms flailing, she caught her balance, and then turned and ran as hard as she could toward the lights of the main street, just running without thought, urged by panic and the certainty that Manfred would kill her without a hint of remorse.

She started sweating and shivering as she splashed up the street. Her hooded sweatshirt wasn't enough to shield her from the cold wind that whipped across Klamath Lake and hammered the city with its winter song.

The light from a mini-mart gas station perched on a corner of the major east-west-street of town offered tenuous sanctuary. She pushed through the front door and skidded to a stop. Standing at the counter with his back to the door was a scraggly looking man she recognized as one of Manfred's dealers.

"Oh Lord," she silently prayed as tears started down her cheeks, "what am I going to do?"

She ducked behind a rack loaded with candy and snacks and headed for the restroom in the back right-hand corner of the store. She didn't take a breath until the pneumatic arm pushed the door shut and the bolt slid into the metal door jamb.

She stood trembling in front of the sink and stared at the frightened, tear-stained face peering back at her from the mirror. Finally, she twisted the faucet and splashed cold water on her face with shaky hand.

Five minutes passed before a knock on the door startled her. A woman's voice said, "Are you okay?"

"Who are you?" Mariah asked.

The lady answered, "I just need to use the restroom. You've been in there quite a while. Are you okay?"

Mariah took a deep breath to steady herself and said, "I'm okay. I'll be right out."

She glanced in the mirror, ran her fingers through her long, uncombed light brown hair, used a paper towel to wipe away the stain of mascara at the corner of her blue eyes, pulled the hood of her sweatshirt over her head, and let it fall almost completely over her face.

She twisted the lock and pushed the door open, brushing by an older, gray-haired woman who reached to catch the door before it closed again.

Mariah looked to make sure Manfred's dealer was gone before approaching the counter.

"So you have something I could write on?" she asked. The clerk, a hardboiled, brassy woman who might have been pretty except for a missing lower front tooth and uncombed dull brown hair, plucked a pen from a plastic cup and pushed a notepad across the counter. The clerk, whose name tag said Dora, worked the 6:00 p.m. to 3:00 a.m. shift and had seen a lot of oddballs, especially after midnight.

"You're out kinda late, honey. Do your parents know where you are?"

Mariah didn't look up as she wrote her home address on the pad. She pushed the pad back across the counter and said, "I saw someone killed tonight...at that address. You should call 911." And then she fled out the door and ran around the end of the store. She squeezed behind a battered dumpster, a cold, shadowy hiding place for her small, sad, quivering self.

The grey-haired lady who had wanted the restroom pushed through the front door of the mini-mart and walked quickly to a dark green Ford Ranger pickup parked alongside the store. The pickup drove around the store, briefly lighting Mariah's hiding place, but the driver was looking down the side street for oncoming traffic. The small dark figure behind the dumpster didn't register on her mind.

A pickup-camper combination pulled off the street and into the gas pumps. Mariah edged forward and peeked around the corner as Dora slowly walked to the driver's door and said, "Fill up? Regular? Cash or credit card?"

Mariah couldn't hear the driver's answer, but she saw an older man slide from behind the wheel and walk around the front of the pickup and head for the store. Dora started the pump and followed him through the pool of florescent light from the pump-island canopy.

The distant sound of a siren galvanized Mariah. Taking a deep breath, she darted though the florescent glare and into the shadow of the pickup. Flattened against the rear of the camper, she tried the camper door. A moan of relief escaped her throat when the door knob turned. Without hesitation, she climbed inside, closed the door as quietly as she could, and then peeked through the side curtains to make sure she hadn't been seen.

The man was still at the counter, gesturing and talking to Dora who nodded and picked up a cell phone. Mariah watched with grim satisfaction when the clerk held Mariah's note to the light and spoke into the phone.

"I hope they get you, Manny," she whispered. "Then you won't beat on me or Babs ever again."

As the wailing of the police siren faded, Mariah plopped down at the breakfast nook and tried to get her pounding heart and her breathing under control.

In a few minutes she heard Dora hang up the pump handle and say "thank you" to the old man. Mariah felt the pickup rock a bit as the old man settled in the driver's seat. The door slammed and the engine started. Mariah braced against the table as the driver eased the pickup out of the parking lot and onto the main street.

Now what? she thought. She fingered the little velvet pouch she wore on a tarnished silver chain around her neck. The lump of cash in the pouch gave her a small sliver of comfort.

She thought once about calling her friend Lacey on the slim cell phone in her rear pants pocket, rejected that as too late at night, and she didn't want to get Lacey in trouble. She settled for a text message instead: No matter what you hear I'm okay. More later. Then she shut the phone down to save battery power.

She felt a touch of guilt at leaving Babs alone, but consoled herself with the hope the police would protect her mom.

12:10 a.m. ~ Klamath Falls

MANNY WAS SURPRISED AT HOW MUCH the body weighed. *Dead weight*, he thought, and giggled a little through his drug induced fog. He propped open the gate, grabbed the inert man under his arm pits and dragged him to the car. Afraid he might be seen loading the body of his now ex-partner in the trunk of the Mazda, he was breathing hard and cussing the dead man under his breath. He struggled with the body, bending and folding Tyson James enough to tuck arms and legs inside the rear trunk area. He grabbed a car blanket from behind the passenger seat and covered the body. And then with trembling hands, he slammed the hatch.

"Now to find that little bitch," he muttered.

He backed the car out of the drive and pointed the car up the street in the direction Mariah had run. He drove slowly, hoping to spot her before she found a place to hide and sicced the police on him. By the time he reached the main street, he knew it was a futile search. *Too dark and too many hiding places*, he thought.

He sped up and headed for the main drag. The white glare of a street light lit the bloody hand gripping the steering wheel. *I've got to get cleaned up*, he thought. As he pulled up to the stop sign by the mini-mart, a groan from the rear of the Mazda startled him. "Damn, it Tyson," he shouted, "why ain't you dead?"

State Highway 97 led a nervous Manny north up the east side of Klamath Lake, toward Chiloquin, eyes glancing constantly in the rearview mirror, afraid he would see flashing lights racing up the highway. He broke into a nervous sweat when he spotted a State Police cruiser parked just north of Pelican Point. He was prepared to run, and in fact had instinctively begun to accelerate, but the big police sedan hadn't moved by the time Manny rounded the corner and was out of sight. His breathing slowed and his heart pumped a little easier when he turned right off of the highway and onto the road the led into the little town of Chiloquin.

Ten minutes later he was headed east on the highway that ran up the north side of the Sprague River. He gave a great sigh of relief when he spotted the sentinel mail box that marked the steep gravel drive to the small two acre bench that was home to a double-wide modular. He turned left and drove up the narrow, gravel track, tires spinning in the snow. He fought his panic, eased off the throttle until the tires caught traction and pulled on up the hill.

Lights were on in the double wide trailer, smoke rising lazily from the chimney. A bright moon peeked through a break in the clouds. Two snow-covered vehicles were parked in the yard. Manny recognized the late model Jeep Grand Cherokee driven by Gordon Tusk, a Native American of uncertain origins. Tusk claimed to be a Klamath Indian when it suited him, or a Modoc when that worked better.

A dog, pillowed on the porch, barked when he pulled up, but it was the half-hearted effort of a guard who only paid lip service to the task.

Manny stepped out of the Mazda and said, "Curly, you ain't much of a watch dog."

Manny's composure was crushed by the rush of a snarling beast that came charging out from under the double wide. He just had time to jump back into the Mazda and slam the door before the big animal was snarling at his window, paws smearing saliva on the glass, and claws digging and cutting through the paint below the window.

The living room curtain parted and a grinning Gordon Tusk looked out. Manny gave him a single single-digit salute, a totally wasted gesture, unseen in the dark vehicle.

The door opened, and the "Tusker," as he was called, yelled at the dog, calling him off. "Come on in, Manny. He won't eat you until I tell him to."

Manny eased warily out of the door. He wasn't afraid of much, but that big brute of a dog scared the crap out of him. He walked to the steps leading to the covered deck on the double wide. Stopped and said, "What the hell is that?"

Tusker laughed and said, "A damned big dog. Old Curly got too fat and lazy to be a good watch dog. My brother over in Blackfoot, Idaho, got him for me. Half wolf, half German Shepherd, and half mean."

Manny frowned and said, "I thought you were Klamath."

"Am. Brother's a Blackfoot." And then he turned serious, his black eyes turning hard, flat, menacing. "I thought I told you never to come here again."

A groan from the back of the Mazda stopped them both. The big wolf-dog growled, the hackles on the back of his neck standing up. Gordon Tusk reached down and petted the big dog. "Easy," he said. "Okay, Manny, what the hell's going on?"

12:17 a.m. ~ Klamath Falls

A UNIFORMED POLICEMAN SLID HIS VEHICLE to a stop in front of Mariah's small house. The officer turned on his spotlight, keeping the front yard awash with a million candlepower of white light that muted the red-blue-white pulse of his emergency lights.

The Rottweiler chained to a post by the front door began barking and growling, straining against the chain wrapped around a porch column. Lights in neighboring houses popped on one by one.

A white Chevy Tahoe, driven by a Klamath City Police sergeant pulled in and blocked the driveway just as an unmarked black Crown Victoria pulled in behind him. The distant wail of a siren announced to the world, "The cavalry is coming."

Detective Mathew Harmon tugged a baseball cap with a KFPD logo over his short cropped brown hair. He slipped out of the seat, adjusted the pistol on his hip and pushed the car door shut. His slipped and slid through wet, slushy ruts to Sergeant Booker's Tahoe. Booker, a beefy black policeman whose mustache was turning grey, powered the window down. He nodded his head and said in a half-mocking tone, "Young Detective Harmon, our rising star. What are you doing here?"

Harmon didn't smile, just shrugged and said, "I was in the neighborhood on other business. I heard the call on my radio. You're out kinda late yourself." When that didn't get any response from Booker, he asked, "What do we have?"

"A 911 call from a woman named Dora Winslow." He pointed north. "Works at the mini-mart on the main drag. Said a girl, a very young girl told her, Dora, a murder had been committed at this address. No. That's not quite right. The girl told Dora Winslow that she, the girl, had *witnessed* a murder at this address."

"Where's the girl?"

"Gone. Dora told 911 the girl bolted and ran out of the store."

"Great," Harmon growled. "Well, what are we waiting for?"

Booker pointed up the street to a patrol car, lights lit up, heading in their direction. "Your vest, and our back-up."

Booker slid out of the Tahoe, pointed at the Rottweiler and said, "And animal control." He sloshed his way to the car lighting up Mariah's front door. The officer powered the driver's side window down, and nodded understanding when Booker said, "Stay here, keep the place lit up, and stay on the radio. As soon as animal control gets the dog out of the way, Harmon and I are gonna go calling."

Harmon popped the trunk, slipped a Kevlar vest over his windbreaker, snapped the buckles, slammed the trunk and walked around his vehicle to the passenger door. He fumbled in the glove box and signaled Booker he was ready. He held up a Taser and pointed at the snarling dog. "I hate to do this, but time's a' wasting. And I don't want to kill the dog. He's just doing his job."

A black and white Crown Vic with two uniformed policemen splashed to a stop in front of Booker's Tahoe. The two patrolmen listened to Booker and then moved around the house and watched the back door, flashlights on, guns drawn, while Booker and Harmon took the front. Harmon talked to the emaciated, snarling beast, trying to get the dog calmed down, until Booker said, "Just do it, Mathew."

The sting of the Taser choked the barking off. The dog twitched and whimpered and then was still. The sudden silence was almost as intense as the dog's barking. Booker stepped over the still form of the dog and banged the butt of the heavy 3-cell flashlight on the front door. "Police! Open up!"

The only movement in the house was the glare and flicker of the TV against the living room window curtains. Booker slapped the door repeatedly with a big hand, the sound like gunshots in the night. "Police! Open up!" When there was no answer, he shrugged, looked at Mathew's six-foot-one-inch frame and pointed at the door. "Your turn, Mr. Harmon."

Harmon's kick ruptured the door frame, scattering splinters of wood into the small living room. He crouched and went left through the door, shouting, "Police! Hands in the air!" Booker followed and went right, flashlight sweeping the room. "Couch!" he shouted. "Someone's on the couch!"

Harmon used his flashlight to sweep the kitchen and hallway as he sidestepped to the couch, gun at the ready. He pulled the worn fleece blanket back and shined his light in a woman's face. She moaned and turned away, but didn't awaken.

"She's out of it," Harmon said.

Booker found a light switch and turned it on. "Okay. Let's clear the house."

12:35 a.m. ~ Mariah's house, Klamath Falls

AN AMBULANCE WITH MARIAH'S MOTHER ON board pulled through a small crowd of gawking neighbors. Lights flashing, the ambulance headed for the Emergency Room at Sky Lakes Medical Center.

Harmon was joined by senior detective Walt Jones, a wiry fifty-year-old with a salt-and-pepper crew cut, who also happened to be Harmon's boss. Jones directed the search of the house and yard. A small back bedroom confirmed that a young girl lived there. Surprisingly, the bedroom was clean and tidy, unlike the rest of the house. A gilt-framed picture of a toddler and a smiling young woman sat on the small dresser in a corner. Harmon couldn't be sure, but he thought it was probably of the girl and her mother.

In a box in the tiny closet Detective Harmon found a scrapbook with school pictures. A three-by-five photo with the sprawled signature in the lower right corner, "Your Friend, Lacey, to My Best Friend, Mariah," gave Harmon a clue to the name of the girl who occupied the room. He pulled it loose and slid it into an inside jacket pocket.

Harmon worked page by page through the scrap book until he found one captioned "Mariah, Age 12." He carefully pulled it loose, gently lifting until the glue gave up the struggle, and then slipped the picture into his inside jacket pocket, companion to Lacey's photo.

He turned and followed a short hallway into the kitchen. The kitchen table held stacks of currency, sorted by Detective Jones and

Sergeant Booker into denominations of fives, tens and twenties. A small caliber pistol, two clips, and several small plastic bags of what Harmon thought could be crystal meth were spread on the kitchen counter.

Jones was searching a small, black handbag. He found a woman's wallet and removed a driver's license, expired, with a photo of the woman they had just shipped to the hospital. "Barbara Caldwell," he said to Mathew, "age 31, brown hair, blue eyes, and" he studied the address, "formerly a resident of the city of Dunsmuir, California."

Booker was busy taking digital photographs of the drugs, the money and the pistol when a uniformed officer yelled down the hallway. "You guys better come outside and look at this."

Bloody snow in the enclosed area beside the garage, and a bloody four-foot two-by-four led Detective Jones to ask his dispatcher to call the State Police Forensics Lab. Dozens of photos were taken of footprints, tire tracks in the driveway, (too indistinct, in Harmon's opinion, to be of value) and drag marks streaked with blood.

Jones, Booker and Harmon huddled in the side yard. "There isn't a body, but somebody left a lot of blood here."

"I'll check with the hospital," Harmon said, and pulled his cell phone from a jacket pocket.

Jones nodded. "We should, but I wouldn't hold much hope you'll find our victim there." He ran the beam of his flashlight randomly over the bloody snow. "I think our witness told us the truth. Someone was beaten here. Brutally."

Harmon dialed Dispatch. A female voice answered, "Klamath Falls Police Department. Is this Detective Harmon?"

Harmon grinned and said, "Well, Brenda, at least it's his phone. How come you're working the late shift?"

He heard her sniff, ignore the question and say, "How may I help you, Mr. Harmon?"

"Please check the hospital ER and see if anyone suffering from a beating has been admitted in the last few hours, and then get back with me. And I nearly forgot, tell the hospital the woman we shipped them is a Barbara Caldwell, but we don't want that information released just yet."

"I can do that."

"Thanks." He shook his head at her cool tone and grumbled quietly to himself, "She's still pissed off. Well, I've been told never to date co-workers. Now I know why."

They had dated casually, at least casually in Mathew's view, for about six months, but when it became clear she expected a more permanent arrangement, soon, an arrangement that included an engagement ring and plans for a substantial future, he stopped asking her out. She was fun, and he liked her. But that was as far as it went.

His reverie was interrupted by an on-looker. "Excuse me, officers," said a young woman as she approached the three policemen.

Booker turned and said, "This is a crime scene, Ma'am."

"I just wanted to know if Mariah is all right."

Jones waved her over and asked, "Who are you, Ma'am?"

"I'm Rowena Norris." She pointed across the street. "I live in the brown house."

"And who is Mariah?" Booker asked.

"She lives there," the woman said, pointing at the house, "Mariah Caldwell. She's thirteen. Once in while she watches my brats for me while I run to the store."

Detective Harmon pulled Mariah's photo from his jacket pocket, turned it to catch some light and held it up to the woman. "This girl?"

"Yes. That's Mariah. Where is she?"

"How old is Mariah?" Harmon asked.

"She's thirteen," Mrs. Norris said.

He pulled the Lacey photo out and showed it to the woman. "And this girl? Have you ever seen her?"

The lady shook her head. "No, I don't think so. Where's Mariah?"

Harmon handed her his business card and said, "If she shows up, keep her inside and call me." And then he took pity on her and said, "Look, Mrs. Norris, I think she's a runaway. So we need to find her and to protect her, to keep her safe."

"May I ask how Barbara is?" Mrs. Norris asked.

Detective Jones said, "And Barbara is the mother?"

"Yes." Rowena hesitated and then said, "Oh, what the hell. She's a damned druggie. That little girl takes care of her when it should be the other way around. Was that Barbara in the ambulance?"

None of the policemen answered. Harmon asked, "Does anyone else live here?"

Rowena Norris looked disgusted. "Yeah. Barbara's live-in boy friend. A worthless piece of crap. He's a druggie, too…and mean to boot."

"What does he look like?" Jones asked.

Fifteen minutes later, the dispatcher had a BOLO issued for one Manfred Giles as a person of interest.

Manfred Giles: Caucasian, approximately 6 feet tall, age mid-thirties, weight approximately 150 lbs, acne scars, long brown hair, diamond stud in right ear, tongue stud, and an eagle tattoo on his right forearm. Photo to follow.

May be driving a 2006 Mazda RX 7, dark blue, Oregon vanity plate MANONE, dented left rear fender. May be armed and should be considered extremely dangerous. Wanted for possession of illegal drugs and for questioning in connection with a possible homicide.

A female officer from Animal Control helped her partner roll the barely conscious Rottweiler onto a litter and carry it to a dog cage in the back of their city pickup. She walked over to the three officers, glared at Mathew and said, "A Taser is for people, you dumb ass. You could have killed the dog."

Mathew was too startled by her aggression to react, but Booker read her name tag, chuckled, and said, "Officer Jensen, the situation called for quick action. We couldn't wait for you to get the dog out of the way."

Mathew watched her stomp over to her pickup, and then shook his head. Booker tapped him lightly on his right shoulder and said, "I believe that nice officer likes you, Mathew."

"Yeah, right," Mathew answered.

A uniformed officer was assigned to protect the scene until the State Police Forensics team arrived, and the neighborhood quieted down as strobe lights went out and police vehicles departed the scene.

Mathew's phone rang and Jones waited until Mathew said, "Thank you, Brenda." He looked at his boss and shook his head. "Negative on any beating victims at Sky Lakes Hospital."

"Why am I not surprised," Jones growled.

"I'd like to talk to the woman at the mini-mart," Harmon said.

12:50 a.m. ~ Klamath Falls

DORA GAVE THEM A DESCRIPTION OF a small, thin girl, maybe five feet tall…or not quite…wearing a dark blue hooded sweat shirt, and blue jeans. "The kind with the embroidery down the seams," Dora explained. "And white tennis shoes."

Dora looked at the two photos Harmon laid on the counter and identified Mariah as the girl who had written the note. He took down Dora's phone number and address, bagged the note, and gave her his card. "I'd like to take a statement from you in the morning. All right?"

"Sure. So there really was a murder, huh?"

Harmon looked at Jones who shrugged. Harmon sighed, and said, "We don't know, but it's a strong possibility. If Mariah shows up here again, please hang on to her. I believe she really did witness a crime, and she could be in danger." He fished his business card from his wallet and laid it on the counter.

"Now," he said, "which way did she turn when she ran out the door?"

"Left."

Jones said, "Let's look."

They found narrow tracks of about a girl's size five or six shoe in the snow alongside the building, and they found marks where she had hidden behind the dumpster. "You know, Mathew, it looks like she hid here for a while and then walked back alongside the store." Jones pointed to a partial print. "Do you suppose she caught a ride?"

"For her sake, I hope not." Mathew paused a few seconds and then said, "I wonder if the security camera caught anything."

When they told Dora what they wanted, she led them to a small office in the back, sorted through a key ring until she found the right key and unlocked the door. She pointed to a monitor linked to the security camera system. Harmon backed up the CD and the two detectives watched the screen until a small girl in a hooded sweatshirt pushed through the door, stopped for a second and then ducked behind a candy rack. Jones said, "Why did she freeze up?"

Mathew said, "It looks like she was afraid of the guy at the counter. We should have the Major Crime Team look at this, see if they can identify him."

They watched as the monitor showed a pickup camper combination pulling into the pumps. It was after the older man who drove the pickup followed Dora back to the store that it got interesting.

"Whoa! Look at that." The camera guarding the pump island picked up the figure of Mariah getting in the back of the camper. Her one quick glance around the corner of the pickup gave them a clear view of her face.

"Yep. That's her." Harmon said.

"I can't make out the license number," Jones said. "We need this at the lab."

Harmon hit the reject button and pulled the CD from the system. "Let's see if the older guy used a credit card."

"We should get so lucky."

Harmon and Jones walked back up front to the cashiers counter. Jones asked, "Do you remember gassing up a pickup-camper combination shortly after the girl ran out of the store?"

Dora nodded and said, "Yes."

Jones nodded and asked, "Did the man with the camper use a credit card?"

Dora shook her head. "No. He always pays cash. But I know he's from Lakeview. He stops in here about twice a month and gasses up."

"Got a name?" Harmon asked.

She shook her head again. "Unless a customer uses a credit card, I hardly ever get a name."

"Well, that's something, I guess." Harmon handed Dora his card. "If he stops in again, get his name and the vehicle license number. Okay?"

Mathew followed Jones's vehicle to the Always Inn, a twenty-four-hour café. Without a word of greeting, a sleepy looking waitress brought them two cups of coffee. She was too tired to pay any attention to Mathew's smile of thanks. She just went back to the counter to continue the chore of folding single napkins around spoon, knife and fork, a "set up" in the vernacular of the restaurant business.

Jones took a sip of the black acid that passed for coffee at the Always Inn, grimaced and put the cup down. He shot a glance at Detective Harmon and asked, "You want this one, Mathew?"

Brown eyes flat and hard, Harmon nodded. "Yes," he said.

"Why?"

Mathew framed his thoughts for a few seconds and then said, "I hate murder, but there are times when you can at least make some sense of the motivation. On the other hand, child abuse is pure, distilled evil. There is no motivation other than evil. And I am enraged when a scared thirteen year old is forced to run in order to stay alive. I need to find that child before this Manfred piece-of-crap does. It's almost certain he'll kill her if he finds her first."

He paused, frowned and rubbed his right thumb over an old scar on his left palm. Jones recognized the unconscious motion. Whenever Mathew Harmon was thinking intently about unpleasant subjects, he rubbed the old scar.

"I'll find her first. Bet on it," Mathew stated flatly.

"Where are you going to start?"

"In about ten minutes I'm going to call the Lakeview City police, then the Lake Country Sheriff's Department and then the State Police."

Harmon pulled the two snapshots from his shirt pocket and reversed them on the table so Jones could see the faces of two young girls. He tapped Lacey's picture and said, "This is Mariah's best friend. I'm betting Mariah will contact Lacey, so what I need to do is find Lacey and convince her to put Mariah in touch with me."

Jones nodded and said, "Do you think this Lacey girl is in any danger from Manfred Giles?"

"I don't know. He might go after Lacey to get to Mariah. But I'll have a better read when I find Lacey."

Jones sipped his coffee and suddenly grinned. "I know the superintendent of schools personally. Beat me out of forty-five dollars playing golf last summer, five dollars a hole for nine straight holes. He's a rotten sandbagger. Let's go rattle his door knob and get him out of bed. He can help us find Lacey before our perp does."

"And you know where the superintendent lives."

"Right. Actually, he's my next door neighbor. His wife Ann and my Linda are best friends."

"And he'll know," Mathew said, "where the kids on Mariah's street go to school." Harmon arched his right eyebrow and asked Jones, "Will he be pissed if we wake him this time of morning?"

"I sure hope so," Jones said and smiled. "I owe him one."

Mathew threw a five dollar bill on the table and said, "Your funeral. Let's roll."

The tired waitress at the Always Inn cleared the table, pocketed the five dollars, and forgot to ring up a charge for the coffee.

12:30 a.m. ~ Dog Lake

IT WASN'T THE FOG GHOSTING ACROSS Dog Lake or the cold seeping through his heavy sleeping bag that brought BB awake. The sudden leap by the little black lab from the foot of his bag, the scrabble of her claws on the frosty planking of Bud's small boat dock, and her angry warning growls did the job.

Pistol in hand, BB wormed quickly out of the big sleeping bag and barefooted up the thin path to Bud's cabin. His heart picked up the pace and his breath sent steaming spirals into the night air.

Molly, a small black Labrador, barked just as BB cleared the willows. Beyond Amanda's 4-Runner, a dark silhouette faded into the night. Molly tore after the intruder, doing her best to imitate a snarling wolf. Her streaking run triggered the motion sensor, and the yard blossomed with light. Over Molly's snarling growl, BB could hear running feet scatter gravel and a man swear softly in Spanish.

A pistol shot ricocheted off the gravel drive, spraying Molly with rock shards. She yelped, and tail tucked between her legs, gave up the chase. BB tried to find the target over the front sight of his pistol, and then slowly lowered his arm without pulling the trigger.

"Damn," he muttered.

The front door of the cabin opened and Bud and Gino stepped out, keeping in the shadows of the small porch that sheltered the doorway. "What's going on?" Bud asked in a loud whisper.

"Intruder," BB answered. "Took a shot at Molly." *Or at me*, he thought.

With a sense of urgency, Gino said, "I smell diesel."

The back hatch of the 4-Runner, Amanda's sleeping place, started to lift and Bud shouted, "NO! Don't open it, Amanda! Something's wrong here."

"What?" she yelled.

"Don't open the hatch!" Gino and Bud shouted almost in unison.

A bullet slammed into the roof of the 4-Runner, followed by the echo of a pistol shot. BB fired his H&K .40 in the general direction of the muzzle flash, pulling the trigger until the slide locked open. "I'm out," he yelled.

Bud motioned Gino around the back, and then dashed to shelter behind a pine tree beyond the cabin. He saw another muzzle flash before he heard the report of the attacker's pistol. He braced his pistol over a limb, held his breath and squeezed three quick shots to the right of the flash, and then quickly moved his sight pattern and squeezed three more shots to the left in a searching pattern. He was rewarded by a yell and the sound of running feet. Gino opened up from the far side of the cabin, four carefully spaced shots.

The racket of a car door slamming and of an engine starting up reached through the scattered pine, and then the killer's vehicle was racing down the road in the direction of Drews Valley. Gino fired again, aiming at the engine block. The sound of pistol slugs punching sheet metal told him his shots were hitting the vehicle, but the engine rpm continued to climb, and then the vehicle was beyond the low dam a long-ago rancher built to raise the level of Dog Lake.

"Did you get him?" Bud shouted.

"No, I don't think so," Gino shouted back. "I hit the vehicle, but I don't think I tagged the driver."

BB was shaking from the adrenalin rush. "Damn, too much fun."

Gino walked back around the cabin and shouted, "Amanda, you stay in your vehicle until we can take a look! I smell diesel, and ain't none of us driving one."

"You thinking bomb?" Bud asked Gino. "I smell it, too." Molly nudged his hand and he absentmindedly stroked her head. "Okay," he said, leading Molly to the cabin door. "Get in there, old girl. It could get rough out here."

BB was suddenly aware of the cold and realized for the first time he was standing in his pajama bottoms and a t-shirt, barefoot, holding an empty pistol. But he too could smell diesel. "We need a flashlight."

Bud sprinted back to the cabin and returned almost immediately with a big 4-cell flashlight. He dropped to his knees, leaned until he could see under Amanda's 4X4 and swept the light back and forth. A dark lump on the ground under the gas tank froze the light. He let out a slow breath and said, "Found it." He scrambled around to the rear of the vehicle and spotted a thin insulated wire running from a 6-volt lantern battery to a suction cup on the rear hatch of the vehicle and back to a detonator pushed into a fertilizer bag. "Bare loop switch," he muttered.

Gino and BB watched him rise, walk around the vehicle and then tapped on the window. "Amanda, climb over the seat and get out on the passenger side, gently. And don't slam the door."

Gino frowned and asked, "What have you got, Bud?"

Bud said, "A lump of something in a heavy plastic bag, and a battery with a bare loop switch."

They watched Amanda slide over the front seat. Bud almost smiled at the sight of her blue Snoopy-patterned pajamas. Pistol in hand, she gently opened the passenger side door and stepped barefoot to the ground. "What's going on?"

"Intruder," BB said. "And a bomb. Maybe. Probably." He took a deep breath and said, "I think you were supposed to open the back hatch and set it off."

She swore softly and felt a sudden fear that left her trembling and slightly sick to her stomach. "Who?" she said, echoing BB's unspoken question.

"I don't know who," he said, "but I can guess at the why. When you popped Ortega, you might have irritated his friends."

"Okay," Bud said. "BB, go get some clothes on and get another clip for your weapon. You two," he pointed at Amanda and Gino, "get behind the cabin. I'm going to disarm this thing."

"What's he going to do, Gino?" Amanda asked.

Gino spoke quietly and explained. "Bare loop switches are simple. Put a dynamite cap in a bag of diesel-soaked ammonium nitrate, attach one wire from the detonator to the negative post on a 6-volt lantern battery, and put another insulated wire through the spring in the center post of the battery. Cut the wire about four inches beyond the spring, and removed the last two inches of insulation.

"That's the only tricky part, keeping the bare wire from making contact. The insulation on the wire in the center spring keeps the bomb from going off. If that same wire is set in the right place, it acts like a trip wire, literally. Any pressure pulls the wire through the spring until the un-insulated part makes contact and completes the circuit. The electric charge sets off the detonator, and boom! Guaranteed.

"And you can buy all of this in a farm supply store," he added.

Amanda shook her head in disbelief, eyes focused on Bud, wondering why she was standing beside Gino instead of hiding behind a tree. "Shouldn't we take cover?"

Gino grinned. "Nah, even a sheriff can disarm this one."

Bud set his spotlight on the ground to illuminate the bomb and then squirmed on his stomach under the vehicle from the rear. He was cramped for room, but his arms were long enough to reach the wire in the center spring of a 6-volt lantern battery. He gently slid it sideways out of the spring, hand clamped around the bare end, and freed the trip wire.

"That ought to do it," he muttered, "I hope." Holding his breath, he pulled the battery to him by the other wire, and untwisted the connection. "I got it," he said, and crabbed backwards out from under the 4-Runner. Cradling the battery in both shaky hands, he got to his feet and offered it to the yard light. "I got it!"

Gino took the battery out of Bud's hand and said, "You don't have to shout. We're right here."

"I told you to get around the back side of the cabin."

"Yeah, and we don't work for you. Besides, when you said 'bare loop,' I knew even you could defuse the sucker. Where's the detonator?"

Bud shook his head. "Still in the bag."

Gino said, "Best pull it, Bud. A stray radio signal could... probably never would...but *could* set it off."

Bud crabbed back under the vehicle, got a grip on one of the detonator wires and gently pulled the blasting cap free of the fertilizer bag. He pushed himself out from under the vehicle and stood up, the blasting cap dangling by the wire in his right hand.

He walked across the driveway and parked the detonator behind a twenty-inch diameter pine tree.

"Damn, it's cold." He said. "Let's get inside."

Amanda stood shivering in her pajamas and pointed at her vehicle. "Is it safe?"

Bud grinned, relief pushing a deep breath from his chest. "Well, without the battery or the detonator all you have is a bag of fertilizer under your vehicle."

"I want my clothes," she said.

"Go for it," Bud said.

When Amanda opened the cabin door, her clothes and make-up kit in hand, she saw Bud using his cell phone and heard him say, "Block the road beyond Drews Reservoir…if you can get there before the perp escapes. I don't have a description, but I'd bet you'll find some bullet holes in the right side of his vehicle."

Sonny Sixkiller, undersheriff of Lake County, asked, "What type of vehicle is it?"

"Hold on." Bud looked at Gino and asked, "Any idea what type of vehicle it was?"

Gino nodded. "Yeah, it was square, sort of boxy-looking, like a medium-sized SUV. A Jeep maybe. Something like that."

"Okay," Bud said into the phone, "you are looking for an SUV, mid-sized probably." He paused and in a frustrated voice said, "Yeah, I know how many SUVs there are in Lake County. But there should only be one on the Dog Lake road this time of morning with a bullet hole in it! And call the State Police. I want a bomb squad out here." He heard Sonny say, "On it, Boss."

BB's big frame shadowed the doorway and he pushed inside, closing the door softly behind him. He had on a hooded sweat shirt, blue jeans and tennis shoes. No socks. His pistol was in his right hand, pointed at the floor. "I'm thinking," he said without preamble, "this guy is parked down the road listening for an explosion. What say we give him one?"

Gino shook his head. "That bomb is evidence. You know… fingerprints, detonator, wire…"

BB grinned. "Yeah, but I got two flash bangs in my old Corvette. What say we walk down to the boat ramp and let him think he got us?"

Bud shook his head. "You just happen to have flash bangs in you car."

"Yeah. Believe it or not, I'm still a detective for the Portland Police Bureau. At least for a month or two. And when I was a Boy Scout, I took the motto seriously: Always be prepared."

"Do it," Bud said. He pulled a heavy coat off a wall rack, jammed a dark hat on his head, and said, "I'll watch the road. In case he comes back." He pushed through the door, Molly close behind and headed around to the back of the cabin, the side paralleling the road.

Amanda took her bundled clothes and her pistol into Bud's small bathroom and pulled the door shut.

About sixty seconds later, two exploding stun grenades echoed across the lake, the concussion rolling like a thunder clap through the timber.

Amanda, dressed in blue jeans and a bulky gray cable knit sweater, came out of the bathroom in time to see the handsome black detective, BB and the shorter stocky Gino walk through the yard lights and up to the cabin, grinning like school boys.

Gino said as he came through the door, "There you go. Now you are dead, missy. No more cartel scumbags looking for you."

She turned to the coffee pot by the sink, started the water to fill the urn, and then stopped. "How do you suppose they found me?"

BB walked over and put an arm around her shoulder. He shook his head slowly from side to side. "And you a Special Agent for NCIS. Come on, Amanda. I'll bet you've been using your credit card. It's a sure bet they have a network that runs through the Northwest."

She nodded without saying anything, turned and poured the water from the urn into the coffee maker, rummaged through cupboards until she found a paper filter, scooped coffee grounds into the filter and closed the lid. "Stupid of me." She hit the On button and turned around, back to the counter.

"When I resigned, I thought, I'm out. I'm free. It never occurred to me that Ortega's thugs would come after me. Or they could find me if they did. I've just been wandering around, looking at the beautiful Northwest."

Gino and BB both were both silent, maybe thinking about their own plans to "quit" police work.

In the stillness, the coffee maker gurgled and a thin stream of coffee dribbled into the pot.

1:15 a.m. ~ Dog Lake

HENRY (BUD) BLAIR, LAKE COUNTY SHERIFF, sat with his back against a small pine tree, not moving, watching the road, thirty minutes of cold working its way through his heavy down jacket and thin moccasins. He was grateful for the warmth of Molly's body as she leaned up against him, grateful for her company for that matter.

He was thinking maybe his vigil was wasted, but he wasn't quite ready to give it up. He shook his head. Bloodstone was in jail, Raul Ortega was dead, and still the cartel sent assassins after them.

Which of us are they after? Not Maretti, even though he shot up that bunch in Bremerton that killed his partner Grandfield. And BB is in the clear. He was a silent partner in the Portland FBI raid on the mosque.

That leaves me and Amanda. And she killed Ortega, so it has to be Amanda. If the bomb kills the rest of us, that's just frosting on the cake. Collateral damage.

He felt the cell phone in his jacket pocket vibrate, pulled it, wincing at the light when he flipped it open. "Yeah?"

Sonny Sixkiller said, "We got 'em, Boss. Sergeant Trivoli hid her vehicle on a side road, and I blocked the road just beyond a curve. When he drove by, Michelle lit him up with her headlights and hit the siren. When he saw my pickup, he bolted and tried to take off through the timber. Too much speed. Smacked a tree hard enough to inflate his airbag."

"Can you ID him?"

"He's got a driver's license. It says he is George Jones. It's phony as hell, and I'll bet he doesn't sing country and western. He looks to be Hispanic. He's not saying anything, but there are three holes in the right side of the Jeep. Bullet holes. I've called for a wrecker to pick it up. We'll get a better look in town."

"Okay. Well, take him to the ER and have him looked at before you lock him up. I'll be in later to have a talk with him."

"What have you got out there, Boss?"

Bud rose, his knees creaking, turned and started walking through the thin screen of trees between the road and his cabin. "If we were in Iraq, I'd call it an IED. He left us a bag of diesel soaked fertilizer, a detonator and a 6-volt battery. That's why I want the State Police out here. Oh, yeah. He also shot at us."

"Us? Who's out there, Boss?"

"There are four of us: our friendly Bremerton City Detective, Gino Maretti, partner to Ron Grandfield, the cop those terrorists killed in Bremerton. That's when Gino was shot. He and my old partner Dell BeBe came down to do some late season fishing, drink a little beer and tell lies. And then Amanda Spears of NCIS fame showed up. She quit NCIS after the Raul Ortega incident. She's the one who killed Ortega when NCIS was taking Bloodstone down. Anyway, when she killed Ortega that put a kink in her career and she just said to hell with it and quit. We were having a nice time until someone planted a bomb."

"And you think?"

"I think Amanda was the target. The bomb was under her vehicle. If it killed the rest of us, so much the better."

"Who do you think?"

"I don't know. Amanda and I both did the Ortega cartel some serious damage. Did you find a cell phone on the guy?"

"Yes. We'll work it."

Phone up to his ear, Bud pushed through the door and into the welcome warmth of the cabin, tail wagging Molly right behind him. "Get an ETA from the State Police Bomb Squad and call me back." He snapped the cell phone shut.

"Got him," he said without preamble.

12:30 a.m. ~ *East of Klamath Falls*

THE COLD PENETRATED THE THIN SHELL of the camper and drove Mariah from the breakfast nook and up into the overshot. The mattress held a double sleeping bag for bedding. She took off her slush-soaked tennis shoes and socks, climbed into the overshot and slid down into the bag. It took a few minutes to warm up, and a few more minutes to adjust to the smelly pillow. Not smelly as in stinky, just smelly like the inside of a hat band that captured old, cotton sweat. Finally, the lulling hum of tires on the pavement and the warmth eased the tension in her thin body and she drifted off to sleep.

It was dream-torn sleep. She tried to run from Manny, but she couldn't get any traction in the slushy street, and the station attendant kept pointing at her hiding place and scolding her for leaving her mother behind. And then Manny was standing over her, a two-by-four raised to hit her head.

She woke with a start, sweating, trembling, heart pounding. It took her a few seconds to remember where she was. And then she realized the camper had stopped. She lay perfectly still and listened. A dog barked and she heard the old man say something and chuckle. She thought he might have said, "Shep, you old rascal. Caught you asleep, didn't I?"

She heard a house door slam, and then listened to the ticking of the engine block cooling off.

Well, she thought, *we must be there, where ever 'there' is.*

She slid off the bed and down to the cold floor. "Now what?" she said aloud.

She tugged her cold socks on protesting feet and slipped into her wet tennis shoes. She found if she pulled the side curtains back, the big security yard light gave her enough illumination to rummage in the cabinets and the camper's drawers. She wasn't sure what she was looking for. Help maybe. Anything that would help.

She found a matchbook, a candle and a flashlight in one drawer, a paring knife in another. An unopened carton of cigarettes was stashed in a cupboard over the tiny sink. She took four packs and left the rest, making sure the cupboard door was re-latched.

The small closet gave her a hooded zipper sweatshirt and a bulky wool jacket, both many sizes too large. But she took them anyway.

Two small cans of Dinty Moore Beef Stew, a can of tuna fish, a can of pork and beans and a box of saltines shared room in a plastic shopping bag. She added two bottles of Evian from the small fridge, and then she was down the metal steps and shivering in the cold night air, the gravel of the driveway grinding quietly under her light steps.

She closed the camper door as softly as she could, and then tiptoed across a narrow strip of brown lawn bordering a barnyard that played host to an open pole barn sheltering big square, five-hundred-pound bales of hay, an equipment shed with three stabled tractors, and to a no-longer-used red-brick milking barn. She was simply searching for shelter and a secure hiding place. She rejected the equipment shed and the derelict milking barn and headed for the pole barn.

She walked quickly around to the end of the stacked hay, out of sight of the house now, and felt her hope quicken at the sight of a medium sized white fifth-wheel trailer snuggled into an alley surrounded on three sides by tall stacks of hay bales. She held her breath and turned the door knob. She nearly cried in frustration when the knob failed to turn. Locked, it was.

She started around the trailer trying the doors to the under-bed storage, the water tank, a general storage boot. A narrow hatch opened to her touch, and the beam of the flashlight lit an interior door to a storage boot. She put her bundles on the hay-strewn ground and squeezed headfirst into the hatch, grateful she was so thin. She rolled over on her back and spun herself around in the narrow space. A hard kick and the small interior door banged open. Warm air flooded the compartment, and Mariah found herself silently crying, tears of relief running down the sides of her face and into her ears.

She snaked through the door and stood in the plush interior of the trailer, plush at least to Mariah, who had never been inside a big fifth wheel. Two minutes later she had her bundles safely inside and the main door relocked. A small space heater sitting on the floor of the kitchen area was keeping the interior from freezing. She spread her cold hands in front of the heater and blessed the warmth.

For a full minute she waited while the heated air blew the chill from her hands and face, and then her fatigue set her to yawning.

She tried the light over the stove and found the trailer was supplied with electric power. The bed in the overshot was made up and covered with a heavy comforter. She slipped out of her shoes, hung her wet socks on the edge of the kitchen counter, undressed and climbed into the large, comfortable bed. She didn't know what the future held, but for now she felt secure…and warm.

1:10 a.m. ~ Sprague River

WHEN MANNY FINISHED HIS TALE, TUSKER just balled his right fist and knocked him off the porch and into the yard. Manny rolled over in the snow and got to his knees, left hand to his bleeding mouth. With his right hand, he reached for the .25 caliber pop gun he kept in his boot, but the sight the big dog standing over him, teeth bared, stopped him in mid-motion. The dog wasn't growling, but the hackles on the dog's neck were standing up.

"That's right, Manny, you dumb ass, you're about five seconds from dead, so just keep still. Don't move or I'll let Lucifer have you, guts and all.'

Manny held his empty hands out to his side, staring at the dog's curled lips in horrified fascination as saliva drooled down the side of the animal's jaw.

Tusker said something, in Spanish Manny thought, and the dog looked at Tusker as if to say, "Are you kidding?" But he obeyed and sat down in the snow, eyes again on Manny. Manny didn't feel a lot safer, but it was a step in the right direction.

"All right," Tusker said, "now slowly and gently take out that pistol you carry in your boot." He waited until Manny pulled the gun with thumb and forefinger from the ankle holster. "That's right. Now toss it over by the steps."

Tusker retrieved the semi-automatic pistol from the snow, popped the clip and threw it as far as he could into the side yard, worked the slide and ejected the round in the chamber. And then he threw the pistol in the same general direction as the clip.

"Okay," Tusker growled, "help me get Tyson into the house. We gonna call 911 and get an ambulance out here. You understand?"

Even with the two of them lifting, Tyson was still heavy and they both puffed and panted with the exertion of getting Tyson up the steps and into the house. They stretched him out on an old Navajo rug in front of a big cast iron wood stove. A built-in fan blew heated air down and across the floor.

Manny's mind was clearing from the meth fog and he realized Tusker wasn't going to help him, was in fact turning against him. *What happened to the good old days? We used to be friends.*

As if reading his mind, Tusker said, "When I was using, we were friends, or at least as much as druggies can be friends. But I'm telling you, man, I'm clean and I've paid my dues. That twenty-seven months I did in the state pen was more than enough. I'm not going down that path again. So here's all that I'm going to do. For old time's sake, I'll give you a head start. I won't tell the cops where you went, but I'm damn well telling them what you did. *Comprende*? And don't ever come back here again or I'll let Lucifer have you."

By the time the ambulance arrived at Tusker's double-wide on the bench, Manny was through the little settlement of Sprague River and headed for the junction of the Sprague River road with Highway 140. "Lakeview or Klamath Falls?" he muttered aloud. The fuel gauge made the decision. He had enough gas to get back to Klamath Falls. He had a sinking sensation, knowing full well that one of two things was going to happen: if the police had a bulletin out on him, he was going to get stopped on the highway; and if he went back to Klamath Falls, he needed to hide himself and the car. "Maybe they won't look for me coming into town instead of going the other way," he said aloud.

At the junction, he turned west and headed over Bly Mountain. The crooked highway and slick, icy corners made for slow going. So it was nearly 2:30 before he finally rolled onto 6th Street, the major east-west street of Klamath Falls. The yellow "low fuel" light was flickering on and off. He needed gas…soon.

At the sight of the brightly lit mini-mart gas station a couple of blocks up the street, he accelerated to forty-five mph to make sure he would have enough momentum to coast into the pumps if the Mazda's tank ran dry.

Dora watched the car roll into the neon glare from the pump island canopy, grumped and silently promised herself, for the umpteenth time, to find a safer, better paying job. *Being alone in this place in the wee hours of the morning has gotten old*, she thought.

She slipped on a flannel lined Levi jacket and headed for the pumps. Manny got out and slammed the door to the car…really slammed it…like he was mad at it. Dora recognized him as the same skinny dude who frequently bought beer and cigarettes at the store. She didn't know his name, but she was wary of him. There was something about him that made her skin crawl. She once told, Spike, the man who double-shifted with her until midnight, "If he had yellow eyes, he'd look like a snake."

Manny answered her, "Fill up?" with a nod and said, "Premium." She started the pump and watched him warily as he crossed the driveway, pushed through the door, and headed to the restrooms in the back corner. She wasn't far off the mark when she muttered, "Probably needs a fix."

By the time the pumps shut off, Manny had the counter loaded with a half case of beer, bags of chips, candy bars, iced coffee, bags of nuts, and two sandwiches from the cooler. He had a half-eaten stale donut in one hand and a hundred dollar bill in the other.

"Give me a carton of Marlboros," he mumbled around a mouthful of donut, crumbs spilling over his lower lip and onto the floor. Dora rang it all up, bagged it and said, "With the gas, the total is $127.39."

Manny said, "Okay," and reached for his wallet. He laid another $50 on the counter.

By the time Dora had counted out the change, he had swallowed the donut and was able to say, "My daughter ran away earlier tonight. I need to find her. She's thirteen, about five feet tall, blue eyes, always wears a hooded sweatshirt. She might have come this way. Did you see her?"

Dora's heart rate jumped, but she was able to control her fear. Her facial expression didn't change even though she knew she was looking into the eyes of a killer. "Did you file a missing persons report, or tell the police?"

"Yes," he lied, "but you know how incompetent those assholes are. I'll have to find her myself."

"I'm sure they are doing the best they can," she retorted defensively.

He grabbed her note pad, took a pen from a plastic cup and scribbled a phone number on it. "Call this number if she shows up. I'll come pick her up." He grabbed the plastic grocery bags in one hand and the beer in the other. "Be sure and call me. I'll make it worth your while."

Dora made no move, just stood behind the counter and waited until Manny's Mazda drove out onto 6th Street and was completely out of sight. Then she hit 911. "I quit," she said aloud while she waited for a 911 operator to answer.

4:30 a.m. ~ Dog Lake, the wee hours of the morning:

AT 4:30 A.M, A THREE-PERSON OREGON State Police bomb disposal team in a white 4X4 Ford Expedition followed a Lake Country Sheriff's pickup into the driveway of Bud's cabin. The pickup headlights swept through the scattered pine, steadied on Amanda's 4-Runner, and then stopped about fifty feet from her vehicle.

A spotlight on the Ford Expedition snapped on, blinding Bud as he came out the door. He held up his badge with his right hand and shielded his eyes with his left hand. Sonny Sixkiller stepped out of the lead vehicle and shouted, "That's Sheriff Blair!"

The spotlight went out, and Bud watched as a third vehicle backed into his driveway, effectively blocking ingress or egress. It was hard to see, but Bud thought he could make out the shape of a Crown Victoria with a light rack.

A small, compact man wearing a dark windbreaker opened the left rear passenger door of the Expedition and stepped down to the ground. The Ford's powered rear hatch lifted. The man hurried over to Bud and stared at the three silhouetted figures peering through the front windows of the cabin. "Got here as quick as we could, Sheriff. Sorry about the spotlight. I think we get a little too jazzed up." He stuck out his hand. "I'm Lieutenant Beltram."

Bud shook his hand and said, "Any relationship with my deputy, Lonnie Beltram?"

"Cousins, actually."

Sonny walked up and pointed at the vehicle blocking the driveway out by the main road. "Want to guess who that is, Bud?"

Bud said, "No. I'm too damn old and too damned cold to guess."

"It's our friend, Trooper Charlie Prince."

"I'll be. I thought he was still on convalescent leave."

"Not any more. His supervisor assigned him as the lead investigator into your bomb…and your bomber. I have a hunch the FBI will also be along sometime in the near future."

Bud didn't say anything, just grunted a "harrumph," to express his displeasure at the notion of any other police organization sniffing around in his county.

State Trooper Charlie Prince walked into the yard lights. The State Police Stetson, and his long stride made him seem even more imposing than his six-foot-six-inch frame. But the grin on his face was obvious as he walked into the yard lights, a big hand stuck out to take Bud's. "Damn, Bud," he said, "Every time I turn around, you throw another party."

"This could have been my last one. How are you feeling?" Bud asked, and pointed at Charlie's stomach.

Charlie grinned as said, "Well, I don't have a spleen any more. The stitches are out, and the doctors said I healed a lot faster than they thought possible. But that shot in the guts gave me pause. Made me think about three things: One, I wish our Kevlar vests were padded better. Two, I'm glad I was wearing one. And three, I think it's time to stop and smell the roses."

Bud nodded. "That's advice we could all use from time to time."

Lieutenant Beltram had been supervising, needlessly Bud thought, as the two disposal experts, one male and one female, pulled big padded protective gear from the rear of the Expedition. "I'm thinking," Beltram said as he walked up, "it might be a good idea for you all to clear out while we deal with the bomb."

"I believe I've already turned it into a bag of fertilizer. The detonator is behind that pine tree," Bud pointed across the driveway, "and the battery is sitting on my picnic table, but you do what you have to." He turned and walked back into the cabin. He grinned without letting Beltram see it, and said, "Grab your jackets... and your coffee cups. Lieutenant Beltram wants us to 'clear the premises.'"

Gino Maretti asked, "Didn't you tell him you disarmed the bomb?"

"Yeah, but...you know...experts. They have their methods and their madness. And I think you have to be a little mad to work bomb disposal anyway. So let's take our coffee out to the road and let them be mad in their own way. My young friend Charlie Prince will entertain us out by his cruiser."

The female technician waddled over in her protective gear and asked, "Could we have the keys to the Toyota? We may have to move it." Amanda dug the vehicle keys from her jeans and held them out. "Good luck," Amanda said.

The young technician smiled and said, "In the theater I think they say 'break a leg.'"

"What do bomb disposal technicians say?" Amanda asked.

"Well, we survivors aren't too sure, but we think it's something like 'oh shit.'" The young woman waved the keys at Amanda, "As Arnold would say: I'll be back."

BB shook his head as they walked out of the light and down the driveway to Trooper Prince's Crown Vic, and said, "Do you remember Slim Pickens riding the A-Bomb in Doctor Strangelove? She sort of reminds me of Slim...minus the cowboy hat."

The wait out by Trooper Prince's cruiser was brief. The disposal techs used their vehicle headlights and hand-held spotlights to inspect the dark lump under Amanda's gas tank, and concluded there were no external wires. So they disengaged the vehicle parking brake, put the key in the ignition to release the transmission, put it in neutral and manually pushed the vehicle forward and off the bomb without starting the engine.

Fifteen minutes later, Lieutenant Beltram walked down the driveway and announced, "All clear."

They all crowded into the cabin, sucking up the warmth. Bud made a new pot of coffee, and listened as Beltram explained, without actually using the term "smart ass," or the term "hot shot," or even saying "dumb shit," why it is always best to leave bombs to the experts. "You see, the obvious detonator and battery combination were real enough. They were actually intended to work. But…my technicians, Wanda specifically, would be pleased to show you a second detonator buried in the bag."

The small woman almost purred at the praise, and said, "The second detonator is a type that can be triggered remotely in case the first detonator is found or fails to detonate the bomb. You did what you thought you had to, Sheriff, and that took guts."

"But?" Bud asked.

"You all got lucky this time," she said, shaking her head.

Bud shared a look with Sonny, shook his head and said, "Lesson learned."

Amanda glared at Gino. "And you said even Bud could disarm a bare loop switch."

Gino shrugged. "But he did, didn't he? Almost."

"What if the perp had triggered the remote detonator?" she asked.

"But he didn't," BB said, "because he heard the flash bangs. Made him think the bomb had gone off."

Thirty minutes later Trooper Prince pulled his cruiser out of the driveway to let the bomb squad out, their Expedition loaded with a bag of fertilizer, two detonators, a 6-volt lantern battery, several feet of fine wire, and two happy bomb disposal technicians, happy because this was hero time. They had done something important. There really had been a bomb. And they had literally defused it.

"Risk, plus success. What more could a bomb tech want?" Lieutenant Beltram mused from the rear seat as the vehicle turned right onto the Drews Valley/Dog Lake road and headed east toward the town of Lakeview, Oregon."The sheriff didn't look very happy when I showed him the second detonator, did he?" Wanda said.

"No," Beltram said, "but he took the lesson to heart." The senior tech, Gerry Willis, a small, skinny looking fellow in his early forties, sporting a military burr for a haircut, squinted over the steering wheel watching for reflected animal eyes in the headlights of the vehicle. He startled his companions by uttering his first words in several hours. "I can't blame the sheriff, but assuming facts not in evidence gets people killed. I wonder if there is an Al Qaida connection. Their IED designs have gotten more and more sophisticated. I read a technical report about our bomb disposal techs in the Middle East finding dummy fuses in IEDs, failing to recognize them as dummies, and then finding the bombs going off in their faces because of a remotely triggered secondary detonator."

Wanda stared at her partner, her senior by nearly twenty years, and her mentor. She found his silence acceptable because she knew his mind was always at work. "You think?" she asked.

He shook his head. "I don't know. But it's got the mark of other Al Qaida bombs. This was rigged for a serious sucker punch. No doubt about it."

Lieutenant Beltram leaned forward and said over his senior tech's right shoulder, "Put your speculation together with a copy of the technical report you just mentioned and write it up, Gerry. I'll want this out as an alert, ASAP."

Gerry tried to stifle a yawn and reached for his travel cup. He took a sip of the cold coffee and placed the cup back in the console holder. "Right after my nap, Lieutenant. Right after my nap."

Trooper Prince, properly introduced to BB, Gino and Amanda, shared a cup of hot coffee, and listened intently as each of the police officers told the "bomb story." He didn't comment when they offered speculation as to whom and as to why someone might want to kill them, just nodded and jotted notes in a leather bound note book. When they had finally run down, and he saw Bud start to yawn, he said, "Thank you. I'd better head for the barn and let you folks get some sleep."

Before heading out to his Crown Vic and the drive to Lakeview, he shook hands with Bud and said, "How about 0900 at your office? I want to interrogate your prisoner."

7:05 a.m. ~ Westside, Lake County

THE MUTED SOUND OF A PICKUP engine woke Mariah from her first dreamless sleep in over two years. Life hadn't been great before Manny moved in with Mariah's mother, but at least she hadn't been exposed to the lowlifes that wandered in and out of the house. When Barbara quit her job at Wal-Mart, she and Mariah were totally at Manny's mercy. Not that Barbara cared. As long as he fed her growing meth addiction, she was fine.

Mariah's independent money came from doing a little babysitting for a neighbor, scooping up loose change in the house, and scrounging bottles and cans for the deposit money. And from petty theft.

Some small convenience stores were careless with the storage of returned bottles and cans. So Mariah would wait until the store was busy and the clerks distracted, and then she would steal garbage bags of bottles and cans and take them to a different store and collect the deposit money. Her best night had seen the same bag of cans sold three times to three different convenience stores for a total of $12.45. The last $4.15 had been right back at the store where she had stolen them to begin with.

The only real risk came from homeless people who were also scrounging for bottles and cans. She quickly learned to drop her bag of cans if she was threatened. The other thieves would take the bag and leave her alone. It only happened twice, but she had learned to be wary of the homeless.

And now I'm homeless, she thought. The faint sound of a screen door banging shut urged her to roll over and lift the bottom edge of the curtain on the window in the front of the overshot.

Without a watch, she didn't know what time it was, but there was enough gray light for her to make out the larger details of a small, fenced pasture divided by a gravel lane that led from the highway to a single-story brick house west of the hay barn. An older woman wrapped in a long car coat was trudging down the lane, her breath creating white puffs in the cool morning air. Mariah watched until the woman retrieved her newspaper from the paper box nailed to the post below a faded silver mailbox. When the woman glanced in the direction of the fifth-wheel, Mariah instinctively dropped the curtain. She held her breath until she heard the screen door bang shut again. And then she sighed, rolled over, pulled the comforter up around her chin and drifted back to sleep.

Bea Johnson frowned and tossed the rolled newspaper on the kitchen table. She thought she had seen something move in the periphery of her vision. But when she glanced at Bob's hay barn and his white fifth-wheel, she didn't see anything out of the ordinary. She went to the kitchen window and looked east across her small pasture to the Roger's place. Sometimes Bob let visitors use the fifth wheel, but it didn't look to Bea like he had any visitors. The only vehicle at his place was his pickup and camper. On impulse she grabbed her cell phone and hit the speed dial.

"Up kinda' early, aren't you Bea?" he growled.

"Sleeping in, Bob?" she gibed.

"Yes. I didn't get home until after 2:00 this morning."

"Why so late? Chemo, again?"

"You mind your business, Bea. I can handle mine. Besides, I wouldn't want to ruin your reputation."

She knew Bob was tired after his treatments, so he probably parked in the Klamath Falls Safeway parking lot and slept a while before heading home. "Bob, you're a mule headed jackass. It's no trouble for me to take you to Klamath. Besides it gives me a good excuse to do some shopping."

"And I appreciate the offer. Is that why you called?"

"No. I was wondering if you have company. I thought I saw the curtain in your fifth wheel move when I went out to get my paper this morning."

"No. Nobody is staying with me right now." He paused, and then added, "I did see a little red fox hunting mice behind the barn. Do you think that was it?"

Bea sighed. "No. I don't think so. Well it must have been my imagination. And since I woke you up, I'm getting ready to cook the kids some breakfast. You want some?"

"No, Bea. Thanks. I'm going to try and get some more sleep."

"Okay. I'll let you go. Sorry to wake you up."

"No problem."

After Bob's wife died, the local wags decided he and "Widow Johnson" were more than just neighbors. That he never took the camper off his pickup was merely grist for the rumor mill. At the Curls R Us, a small beauty shop run by a young Brenda Darling out of her converted garage, Bea caught the tail end of a story that died out as she opened the door to the shop. "...and they sneak off in his camper." Bea heard the shop owner, Brenda Darling say, "Good for them," before a heavy pall of guilt silenced the gossipers.

When Bea told Bob about it, he chuckled and allowed he had never had to protect the reputation of a sixty-year-old woman before. "But it won't do mine any harm," he grinned.

"It's not funny," she snapped.

He had held his hands up in front of his face in mock protection, and laughed until she actually swatted him on top of the head with a rolled-up newspaper. They finally agreed they would never be gone from the Goose Lake Valley at the same time. Bob had an eyebrow cocked in speculation when he finally nodded his okay. In the privacy of his mind, he admitted Bea's trim figure and exceptionally deep blue eyes were damned attractive. *Maybe*, he thought, *those old biddies have a good idea.*

When Bob was diagnosed with prostate cancer and needed several trips to Klamath Falls for his treatments, Bea simply ignored the wags and nursed him after each of his sessions.

Bea plugged in the old waffle iron, shook her head and muttered, "Damned bull headed fool," and wandered down the hallway. She knocked on the first bedroom door and hollered, "Rise and shine. School bus will be here in an hour." Without waiting for an answer, she knocked on the second door. "Cody, it's time to get up."

A thirteen-year-old girl, red hair sleep tousled, peeked out from behind the door of the first bedroom. "Gramma, can't Cody drive us to school?"

"No, Colleen. I need the pickup this morning. You kids will have to take the bus."

7:30 a.m. ~ Klamath Falls

HARMON HADN'T GOTTEN TO BED UNTIL after 3:00 a.m. A phone call to the Lake County Emergency Services Center asking them to track down "an older unknown Lake County man who had a camper on a dark blue or black Dodge pickup" had taken a good half hour of his time. He winced when the dispatcher said, "Thank you so much for such detailed information." It was almost 2:30 a.m. before he made a trip to the Sky Lakes Medical Center to check on Mariah's mother.

A person wandering through a coma doesn't share much, so in a very real sense Barbara Caldwell didn't have anything to say. The uniformed officer watching the hallway into the ICU just shook his head when Harmon asked how she was doing.

He drove home, shaved and showered before setting his alarm three hours downstream. Jones called him a little before six a.m.

and told him to get his lazy ass out of bed and down to the station. He was to hook up with Officer Christine Downing, a blond woman who looked more like a high school student than a police officer. She was often the lead called on to investigate child abuse complaints.

When he walked into the station at 6:30, Jones told him the Superintendent of Schools had called ahead to let Lacey's parents know Harmon and Downing were going to pay them a visit.

Lacey's parents were wary of Detective Harmon, especially at 7:00 in the morning. But the presence of a uniformed female police officer and a close study of Harmon's badge gave them some assurance that Harmon really was a police officer. *Maybe it's my bloodshot eyes that make them suspicious*, he thought.

The parents finally let the front door swing open and invited the two officers inside and off the wind battered front porch. The short, trim woman Harmon assumed was Lacey's mother was dressed in slacks and sweater. *For the office?* Harmon wondered. The husband was medium height, dressed in military trousers and blouse, lieutenant colonel insignia on his collar points.

"Lacey's getting ready for school," the mother said nodding to the stairs leading to the second floor, "but she should be down in a few minutes." She closed the door and asked, "What's this about? Lacey hasn't done anything wrong that I know of."

"No. I'm not here about Lacey." Harmon said, "But her friend Mariah Caldwell is missing. We're hoping Lacey can give us an idea of where to start looking for her."

The mother frowned and asked, "How did you know Lacey and Mariah were friends?"

"That's a good question," Officer Downing said, looking at Harmon.

He grimaced and acknowledged he had neglected to share that information. "Sorry."

Harmon pulled the two photos out of a small, zippered notebook and handed them to the mother. "I found this picture of Lacey in Mariah's scrapbook."

She looked at the photo and read the inscription, *Your friend Lacey, to my best friend, Mariah.*

"Last year's photo," she said and handed it to her husband. He took the photo, nodded and said, "I think we better offer these folks some coffee," and walked through the small foyer, down a short hallway and into a back kitchen. He pointed at a breakfast bar with two stools. "Have a chair."

Taking charge, or at least trying to, Harmon thought, and then he mentally shrugged. *Whatever it takes.* During his tour with the Coast Guard, the officers he knew were almost always "take-charge" kinds of people.

Lacey's father pulled two mugs from a cupboard, poured coffee and set them on the breakfast bar. "Cream? Sugar?"

They each said no and settled onto the stools. "I'm sorry to be rude," Lacey's father said. "I'm Don Largent, and this is my wife Eleanor." He paused, "What can you tell us? If Mariah is in danger, does that mean Lacey is in danger as well?"

The two officers glanced at each other and Harmon said, "We don't know. Was Lacey ever at Mariah's house? I guess I'm asking if the man who lived with Mariah's mother would know Lacey and would know where she lived."

Eleanor said, too quickly, Harmon thought, "Lacey was never at Mariah's house. They were friends at school. And Mariah came here after school sometimes." She paused and then without really knowing why added, "I felt sorry for her. Lacey told me about Mariah's mother. And I made the mistake of offering her some of Lacey's old clothing once…a really nice sweater and some other things. Mariah gave me a look that would have frozen Klamath Lake. Then she said "No thank you" and left the house. I just felt like crap. I didn't mean to be insulting."

Lacey was a tall, thin young girl, braces on her teeth, hair in a blond pony tail and wearing a Henley Middle School sweatshirt. At age thirteen she stood an inch taller than her mother's five-feet-three inches, and gave promise of someday being even taller. She was nervous, but she had the natural poise of someone whose life has been blessed with loving, indulgent parents.

Officer Downing introduced herself and Detective Harmon, and then said, "We are looking for your friend, Mariah. She's missing and we need to find her. Do you have an idea of where we should look?"

Lacey firmly denied knowing where Mariah was, and just as firmly denied having any recent contact with Mariah. She also denied ever meeting Manny or being at Mariah's house.

Officer Downing pushed Lacey's photo across the breakfast bar and said, "If you really are her best friend, you'll want her to be safe. Right now her mother is in the hospital, in a coma. And we believe Mariah witnessed a murder. If she did, it's possible, in fact it's likely the killer will come after her. We need to find her first."

Lacey's mother stared hard at her daughter and said, "Lacey, if you know anything, you need to tell us."

Tears in her eyes, Lacey looked up at her father. "Please, Daddy, don't make me tell."

Colonel Largent said gently, "Loyalty is commendable, Lacey, but in this case it might be misplaced. Come on, Button. What do you know?"

Lacey put her backpack on the counter and unzipped an outside pocket. She took a rose-colored cell phone out, turned it on, fiddled with it and pushed it across the breakfast bar to her father.

He read the text message and then handed the phone to Officer Downing. She read the text message and then looked at Harmon. "This was sent about fifteen minutes after Mariah talked to the clerk at the mini-mart. So we know she was safe then."

She pushed the phone back to Lacey and said, "Will you send her a text message and ask her to tell you where she is. Tell her we want to send a police officer to take her to a place of safety. Also, tell her that her mother is in the hospital. If she lets us, we'll take her to visit her mother. Can you do that?"

Lacey nodded and wiped her tears with the sleeve of her sweater.

Harmon waited a few seconds and said, "How about right now?"

When it was obvious that Mariah wasn't answering any text messages right then, Harmon sighed, pushed his business card across the counter to Colonel Largent and said, "As soon as...?"

Colonel Largent said, "You bet," and nodded toward the front door. "Can I talk to you privately?"

He led them into a small office off the entry and closed the door. "Okay, who is this guy that may be after Mariah?"

Harmon paused a few seconds and then pulled a copy of the BOLO out of the inside pocket of his windbreaker. "We don't have a picture yet, but we expect DMV to send one soon."

The colonel read the BOLO and shook his head. "The things we do to our children. Okay, that's it then. I'm sending Lacey and her mother to visit my in-laws. I won't take any chances. Now...I assume you have people watching the school for this scumbag, and I assume you have someone watching the mother."

Harmon smiled and asked, "Were you ever a cop?"

"Air Force intelligence."

"Good for you. Normally I wouldn't share our plans, but in this case... yes, we have watchers at the hospital, at the school, and at his house. We might get lucky."

Colonel Largent showed them to the door and shook each of their hands firmly. "Thank you. Let me know when you catch that scumbag." He handed them a business card with a Kingsley Air Base phone number.

A cold wind pushed them down the walk and to the car. When the engine started and the defroster cleared a hole in the fog on the inside of the windshield, Harmon engaged the transmission and pulled away from the curb.

"What else haven't you told me?" Officer Christine Downing asked.

"When we get back to the office, I'll show you the security camera pictures from the mini-mart. It shows a girl I'm betting is Mariah getting into a pickup camper. We know the driver of the pickup is an older guy, maybe in his sixties, no name, lives in the Lakeview area and comes to Klamath a couple times a month. We do not have a license number or other ID on the pickup except that it's a Dodge 4X4, regular cab, made sometime after 1994. That's when the Dodge pickup model changed from square box to something a little sleeker. It may be dark blue or black in color. But we don't know that for sure either. The Lakeview City Police and the Lake County Sheriff's office will be out looking for "whoever" later today, or at least looking for a pickup-camper combination."

"Whomever," she corrected.

"What?"

"It's whomever, not whoever."

"And that's relevant?"

Officer Christine Downing looked over at Harmon and grinned. "Not really. But my mother was an English teacher."

"Terrific."

Downing nodded and said, "Back to Mariah. I'll give her credit for this much. She's resourceful."

Harmon said, "Or just desperate. I can't believe she knew where the pickup was going, but she got in anyway. I'm hoping she'll contact Lacey again."

Downing nodded affirmative. "She will. She has a phone, she has a best friend, and she's a girl. Odds are one hundred percent."

"For all of those reasons, huh?"

"Throw in 'alone' and you have four compelling reasons."

Harmon turned into the Klamath Falls Police Department parking lot, maneuvered into an empty slot and killed the engine.

"Are we partners in this? Is that what Detective Jones is doing?"

"Yes. Didn't he say anything to you about it?"

"No. Only that you were going with me to interview Lacey. He said you were the best he'd ever seen at interviewing children."

She frowned and then looked quickly at Harmon. "I do all right with kids. It's adults I have problems with."

He keyed in on the serious, introspective look on her face...a lovely face he decided...and failed to stifle a grin. "That's okay. I don't like big people very much either." He paused and waited until a smile tugged at her mouth before adding, "but I think you and I will do just fine."

He opened his door and stepped out into a slush pile and said, "Come on partner. We need to move fast on this."

"Quickly," she corrected.

7:30 a.m. ~ Dog Lake

THE QUIET RUMBLE OF BB'S CORVETTE idling in the yard finally broke Bud's sleep. The alarm's incessant buzz had failed to wake him at his normal 6:00 a.m. He twisted out of bed, slipped on a pair of old, floppy fleece slippers and pushed his arms through a big blue terry cloth robe, a gift from Nancy that brought a fresh wave of grief each time he saw it. But he couldn't bring himself to give it away.

He opened the door to his upstairs bedroom and smelled coffee and bacon and the aroma of fresh biscuits. BB's baritone was quietly filling the room with tales of his partnership with Bud when they were both young detectives for the Portland Police Bureau. Bud overheard BB concluding with, "Hell, we both spent too much time at the Greeks drinking beer and eating olives…much too often." BB chuckled and said, "That's probably why my first and last wife left."

Bud growled down the stairs, "Understandably."

"Now don't go get on your high horse, Sheriff. Just telling it like it is."

"Was."

"What?" BB asked.

"Was," Bud repeated without any heat whatsoever. "Past tense. Remember what I told you, BB: spend too much time in the past and it becomes a parking lot."

"Speaking of which," BB said, "I think I best get on the road before that gas guzzler out there runs dry." He rose and extended his big hand to Bud. "I'm headed home. I like y'all, but I don't have the resources I need to work this case."

Bud nodded, shook BB's hand and said, "Heck of a fishing trip. We'll have to try again next summer. Right?"

BB smiled and said, "Sure. Right after I get my new summer house built," he pointed at the south end of Bud's A-frame, "right over there."

"I don't know if you want to do that, BB," Bud said. "This has gotten to be a rough neighborhood."

BB chuckled and said, "That's why you need me, Bud."

Gino Maretti slid from behind the small table and shook BB's hand. "Drive safely, my friend. I'm heading back to Bremerton as soon as I clean my kitchen."

"You cooked?" Bud asked.

Gino ignored the question. "You know," he said looking only at BB, "we are going to have to cut the head off the snake or else these two," he pointed at Amanda and Bud, "will have to go into hiding for the rest of their lives."

BB said, "You gotta plan?"

"I'm working on it."

"Call me," BB said. He turned and gave Amanda a big hug and a warm smile. "Think I'm gonna call you Flash-Bang from now on," he winked, "but only in private." He dug into his wallet and fished two one-hundred dollar bills from the wallet's hide-out. "Use this until you can get to a bank." When she started to protest, BB pushed the bills into her hand. "You can catch me up next time we meet. In the meantime, cash and carry, Flash Bang, cash and carry."

Molly followed BB out the door to where the Corvette idled, the exhaust wrapping the car in wisps of vapor. BB patted Molly and slid behind the wheel. He waved in the general direction of the cabin and reversed out of the driveway.

They listened until the rumble of the tuned exhaust system faded from their hearing. Bud sipped a cup of coffee, piled strips of bacon on a biscuit and took a bite. He realized suddenly how hungry he was.

"Good," he muffled around a mouthful.

Gino scraped plates, and with his one good hand plunged them into a steaming sink of suds to soak. Amanda started to help and Gino said, "Not enough room. Sit."

Bud eyeballed Amanda and asked, "Where you gonna go?"

She looked up at him, staring at his bloodshot hazel eyes, the small scar running through his left eyebrow, and at the heavy five o'clock shadow on his jaw. BB had warned her Bud was still carrying the torch for Nancy Sixkiller, but she suddenly thought, *To hell with that. She left and I'm here.*

She came close to batting her eyes at him, but with quick insight, decided that would be a mistake. She settled for a flat statement. "I might just stay right here for a couple of days, if that would be all right."

Bud shook his head and said, "We can't protect you out here. I don't have enough people to spare."

"Not necessary," she argued. "Look, as far as Ortega is concerned, I'm dead. No one will come looking. I think I'll be safer here than in town."

Bud finally shrugged and said, "Okay. I'll bring some groceries out tonight so you won't starve to death. You want Molly for company?"

Amanda nodded, her eyes bright with unspoken triumph. "Yes."

Gino grinned. He winked at Bud over the top of Amanda's head, dried his hands on a kitchen towel and handed it to Amanda. "In that case, you can finish the dishes, Missy. I'm out of here."

Gino gave Amanda a quick shoulder pat and whispered, "You take care of our boy." She nodded even though she wasn't exactly certain what Gino meant by "take care of."

Gino shook hands with Bud and said, "You'll be hearing from me. See that you both stay alive. And don't worry. Me and BB…we gonna take care of the Ortega thugs." He gave a mock salute, patted Molly's shoulder and said, "You stay alert, old gal. They might need you."

Amanda and Bud listened to the crunch of the tires from Gino's Ford Mustang as he reversed and drove out to the main road. For both of them it was suddenly silent, oppressively silent until Molly padded to the door, wanting out.

7:45 a.m. ~ *Westside*

MARIAH HAD FALLEN BACK TO SLEEP after the older woman had gone to fetch her newspaper, but the sound of Bob Rogers shutting the door on his Dodge pickup, followed by the muffled start-up of the engine, brought Mariah awake again. She listened until the crunch of tires on gravel ended as Rogers drove out onto the paved road.

Mariah pulled the heavy comforter up around her ears, and tried to think about her next step, or if there even was a next step. She pulled her cell phone from under her pillow, turned it on and frowned at the "battery low" message. She checked her text messages and saw she had one from Lacey. Encouraged and suddenly less lonely, she tried pulling up the message. Her only reward was to watch the small screen turn black.

"Great. I don't even know where I am, and my phone dies."

The screen door of the ranch style rambler across the small pasture slapped shut and she could hear voices that sounded like a girl and a boy talking. Mariah rolled over and slowly pulled the front curtain back an inch or so. She watched a boy she guessed to be about seventeen or eighteen and a smaller redheaded girl, each wearing zipper sweatshirts and carrying book bags, walking out to the main road. The boy said something Mariah couldn't make out, and then skipped out of the way as the girl tried to smack him on the shoulder with her fist. Mariah heard him laugh and say something else that caused the girl to pick up a marble sized rock and fling it at him. His "Hey, now," was clear enough to Mariah. She wondered what it would be like to have a brother.

A school bus eased to a stop at the end of the Johnson driveway, red lights flashing, one brake pad squealing a little. She watched the teenage boy and the younger girl cross the road and board the bus. The bus pulled away. And then it was quiet again.

She lay back down and pulled the comforter up under chin, tears pooling at the corners of her blue eyes. For some reason she couldn't explain, the friendly, innocent antics of the boy and girl suddenly flooded her soul with a great wave of grief and sorrow.

She allowed herself a full five minutes of tears and pity. And then she started getting angry…angry at her mother for being so weak…for her addiction…for taking up with that scum Manny…angry that she had been forced to run…angry at an adult world that couldn't see she and her mother needed help…angry that she couldn't have a normal life…or even a childhood.

"Damn it, Babs," she almost shouted, "you screwed up big time. First Manny, and then the drugs." She pounded her small fist into the comforter.

She sat up, wiped the tears from her eyes, and said to herself, "Okay. I need to find a battery charger. Then I need to find out where I am. I know we went east from Klamath Falls…but how far?"

The sound of a powered garage door opener drifted across the small pasture. She rolled over and peeked through the front curtain in time to see a maroon pickup back out of the garage, reverse on the big gravel parking pad and head down the lane, a thin cloud of exhaust vapor trailing behind. The garage door closed, and the pickup turned left onto the main road.

There must be a town in that direction, Mariah thought.

She slipped out of the bed in the overshot and pulled her jeans and sweatshirt on. He socks were dirty, but they were warm and dry when she slipped them on…and the fan in the small heater blowing warm air across her tennis shoes had driven the moisture out…almost. But they felt better than they had.

She emptied a bottle of distilled water into a sauce pan and lit the gas burner with the self-starter button. She hadn't found any coffee in the cupboards, but she did find some tea bags...and some packets of sugar. Aloud, she said, the vague outlines of a plan forming in her mind, "I wonder if those people across the field have a phone charger?"

8:05 a.m. ~ Klamath Falls PD

DETECTIVE JONES WAS WAITING IN THE hallway beyond the reception area when Detective Harmon and Officer Downing pushed through the security door. "Come in," he said, pointing to his office door. "Want some coffee?"

Mathew shook his head and Officer Christine Downing said, "No."

"Have a seat," Jones said, pointing to a couple of battered, wooden visitor's chairs.

"How was your interview with Mariah's friend?"

Downing said, "She wasn't wanting to rat on Mariah, and she really didn't know anything except Mariah had sent a text message saying she was all right and that she would get back later."

She glanced at Harmon who shrugged. "So," she continued, "we had her text Mariah back, ask he where she was, tell Mariah her mom was in the hospital, and say we wanted to protect her. Mariah hadn't answered back by the time we left."

"Is her friend Lacey in any danger?" Jones asked.

"According to the mother," Harmon said, "Lacey was never at Mariah's house. So...we don't think so. But Lacey's father, who is a Colonel at the air base, is sending both the mother and Lacey to stay with grandparents until we catch Giles."

Jones nodded and said, "Good. Now, I have three things for you. First, a man named Gordon Tusk, who lives up the Sprague River east of Chiloquin, called 911 in the wee hours of the morning, asking for an ambulance. The ambulance brought one Tyson James to the ER, brutally beaten, but still alive as of about thirty minutes ago. His condition is critical. I ran him and he has a prior conviction for drug use and for drug dealing. Known associates include our boy Manfred Giles."

Harmon interrupted, "What about Gordon Tusk? I seem to remember he did some time for dealing drugs."

Jones nodded. "He did, but from what I'm hearing, he has cleaned up his act since he finished his sentence. According to the Chiloquin

City Police, he cut his ties to the drug world, has a job at the Casino, cuts firewood for extra money, raises a couple of calves each year for beef. They make him sound like an upstanding citizen."

"Got a phone number?" Harmon asked. "I want to talk to him."

Jones slid a business card across the desk. "On the back."

"To continue," Jones said. "Dora Winslow, the woman we interviewed at the mini-mart, called in with a tale of a man fitting Manfred Giles's description, driving a blue Mazda, and asking about Mariah. He promised the Winslow woman some cash to call him if Mariah shows up. Claimed Mariah was his daughter. Sergeant Booker is on his way to the mini-mart to collect the surveillance video."

"Doesn't Booker ever sleep?" Harmon asked of no one in particular.

"Did anyone try to find Giles?" Officer Downing asked.

Jones winced and said, "Everyone on duty was working an injury vehicle accident up by the college. By the time we shook someone loose, Giles had apparently gone to ground."

Harmon nodded and then said, "I'm thinking he's hiding in or near the city. I'm also thinking we need to continue to stake out his house and to keep security up and running at the hospital."

"Has anyone tried the number he gave Dora Winslow?" Officer Downing asked.

Jones shook his head. "Not yet, but I want you two to plan an operation that involves Dora Winslow making the call and luring Giles to someplace we can safely arrest him."

"Okay," Harmon said and glanced at Officer Downing, "we can do that." He paused, looked directly at Jones and added, "You said there were three things you wanted to talk about."

"Yes. Yes I did. I wanted to let you know that Mariah's mother regained consciousness an hour ago." He looked at Officer Downing, "Someone needs to interview her. Find out if she might know where Mariah would run to, and if she knows where Giles might try to hide."

Detective Harmon frowned and looked sideways at Jones. "Boss, I thought I had the lead on this."

"And you think I'm butting in?"

"Yeah, I do, and you are. First you don't tell me I'm teamed with Officer Downing, then you start giving us assignments." Harmon's voice rose in volume a bit in emphasis of his last point. "Either you run this investigation or get out of my way."

Jones tried not to smile and then quit trying. "Sorry Mathew, but the information came my way and I just sort of ran with it. We haven't had a lot of time to get organized, but I'll let you…and Christine…take the lead on this. Okay?"

Harmon nodded and finally smiled. "Okay, Boss. We're on it."

8:15 a.m. ~ Westside

MARIAH FOUND THE SIDE DOOR TO the garage unlocked. Unlocked doors were an unfamiliar practice in her Klamath Falls neighborhood, but one she welcomed here with a sigh of relief. She slipped through the garage and into the mud room, tiptoeing past the wall rack of jackets, sweatshirts and coveralls.

The faint, cold smell of cooked bacon, waffles and maple syrup in the kitchen set her mouth to watering, and she eyed a cold leftover waffle on a small plate. Hunger drove her good sense into the right side of her brain where it warred with her left brain survival instincts. She argued in her mind, "There are three of them. They won't even notice if it's gone." She looked at the unwashed dishes stacked in the sink and gave into temptation.

She heated the waffle and its plate in the microwave and searched the cupboards for syrup. Maple syrup is what she craved. When she couldn't find it, she opened the fridge and looked. Lying next to a bottle of Log Cabin syrup was a baggie stuffed with leftover bacon strips, nice crunchy mouth watering bacon strips.

"Ah, hell," she said and stuffed the baggie in the pocket of her sweatshirt. *Not smart*, she thought.

The microwave dinged its proud announcement that the waffle and the plate were warm. She couldn't find any butter, but by then it didn't matter. She was suddenly ravenous. She poured cold syrup on the waffle, wolfed the waffle down, poured herself a small glass of milk from the gallon in the fridge and suddenly felt better than she had since midnight.

She rinsed the plate and the glass and added them to the dish pan in the sink. *Please don't let them notice*, she prayed in silent entreaty to God.

The search for a charger was simple, short and sweet. A phone charger lay on the counter, plugged into a wall socket on the end of the sink counter. She compared the connection with her cell phone, and, satisfied it would work with her phone, hesitated for almost a full twenty seconds before unplugging it and sticking it into the belly pocket of her sweatshirt, companion to the bacon.

"That is enough disturbance," she whispered to herself. She made sure the syrup bottle was precisely where she had found it, and then wandered through the living room and down the hall. The first door on the left opened to the young girl's room. Mariah took clean socks and clean panties from a drawer, hesitated and then slipped her money pouch over her neck. She placed a ten dollar bill under the neatly folded stack of panties. "I'm not a thief," she told herself.

Then it was back through the kitchen and out the mudroom door. She was reaching for knob on the side door when the garage door opener hummed and began to ratchet open. Trapped, heart suddenly pounding, she spotted a door in the corner of garage, ran to it, and slipped into a small furnace room. She prayed she hadn't been seen.

She heard the pickup engine shut down, the driver's side door open and heard Bea Johnson mutter, "Getting forgetful in my old age. I thought I had the checkbook in my purse." The vehicle's door slammed shut and Mariah heard the older woman open the door to the mudroom. She was gone almost five minutes before she came back out, slammed the mudroom door and crawled back into the pickup. The engine started, and Mariah heard the crackle of studded tires as the pickup backed out and the garage door slowly ratcheted down again and closed.

She let out a deep breath and felt her pounding heart slow down, headed for a more normal rate. She opened the door and thought of one more thing. In the recycle basket by the back door, she found an old newspaper. She slipped out the side door, hesitated for a moment, listening for vehicle traffic. Reassured by the quiet, she ran across the pasture, squeezed between the barbed wire strands and scooted into the shelter of the pole barn.

Once the trailer door was locked, she plugged the phone charger into a wall socket and attached it to her cell phone. A reassuring beep told her the phone was charging.

She sat at the breakfast nook table, spread the newspaper out and nibbled on the thin, crispy bacon strips. The masthead proudly displayed "The Lakeview News."

"Okay, that makes sense. We traveled east out of Klamath Falls," she said aloud, unconsciously including the old man driving the pickup in her flight from Manny.

"And town must be that way," she added, pointing east.

The cell phone chimed the news she had a text message. She stuffed the last piece of bacon in her mouth, wiped her fingers clean on a paper towel and picked up the phone. There were two messages from Lacey. The first told her that her mother was in the hospital, the police wanted to know where Mariah was, to let them know and the police would pick her up, keep her safe, and take her to see her mother.

The thought of seeing her mother bothered her. That wouldn't be smart. Manny would be watching. "Too dangerous," she said aloud.

The second message said, Cops here. Dad sending Mom n me way till it's safe. Keep ur fon on. Made me tell we txt. Promise Dad wud let hm no u r ok. RU?

Mariah hesitated before typing, Im ok. No cops. Near Lakeview. Don't tell anyone.

The reply was almost instantaneous. Have to. Sorry.

Go ahead. Won't find me anyway.

What about your Mom?

Is she alive? Mariah asked.

Lacey replied, Yes. Still in the hospital.

Mariah typed in, Good. She needs help. Bye. With that she shut the phone down, sick at heart, terrified again that Manny might find her.

9:00 a.m. ~ Lake County Sheriff's Office

BUD BUZZED HIMSELF THROUGH THE STREET side entrance into the booking area of the Lake County Sheriff's office. The business of policing the county was carried on in a wing of the L-shaped County Courthouse, a two story building that occupied a big tree shaded block near the center of the small city of Lakeview.

The courts, district attorney, the county library, and the functionaries of Lake County occupied the other portions of the Courthouse.

Karen Highsmith's short curly brown hair was barely visible behind the booking counter. She worked as Bud's technical deputy in charge of the jail, and as his unofficial administrative assistant. She looked up and said. "Good morning, Boss. Judge Lynch and Howard are in your office. And," she winced at the sound of Sonny Sixkiller's flat hand slapping the conference room table, his angry voice floating through the closed door, "Deputy Superintendent Benson from the Warner Creek prison is meeting with Sonny, Michelle, and Trooper Prince."

"About what? Doesn't sound friendly."

"It isn't. George Jones turns out to be an inmate of the Warner Creek prison. According to their records, he's still there."

Everybody in Lakeview knew she had a long term crush on the sheriff...except the sheriff, of course. Her voice softened when she asked, "What happened out there, Bud?"

"I'd be guessing, but I think Ortega's brother sent someone after Amanda Spears. We found a bomb under her vehicle, and somebody took some shots at us."

"Jones?"

"Probably." He paused a couple of seconds, and then asked, "Did Sonny and Michelle find any weapons on the guy?"

"Yes. A semi-automatic pistol."

He shrugged his shoulders and said, "Well, maybe we can find a slug and match the pistol to the one he was trying to shoot us with. You got anything else?"

"Yes. Deputy Hildebrand and Deputy Holcomb would like to speak with you."

He turned down the short hallway. "Later," he said and walked to his office. He stopped when he heard the murmur of voices behind his office door. He recognized the deep basso voice of Howard Finch, District Attorney and the higher pitched voice of Judge Lynch, elected official in charge of county administration.

Bud opened the door and the discussion stopped cold. The tension between Howard and Judge Lynch told Bud he was the subject of the conversation.

Dressed like the cowboy rancher he truly was, complete with polished Justin boots, Lynch was tall with wavy silver hair that managed to compliment a handsome, weathered face.

Bud suppressed a smile and nodded. "Good morning, Judge. Howard. What's going on?"

Howard was red in the face. "I'm 'disgusting' you with our esteemed asshole judge."

"Disgusting me? I see. About something I've done, no doubt," Bud said.

The Judge held up his hand and interrupted, "Now damn it, Howard. That's a crappy attitude. I know you are both elected officials, so I can't fire either one of you…except for malfeasance… but if we can't have a civil conversation, I sure as hell won't give you my endorsement for office come election time."

Howard retorted, "And you'll want us to support you when you run again?"

Bud growled, "Enough! What the hell is going on?" He leaned against the wall and crossed his arms, staring hard at both of them.

Lynch harrumphed and said, "Now understand I'm just the messenger. Certain citizens of the county have asked me to tell you they are wondering if it wouldn't be safer for all of us if you were to resign. You seem to attract the attention of some really bad people."

Bud turned red in the face, unconsciously balled his right fist and said, "You son-of-a-bitch." But he said it quietly, and it somehow seemed deadlier and more threatening than if he had shouted. "I think it would be a good idea if you got the hell out of my office. Now."

Lynch looked embarrassed, but he stood up to leave. He was taller than Bud by a couple of inches, but he knew he didn't have enough resolve to whip someone as coldly angry as the sheriff. Although for a split second, he did think about it.

Bud opened the door for Lynch, glaring as the Judge stomped through the door and down the hallway.

He controlled his temper enough to keep from slamming the door, but he couldn't resist smacking the cork board on the wall behind his desk. Bud shook his hand and said, "Damn it!"

He glared at the Lake County District Attorney. "Okay, Howard. Disgusting me? That's the best you can do?"

"Actually," Howard smiled, "I thought it was pretty good." And then he broke into a laugh that bounced his unruly mop of curly blond hair.

Bud smiled tightly and asked, "Who's behind this 'get the sheriff out of Dodge' business?"

"I honestly don't know. Everybody likes the job you've been doing. Nobody even ran against you in the last election."

"And to think a few short weeks ago, the city council, the county commissioners, and the whole town were treating me like a hero."

"Maybe they are just afraid now," Howard said. "I know I get nervous thinking about cartel messengers blowing things up. I don't have an armored office like you do."

Bud thought about it and then nodded slowly, thoughtfully. "I know. We all get a little spooked by the drug thugs, but I can't believe the people of this county would turn tail and run. I'd sure like to know who's behind this 'get rid of the sheriff and every thing will be all right' business.

"Well, let's go see what Sonny is raising so much fuss about."

The hunger for jobs in Lake County outbid the grumblings of the neighbors living closest to the site. In the few years of the prison's operational life, there had been no instances of escape or of other problems. And the citizens of the county had grown used to the sight of small crews of inmates working under the loose supervision of a Correctional Officer, cutting brush and cleaning litter from the roadsides and sprucing up BLM and Forest Service campgrounds.

A much-coveted annual project for prison crews was opening up the trails into the Gearhart Wilderness. And most citizens thought it was a good use of inmate time.

Hugh Benson, all five feet six inches of him, worked as the Deputy Superintendent at the Warner Creek Correctional Facility, a new prison built out in the rolling sage covered hills north and west of town. Locally it was known as the "pucker brush pen."

Benson was sitting behind the conference table, his back to the corner of the room. Psychologically, and physically, he was trapped by the lean, six-foot Sonny Sixkiller, Bud's undersheriff, and dark-haired Sergeant Michelle Trivoli, who, at nearly five-ten, came close to matching Bud's five-eleven. Both Lake County Deputies looked pissed off.

Sonny was leaning over Benson, one hand on the butt of his pistol, while Sergeant Trivoli blocked the other avenue of escape and had the look that earned her the nick name of Trigger True Shot. And Trooper Prince, big man that he was, sat like he always sat—knees lifting the table slightly—taking notes, making no effort to interfere with the actions of Sonny and Michelle.

As they opened the conference room door, Howard and Bud heard Sonny say, "And you lost him?"

Benson looked in the direction of Bud and Howard. "Sheriff," Benson started in, "am I glad to see you. Your officers seem to think I'm the enemy."

Bud frowned at Sonny and Michelle and they backed away. "Why don't we offer Hugh some coffee?"

Michelle blinked and then asked the Deputy Superintendent without a hint of warmth in her voice, "Black?"

Benson liked a little cream in his coffee, but he decided any peace offering was welcome. He looked warily at Michelle, but he nodded. "Black would be fine."

Sonny looked at Benson, shook his head and pulled a chair away from the table. He sat down, effectively blocking Benson's path to freedom.

Bud suddenly found the whole scene humorous. He moved down the side of the table and tapped Sonny on the shoulder. "Why don't you get some coffee and then come back." When Sonny had cleared the aisle between the table and the wall, Bud walked over and held out his hand to Hugh Benson who rose and shook hands with some relief.

Benson gave Bud a wry smile and said, "I thought maybe I was about to be served on a platter."

Trooper Prince chimed in. "I wouldn't say it was that serious, but you can see why we might be suspicious." He turned to Bud. "We ran his prints and it seems our George Jones is an inmate at Warner Creek. There he's known as Jésus Mendoza. In fact, the records show Jésus is incarcerated there right now. The problem with that is, of course, that the same Jésus, a.k.a. George Jones, is locked in your jail."

Howard Finch sputtered, "How the hell did that happen?"

Deputy Superintendent Benson said, "I don't know, but we'll be looking into it. I'll send two of my CO's to take him back to Warner Creek."

"Not until we sort this out, you won't," Bud snapped. "He seems to have escaped from your custody, equipped himself with a vehicle, bomb materials and a hand gun."

Lord, Benson thought to himself, *another hard-ass..* Aloud he said, "I can't tell you how that happened. I refuse to believe any of our CO's would help him escape."

Trooper Prince interjected, "Until we know how that happened, the Oregon State Police is asking the Sheriff of Lake County to hold him for the next 24 hours while we investigate. That will include a look at Warner Creek personnel. You can't have him."

District Attorney Howard Finch added, "In the meantime, Lake County is looking to charge him with attempted murder, bomb making, assaulting police officers, a felon in possession of a fire arm, attempting to elude police officers, and escape from custody."

Benson's cell phone rang just as and Sonny and Michelle opened the conference room door. Benson pulled his cell phone from his shirt pocket and glanced at the screen. "My office," he said and took the call.

The side of the conversation Bud and the others could hear was, "Judas! I can't believe that. I'll get with you." When Benson hung up, they were all staring at him. He took a deep breath and let it out with a heavy sigh. "It seems that one of our Correctional Officers left his station early this morning and hasn't been seen since. His wife called and wanted to know if he was working overtime this morning. He didn't come home last night."

State Police Trooper Charles Prince snapped his notebook shut, stood up and said, "Mr. Benson, we'll want whatever information you have about your correctional officer…name…photo…distinguishing marks…vital statistics…the vehicle he drives…the whole nine yards. I want a BOLO out on this guy within the next thirty minutes. Can you handle that?"

Benson nodded and said, "Yes. This is damned embarrassing. You'll have our full cooperation. I'll send the information to the sheriff electronically"

Benson scooted around the table and down the hallway.

Bud took the cup of coffee intended for Benson and sat down. "I'm a little punchy this morning…too much excitement and too little sleep…but the way I read it, someone bribes a guard. The guard lets 'George' out. George's job is to kill Amanda.

"That done, George goes back to the prison, the guard lets him back in, and George Jones becomes Jésus Mendoza again. What better alibi could you have than to be locked in prison? And the guard was probably thinking the guy just wanted drugs or a woman or was engaged in some lesser criminal activity, so why not? But George doesn't show back up at the appointed hour, and our missing guard panics and runs."

Bud looked at big Charlie Prince. "You mind if Sonny and Michelle go talk to this guy's wife?"

9:30 a.m. ~ Klamath Falls

FOR OVER TWO YEARS, MANFRED GILES had leased space in an industrial building, a long metal structure sheeted in green aluminum siding, trimmed in white and divided into individual units, each with an office, toilet, and a truck-size overhead door for access and delivery. Except for the address numbers or the business signs on the front of the units, they all looked the same. Manny's unit also had a rear overhead door so delivery trucks could drive into the building, unload and then drive forward to exit from the back door and return to the main street via the alley.

Hanging in the front window of Manny's unit was a cedar slab, maybe two feet by three feet in size. In carved relief, the warm grains of the varnished cedar carried a teepee, three horses grazing near a willow lined creek, and Mt. Shasta in the background. A lizard, a snake, a crow perched in the willows, a coyote stalked a mouse, a badger, a soaring eagle, and a fox lived in the edges of the carving. Most people who saw it fell in love immediately. It was simply stunning.

On one of his supply delivery runs to Bend, and for reasons he could never explain, Manny had stopped to look at the chainsaw carvings of salmon, bears and eagles on display in front of a small wooden workshop on Highway 97 in the town of Chemult. He hadn't purchased any of the carved figures sitting on stump pedestals.

Instead, he had spotted a dust-covered carving leaning against the wall just inside the door, and something in his drug-perverted soul told him he had to have it.

In an atypical fit of generosity that belied his normal atavistic behavior— meaning he didn't plan on stealing it—Manny actually paid the artist fifteen hundred dollars for the carving. He took it back to his leased office, hung it in the window and had gold letters painted on the glass half of the front door that declared the establishment as "Indian Art, Import and Export." What he really imported and exported, of course, was a variety of drugs centering primarily on marijuana, crack cocaine, and Ecstasy. But he took perverse pride in the carving.

Last night, after talking to the woman at the mini-mart, he had bolted for his "import-export" shop. Manny knew he had to keep the Mazda out of sight…at least for now. He breathed a deep sigh of relief when the shop's overhead door cranked down and closed behind him.

He popped the tab on a beer, smoked a joint and then tumbled onto the camp cot he kept in the office. Befuddled and slightly amazed at his fall, thinking of an earlier more innocent time when his whole family had camped and fished at Lake of the Woods, he drifted into a dream-wracked sleep.

9:45 a.m. ~ Christmas Valley Lodge

WALTER (WALLY) PIDGEON SAT AT THE counter drinking coffee, compliments of his friend Billie Thompson, chief cook and bottle washer as well as the owner of the Christmas Valley Lodge, an attractive stone-fronted, single story restaurant and bar with a modified A-frame dining room and lots of high windows.

Wally liked the short walk from his house for his morning coffee and conversation with Billie. The landscaping around the Lodge gave him some relief from the monotony of sage and rabbit brush and scattered juniper trees that filled the expanse of the old lake bed that now supported big circle irrigation systems, alfalfa hay fields, and cattle ranches. Except for the trees and evergreen shrubs around the Lodge and the motel next door, there wasn't a lot of vegetation in Christmas Valley.

Billie's cook had the day off, so Billie was in the kitchen frying bacon and pouring hot cakes on the grill for an older couple sitting at a corner table.

Californians, Wally figured, because the only car in the parking lot had California plates. *What a detective!* he mocked himself, and then wondered what brought them to Christmas Valley so late in the year.

Through the serving window, Wally could see Billie's movements, a kind of "chef's dance," a rhythmic pirouette of reach and turn, and then the slide of two warm plates of hot cakes and bacon onto the metal service bar in the window between the grill and the dining area. The warm smell of fried bacon made Wally's empty stomach growl.

Billie came through the kitchen door and down the aisle between the counter and the dish cupboard. She slid the plates off the service counter, perched one on her arm, balanced against the other plate in her hand, and grabbed the coffee pot before heading to serve her only paying customers.

Wally picked up Billie's copy of the *Bend Bulletin* and scanned the headlines, listening to the California couple ask Billie if she knew of any property for sale in Christmas Valley. He was half amused when they told Billie they were living in Ontario, California, and were sick of the population pressures, the buildup of racial tensions, and the asshole politicians running the state. He almost snorted when they described San Francisco and L.A. as the "Sodom and Gomorrah of the Left Coast."

Billie gave them a business card from the Christmas Valley Realty, and suggested they talk to Raymond. She started to turn away and then stopped. She asked, "Why Christmas Valley?"

The man laughed and said, "Well, the name is pretty, the web says you have a golf course and the town is unincorporated. That's three good reasons to look."

"And," the man's wife added, "winter is a darned good time to see if a place is livable. Besides, our son and his wife live in LaPine. We looked there, but something about the place just didn't feel right. So here we are. Looking."

Billie smiled, set the coffee pot on a nearby table and held out her hand to the man. "Billie Thompson. I'm the chief cook and bottle washer, bartender, swamper, and owner of the Lodge. Rocky, my chef, is off today, so I'm it."

"Stan Snyder, and this is my wife Lucille."

"Well, nice to meet you. If you decide to settle here, the first dinner is on me," Billie said, shaking hands with each of them.

Wally shook his head and marveled at his own decision to live in Christmas Valley. He didn't play golf, but his reasons for living there were nearly identical to those of the Snyder's. Nearly.

His reverie was interrupted by the crunch of tires on gravel and the low rumble of a diesel engine. He turned and watched a white Lake County pickup with a Sheriff's decal back into a parking spot near the walkway leading to the front door of the Lodge. One of his all time favorite people, Deputy Larae Holcomb, now last name Bernard, stepped out of the passenger side door, straightened her uniform, slammed the door and joined her partner, wide-bodied Deputy Roger Hildebrand, who was headed down the walk to the Lodge.

Wally's feeling about Larae's marriage to John Bernard, retired special agent for NCIS, were somewhat ambivalent, but when the two of them had announced the purchase of a small ranch between Fort Rock and Christmas Valley the previous Fall, he felt better. At least she would be staying in the area.

A hint of a smile flickered on Larae's face when she pushed the door open and saw Wally grinning at her from the counter. "You old reprobate. How are you doing today?" she managed.

"I'm fine. And how are North County's finest today?"

Roger Hildebrand eased his stocky frame on a red vinyl stool. "Damned frustrated this morning, Wally. Someone tried to kill Amanda Spears and Bud last night. Another damned bomb again. Sons-a-bitches!"

"So tell me," Wally ordered.

Larae looked at the California couple staring in interest at Roger's none-too-discreet cussing, and then nodded in the direction of the empty bar. "Let's go in there."

When they finished the tale, Wally looked at Larae and said, "I need to talk to your husband."

"Why?"

"Well, actually, I need to talk to 'Gar,' not John Bernard. We need to conference about this drug cartel."

"He's retired, Wally," she said sharply.

"Well...a retired race horse is still a race horse. You can't take that out of them. And Gar is still Special Forces, retired or not." He paused, looked at Roger, "Just like our friend Deputy Hildebrand. Right, Roger?"

Roger stared daggers at the old man and finally, reluctantly nodded. He asked "What would you know about that, Wally?"

Wally stared past them out through the back sliders that gave way to a cold, snow-dusted patio. "Once, when I wasn't quite this old, I worked in law enforcement in Southern Arizona. Loved that part of the world. Still do."

Larae was amazed at the transformation. Wally suddenly wasn't the charming old coot who teased and kidded and called her "Sweet Mama." He was articulate, focused and deadly serious.

"Grew up in Sedona when it was still a backwater. Graduated and moved to Tempe to attend college. Fell for Gwynn, lovely young woman. And got hooked on the study of criminology. Graduated fairly high in my class. But mainly, I think, because I spoke the Spanish my Grandmother taught me as I was growing up, I found myself much in demand. CIA, FBI, Arizona highway, Coast Guard, military intelligence, and I don't remember who else.

"I thought about it a lot, and finally decided I liked the mission of the DEA a lot better than what the others were doing. And the job promised to keep me closer to home. Which it did...at first. Gwynn and I had a baby girl, bought a nice adobe hsouse in Tucson. Socialized. Lived the good life.

"And then I went undercover in Mexico as 'Guillermo Peña.' Three months turned into six which turned into a year, which turned into a lot of nights in the Ruby Hotel cantina. When I finally got home, my house was empty; Gwynn had filed for divorce and moved herself and my daughter back to Minnesota. I saw my daughter at her high school graduation, and at her commencement from the University of Wisconsin where I discovered I had sired a damned communist. That was eighteen years ago.

"Anyway, I went back undercover, lived in the American Community in Guaymas, and frankly got rich off the drug lords while I ratted them out to the DEA. I was pretty cynical about the whole thing.

"And then I was called on to testify as Guillermo Peña against one of the Ortega brothers. And of course the Ortegas paid some young thugs who were supposed to kill me. I was better than they were that day, but it put a bee in the DEA's bonnet, and as soon as the trial was over, I was whisked away to a safe house.

"I was offered witness protection, refused, and looked for a place to retire. The words Christmas Valley sounded very nice. I came, I saw, I settled."

Larae shook her head. "That explains your comment about me being a pro when I pinned Cowboy's arms during that bar ruckus a while back. You almost gave yourself away, didn't you?"

"A slip up on my part," Wally admitted.

"And now you want my just-retired, small-rancher husband for some kind of move against the Ortega Cartel. Is that right?"

"No. I don't want your rancher husband. I want that Special Forces guy who goes by strange names like "Gar" or "Stone Fly."

But really, I just need him for his NCIS contacts. I can arrange the rest."

Both Roger and Larae stared at Wally like they were seeing him for the first time.

Wally waited until the two police officers finished their coffee and headed back outside to their county vehicle. When they had driven safely out of sight, Wally zipped up his dark blue down jacket and said, "I'll be back later, Billie. Thanks for the coffee."

Billie frowned. "Thanks for the coffee?" she said aloud. She looked at the California couple and said, "Something's going on. He never says thanks."

The husband asked, "Does he come in here often?"

Billie laughed and said, "Almost every morning. Drinks my coffee, teases my few breakfast customers, tell stories, and threatens to buy me some really good coffee beans."

"And he never pays?" Lucille asked.

"No. Not directly. Says he pays by gracing me with his good company or some such prattle."

The husband said, "It sounds like you are good friends."

Billie nodded, "I'd miss him if he didn't come in each morning. You know, if I really needed help, I know I could count on him." She shook off some fleeting sense that her time with Wally was about to change. "Besides, some mornings he's my only customer." She chuckled, but the notion that all was not right in her world wasn't easy to dismiss.

"The big guy, the deputy, mentioned a bomb and said 'again.'"

Billie rinsed the cups and the pie plate and slotted them into the dishwasher.

"You may have read about that in the papers or seen it on TV. Some terrorists were smuggling explosives through the county in a hay truck. Larae's husband got wind of it, shot the tires off the truck, and then Roger Hildebrand, that's Deputy Hildebrand, our Undersheriff Sonny Sixkiller, Deputy Larae Holcomb, and a state trooper whose name I can't remember, caught up with them…some Arab guys. There was a gun fight.

"The state trooper was shot. The word is his vest saved him, but he lost his spleen.

"Anyway, the terrorists set off the explosives. Larae had her ankle broken and was cut pretty bad by some by rock chips. A big chunk of rock smacked Sonny, another officer on the head, and the explosion knocked Roger for a loop.

"When they came to, there wasn't much left of the truck. And the terrorists had been blown to smithereens. End of story."

The wife looked pointedly at her husband before she asked, "And does this kind of thing happen often?"

Billie could see where the woman was going. "No," she said, "I've been here sixteen years and we've never had any problems like this. Drunk driving, maybe. Family quarrels. Hippy dope smokers. Stuff like that, but no major crime. I don't even lock my front door."

"What about last night?"

Billie shook her head. "First I've heard about it."

There was a hint of disgust in the man's voice when he said, "Hell. I don't know where to go. This place sounds a lot like where we're living. Drugs, guns, human slaughter."

Billie nodded. "But at least here we know our neighbors and we all have guns. Besides, we catch our bad guys. Well…the Good Lord does, at any rate."

Wally's short walk home west from the Lodge took less than a minute, just long enough to remind him to wear a cap next time. His thinning hair just wasn't the warm comfort it once was. He locked the front door behind him, probably for the first time in over a month, walked through the living room and down a short hall to the mudroom off the garage.

His gun safe was a large, five-hundred-pound model with a heavy door and a keypad combination lock. The safe was attached to the floor by four three-quarter-inch concrete anchor bolts that had been driven into epoxy-laden bolt holes. It could be moved, but only with a cutting torch, cables and pulleys, and not easily at that.

He tapped in his personal code, pushed down on the handle and pulled. The well-oiled door swung out and Wally was in business.

A smaller safe sat on the bottom of the gun safe. Wally worked the combination and opened it. Neatly bundled stacks of fifty-dollar-bills, each worth $500 filled the safe. Wally hadn't counted it for quite a while, but he knew his ready-cash reserves were close to one hundred thousand dollars…just in this one hidey-hole. His other "reserves" were in a safe deposit box in a Sedona, Arizona bank.

His nest egg savings were also in an open account in Sedona. Each month he wrote a draft against his Sedona checking account and deposited it in the little Jefferson State bank in LaPine. The cartel might watch the Sedona bank, but unless they bought someone off, they couldn't trace the draft to Oregon.

He took twenty bundles of cash and put them in a small carryall, and then from a half-dozen pistols hanging on pegs at the back of the gun safe, he selected a dull-finished, black 9mm Beretta and four clips, each of which held fifteen rounds. He hand-fed rounds into a fifth clip, slapped it home, worked the slide and chambered a round. He ejected the clip and added a fresh round to the clip before reseating it. The pistol went into a black nylon holster and then followed the money into the carryall. He looked longingly at the 10 gauge shotgun, but knew he could never smuggle that into Mexico.

11:00 a.m. ~ Dog Lake

AFTER BUD LEFT FOR TOWN, AMANDA spent the morning looking through his bookcase, trying to become better acquainted with this man she found so attractive. She was surprised by the half-dozen volumes of western philosophy, a well thumbed "Collected Works of William Shakespeare," a book of Robert Frost's poems, several contemporary novels. The numerous CDs were an eclectic assortment of jazz, including a lot of old Dave Brubeck and Miles Davis, a few country western, heavy on George Strait, and heavy on groups from the seventies and beyond, groups like the Eagles and Chicago.

Coupled with Bud's numerous wildlife pictures, mounted and hung on nearly all of the flat surfaces in the cabin, including the sloping ceiling of the bedroom in the loft, her mental picture of Bud changed from someone good at law enforcement to one of someone who would be good at anything he set his mind to. She was especially drawn to one photo of a mother beaver and her baby sleeping on a sunny rock in the middle of the Rogue River. That earned a smile, and on impulse she grabbed one of Bud's jackets from a hook near the door and said to Molly, "Let's go see the lake."

Amanda's selection of a ring tone sounded like the opening phrase of Beethoven's Fifth Symphony. It rang a "bah-bah-bah-boom" just as she and Molly neared the cabin after a leisurely walk past the boat ramp and around the point. She ignored the call…and the caller. *Leave me alone*, she thought.

Amanda's binoculars hung from a strap, and she lifted them to focus on a late formation of forty or fifty southbound geese as they fled across the slate gray sky, their calls to each other somehow encouraging and mournful at the same time. She stood perfectly still, watching the beat of their wings and listened for each new call. And somehow, in some unknowable way, the lake, the geese and the solitude calmed her soul.

The V formation of the big Canada honkers wasn't perfect, but darned near, and as she watched, a big, strong goose relieved the leader and became the apex of the formation. She watched in quiet fascination until they had flown over the ridges and out of her sight, and then put her binoculars down and looked for Molly. She spotted the little black Lab, nose to the ground, tail wagging, hunting the willows along the shore. A breeze ruffled the surface of the lake, and Amanda shivered even though she wasn't really cold.

"Molly," she called. "Let's go in."

Muffled by her pack, the phone's "bah-bah-bah-boom" vied with Molly for Amanda's attention as she shut the cabin door. The heat from the wood stove felt good, and she held her hands out to it. The phone stopped ringing and then after a short pause started in again. She dug the phone from her pack and then sighed when she recognized the number. It stopped ringing and she was about to put it away when it started in again.

She answered, "Hello?"

A familiar voice pounced. "Amanda, where the hell have you been? Are you okay? Why don't you answer your phone!"

"Well, Denny, I'm fine. Thanks for asking. And how are you? And I might add, in case you've forgotten, I don't work for you any more."

"Not true, Amanda. I'm sitting here in Springdale looking at your letter of resignation. Nice try, but it was never processed. Haven't you checked your bank account recently? You're still on the payroll."

"What do you mean, it was never processed?"

"The SAC told me to just sit on it. So we put you on paid administrative leave, and now we want you to come back in. We heard about the bomb."

"No," she said. "I won't. I did resign whether you processed it or not. And the Ortega's think I'm dead now...because of the bomb. I'm safer here than I would be with you." *And I think I'm in love.*

Dennis Moore, Assistant Special Agent in Charge, all six-feet four inches of him, felt an unfamiliar degree of frustration. He ran a hand through his curly dark hair, a head of hair the women in the NCIS office admired and envied, as it registered with him that someone had the grit to defy a direct order.

"Amanda," he said, "you are still an NCIS agent, like it or not. When Thompson heard about the bomb, he said to get you back in here. He wants to plan an operation for NCIS to put an end to the Ortega Cartel." He paused, took a deep breath and said the magic words. "We need you."

10:30 a.m. ~ *Klamath Falls*

AFTER INTERVIEWING LACEY AND LACEY'S PARENTS, Detective Mathew Harmon and Officer Christine Downing spent the next hour getting Manfred Giles' DMV photo attached to the BOLO sent out during the night, and then resent the amended version. The DMV photo was also blown up and glossy prints given to each officer in the KFPD along with the BOLO.

That done, they headed to the Sky Lakes Medical Center to check on the condition of Mariah's mother and on the condition of the injured man brought in during the wee hours of the morning.

The nice volunteer at the "Check-In-Here" counter refused to tell them anything about either Barbara Caldwell or Tyson James, citing orders "from the police," until Mathew produced his badge wallet. That accomplished wonders, and in addition to directions to the ICU where both victims were cared for, the suddenly nice lady offered to get them coffee "from the nurses' break room. Really good coffee."

Officer Downing smiled and said, "No. We're fine, thank you."

As they walked down the hallway, Christine smiled and said, "I felt like patting her on the head. Do you do that to all the girls?"

"What are you talking about?"

"She turned into a puppy dog once you showed her your badge. I just wondered if all of your girls behave that way?"

He pursed his lip and frowned. "There are no *girls* in my life right now. So drop it."

She didn't let him see how smug she felt, but she failed to prevent a self congratulatory thought. *I really am a good interviewer, aren't I?*

The uniformed policeman sitting in a chair in the hallway appeared glad to have something, anything to break the monotony of baby-sitting the ICU. He recognized Harmon and Downing when they turned the corner and headed his direction. He stood up and was suddenly aware that he desperately needed to use the bathroom.

"Boy, am I glad to see you guys. I've had to pee for an hour. I'll be right back."

Harmon grinned and said, "Have at it, Ken. We'll hold the fort until you get back." He shook his head and looked at Officer Downing. "You ever do any stake out?"

She shook her head, "No."

"I have, and it's monotonous, tedious work. I find that if I know how long I'm going to have to wait for something, I'm okay. But if I don't have an end time, it's almost painful. And one of the worst things is being afraid to take time out for bathroom breaks."

Officer Downing nodded and then looked back down the hallway over Harmon's shoulder. "Don't look now, but I think we have trouble coming this way."

Harmon didn't react except to let his arm slip slowly to his side, hand close to his pistol. "What do you see?"

"A man, Caucasian, about 25 or so, six feet tall maybe. He's wearing a hooded windbreaker, clean shaven, but lots of acne. Has his right hand in his pocket. Weapon, maybe? I can't tell."

"Okay, Officer Downing, we're going to separate. You move to the right slowly, and lean against the wall. I'm going to turn and confront this guy." He noticed a slight tremble in her hands. "You ready?"

She nodded and moved to the wall. When the man was about twenty feet away, Harmon turned, gun drawn and shouted, "Police! Hands in the air! Get your hands in the air." Before he could repeat his order, Officer Downing, gun pointed at the startled man's midsection, closed in, kicked him rudely behind the knee and had him pinned to the floor with a knee in his back. She put her pistol against the back of his head and shouted, "Freeze, sucker!"

An amazed Harmon holstered his pistol and pulled the man's arms behind him to snap stainless steel handcuffs on the man. When he pulled the man's right arm out from under the man's chest, a small pistol went skittering across the tile floor. "Shit," Officer Downing muttered. She ran to a nurse's station, grabbed a latex glove from the box on the counter and scooped up the pistol.

By the time the uniformed officer came back out of the bathroom, it was all over but the shouting. Harmon said, "I want you to call for two officers and a unit to take this guy in. ASAP."

The officer nodded and started speaking into his lapel mike. "And, Harmon continued, "I want to double the guards here. One ain't gonna cut it." He grinned at a still breathless Downing, blond hair awry for the first time that day, and said, "Cause a man's gotta do what a man's gotta do. Or is that 'A woman's gotta do what a woman's gotta do?'"

She was still shaking slightly from the adrenalin rush when he put his hand out and said, "Nice work partner, but maybe a tad reckless, don't you think?"

She shook her head. "No. I knew you'd shoot the bastard if he tried anything."

"Listen, pardner, I can't hit the broadside of a barn with a pistol. I'm an okay rifle shot, but up close I prefer shotguns."

She started to say, "I can teach…" but when she saw the corners of his mouth tugged by a stifled grin, she stopped and simply shook her head. And then she remembered Harmon winning the Department's Pistol shoot last year.

Before two burly uniformed officers hustled the would-be assailant down the hallway, and out to a waiting Crown Vic, Harmon said, "Tell the Lieutenant we'll be in shortly to question this guy."

Dick Savage, the senior officer, and a man Harmon knew from his days in uniform said, "You sure get around."

Detective Harmon just shrugged and pointed to his smaller, blond, female partner. "She did it."

Reassurances were given to a worried medical staff that the guard would be doubled and maintained around the clock until either Barbara Caldwell was released or her boyfriend was caught.

Harmon found himself saying to a circle of doctors and nurses, "We know who the perpetrator is. We know he's still in town someplace, and every officer in the city, the county and our local State Troopers know what he looks like. I believe it is a matter of only a few hours before we apprehend him."

A young female doctor grumbled, "But *we* don't know what he looks like."

"Wow," Harmon said in a quiet aside to Christine, "How did we miss that?"

Officer Downing reached into her small handbag and took a folded BOLO from a side pocket. "Can one of you copy this?"

An eager nurse, a muscular man an inch taller that Harmon's six-feet-one, practically snatched it from her hand and said, "Can do."

The floor supervisor, a severe looking RN about forty-five years old said to her medical staff, "Okay. We'll get the photo to each of you. Let's get back to work."

She looked at the two police officers with something like disapproval on her face and then relaxed enough to smile. "Dangerous times, officers. Dangerous times. Now then. How may I be of assistance?"

When they asked about Tyson James, she told them, "He's still in a coma, but his vital signs are strong. The doctor believes he'll live. The only question is the amount of brain damage he might have suffered."

They also learned Barbara Caldwell was sleeping. She was described as being in a guarded condition. "She has the look of a heavy meth user," the floor supervisor said. "One side effect of meth addiction, other than death of course, can be a stroke. We are in a 'wait and see' posture right now."

"I was told she was conscious," Harmon said.

"She was awake for a short period of time, but her speech was incoherent."

"Well crap," Harmon said. He pulled a business card from his shirt pocket and said, "If she wakes up, please let us know. We are trying to find her daughter, and I'm hoping she might tell us where to start looking."

"Will do."

On their way back to the station, Harmon said, without taking his eyes off the road, "Nice job, Christine. This partnership might just work out. You smile and seduce the bad guys, I'll hold them at gunpoint, and then you kick the shit out of them." He paused before adding, "Where did you learn that stuff? You know, that kick 'em behind the knee stuff? At the academy?"

She glanced at him, struck again by how good looking he was, and said, "I told you my mother is an English teacher. But I didn't tell you Dad is also a teacher. He teaches chemistry, and coaches wrestling. But his true passion is martial arts. He's been teaching me self-defense moves since I was in kindergarten."

"And 'freeze, sucker?'"

Christine shrugged. "I always wanted to use that line. I get a kick out of watching cop shows."

Detective Harmon just gave her a nod and signaled a left turn into the station, but he had definitely filed her information away for future reference.

9:30 a.m. ~ Lakeview

THE INTERVIEW WITH JÉSUS MENDOZA, A.K.A. George Jones, went like Bud thought it would. Jésus refused an attorney, but he also refused to answer any questions put to him. Bud watched through the one-way window as his undersheriff, Sonny Sixkiller, an expert interviewer, and Trooper Charlie Prince took turns. Each cajoled, threatened, promised protection, promised mayhem, offered Jésus coffee, a reduced sentence, or a one-way ticket to Mexico without any results.

For over an hour, Jésus refused to say anything…either "yes" or "no" or "kiss my ass." He just stared at the two police officers without expression. He didn't even shake his head or nod. The bruises around his eyes from the impact of the airbag deployment partially hid the little teardrop tattoo near the corner of his left eye.

Bud noticed the first tiny flicker of emotion when Sonny told him the DA would be prosecuting him for murder. Sonny was standing behind Jésus when he said, "We have enough residue from the bomb and enough fertilizer residue from the steering wheel, transferred there by your hands, to make it stick. You killed a federal officer. That means you get the needle.

"Now maybe, just maybe we can get you a better deal if you work with us. Tell us who hired you, who you called on your cell phone, where you got the gun, the fertilizer, the detonator. We know you didn't get those things from prison."

A thin smile flickered on Jésus' face and then died. He couldn't keep from saying, "Are you sure?"

Trooper Prince tried a different tack. "How much did you pay the guard to turn you loose?"

Bud finally grew tired of the game and walked down the short hall to the interview room door. He knocked and pushed the door open. Without preamble, he said, "Jésus, I've had it. Talk or don't talk, I don't care, but we *are* going to ship you to the state pen in Pendleton. You will be housed with criminals doing hard time. And we will tell them you ratted out the Ortega Cartel to save your hide.

"That will give you a life expectancy of about twenty-four to forty-eight hours, after which the State of Oregon will box your remains and ship them to your family...if your family is still alive. Otherwise, it's into the furnace with you."

A bead of sweat broke on the little killer's forehead, ran between his eyes and dripped from the end of his nose. And for the first time he swallowed...hard. Bud pushed a bottle of water across the table. "Drink," he ordered.

In perfect, unaccented English, Jésus said, "You don't understand. If I talk they will kill me anyway and then kill my family just to make sure I didn't tell them any thing. These *ombres* are *muy malo*, very bad people."

Sonny said, "Looks like we're the only chance you got. Think about it. We'll be back."

And with that the three officers left the interview room and locked the door.

Trooper Prince said, "You think he'll cooperate?"

Sonny nodded. "He's trapped. The only deal he can make to stay alive is with us."

"Yeah," Bud said, "but he didn't kill anyone. He just *tried* to kill us."

Sonny gave Bud a tight smile and said, "He doesn't need to know that just yet. As long as he thinks he killed Amanda, he'll cooperate."

"What happens when Ortega sends him an attorney?" Charlie asked.

Bud slapped the big man on the shoulder and said, "We'll cross that bridge when we get there. In the meantime, I'm going to let you two milk him for what you can get…before the FBI gets here."

"Think they will?"

"I know it. Bombs and bomb makers get the FBI all excited. Dutch Vanderlin, the Portland SAC, called. They are flying two agents down here this afternoon. ETA 1400. You have until then to break this guy. After that he belongs to the FBI. So get to work. While you're doing that, I'm going to run some groceries out to Amanda. I'll be back as soon as I can."

Sonny shook his head. He didn't like the idea of the boss being gone at a critical time like this, but once Bud made up his mind about something, he could be stubborn as hell. So Sonny settled for a terse, "Use the lights, Boss, and get back as quick as you can."

Bud pulled into the cabin's driveway, just in time to see Amanda loading Molly into the back of her 4-Runner.

He pulled up beside her and powered the window down. "You going someplace?"

"Hi, Bud. Yes, I find that I'm still an NCIS agent. SAC Thompson didn't process my resignation. Just put me on paid administrative leave. They are planning an NCIS operation to put the Ortega Cartel out of business. So…I was going to drop Molly at the station, and head for Silverdale.

"When I left, I paid six months in advance on my little house, so I'll just move back in and go to back to work."

"Okay. Well, dang…or maybe congratulations or something like that. Let me put my groceries away and you can follow me back in."

Molly hopped out of Amanda's vehicle and followed Bud into the cabin, tail wagging while he put perishables in the fridge and the steaks in the freezer compartment. He looked at Molly and said, "Well, old gal, let's get back to town."

Amanda waited while he locked the cabin, and then opened the pickup door so Molly could hop in.

He held out his hand to Amanda and said, "Well, good luck and keep in touch."

On a sudden impulse she ignored the hand, gave him a hug that lasted too long, but maybe not long enough, and kissed his stubbled cheek.

Bud was startled, and, he would admit to himself when it was too late to do anything about it, disturbed by his impulse to return the kiss. Instead he simply released her and turned away before she could read the emotion in his eyes.

Amanda cussed NCIS almost all the way back to town. She had some notions about her stay at Bud's cabin that would just have to wait, and she had a fleeting sense of a missed opportunity she hoped she wouldn't live to regret.

"Damned career," she muttered under her breath, as Bud's pickup, emergency lights flashing, pulled further and further ahead of her and then was gone.

The first snow of the year in the Goose Lake Valley dusted the landscape, pelting her windshield with hard granules of dry snow. By the time she reached Five Corners on the main highway a couple of miles west of Lakeview a strong wind was blowing snow in a nearly horizontal line, and visibility was down to less than a hundred yards. She turned the defroster on and increased the fan volume. Then she asked her OnStar system for directions to Silverdale, Washington. OnStar told her to proceed west on Highway 140 to Klamath Falls.

A strong gust of wind spooked her when it rocked her 4-Runner, and she began to rethink her decision. "Wouldn't it be better to outwait the storm?" she wondered. "My snow driving skills are non-existent. In fact, this is the most snow I've ever driven on." On impulse she turned east and drove slowly down the highway in the direction of Lakeview. "I'll find a motel for the night," she told herself, but apart from her fear of the storm, she knew Bud Blair was a bigger draw than NCIS in Silverdale.

12:30 p.m. ~ Westside

MARIAH OCCUPIED HERSELF WITH MINOR HOUSE-KEEPING chores, boiling water for tea, heating a small can of beef stew, and doing her best to make sure she left no telltales that she was ever in the trailer. Her paranoia was such that she took a paper towel from the roll over the sink and wiped all the surfaces clean to remove her fingerprints.

She didn't know what she was going to do next, but she knew she wasn't going back to live in the same house as Manny. "Never again. I'll kill him first," she told herself. "Wait until he's asleep and smack him with a baseball bat.

Yeah, and then go to jail. No. It's just better to keep away. Babs is on her own."

In spite of her self-lecture, she yearned for an earlier time when her mother curled up with her in bed and read her stories. Mariah remembered her mother's wet hair and the scent of shampoo, and her soothing voice as she worked through volumes of Dr. Seuss. And then the tears came again.

"Won't do any good," she said aloud, but her deep sorrow was too much to bear and so she climbed onto the bed in the overshot and sobbed into the pillow until she was emotionally spent.

Ears, keener than human ears, detected the faint sobbing coming from the pole barn. Bea's old mama cat, curiosity aroused by something more interesting that the idle hunt for mice in the pasture or in hay stacks, stalked her way through the first dusting of snow, under the fence and across the pasture, her two white stocking feet in syncopated rhythm with her black rear paws. When she heard Mariah lecturing herself to "Be brave, girl, be brave," the old cat hopped up on the first step of the fifth wheel and meowed.

At first Mariah didn't hear the mewing over the racket of the wind rattling the metal roof of the pole barn, so the cat increased the volume to a more insistent mewl...almost, but not quite a screech.

Mariah stopped and listened and when the black meowed again, she slipped off the bed and walked to the door. Again the cat meowed and Mariah cautiously opened the trailer door.

A saucy black wraith hopped up the next two steps and into the trailer, a soft swirl of dry snow trailing behind. While the cat rubbed against her legs, Mariah closed the door and said, "What a nice kitty. Where did you come from?" And then she picked up the cat and cradled it in her arms, brushing the dry snow from her fur. When the cat started purring, Mariah sat at the breakfast table and petted, and petted the old cat...who seemed quite content with the whole arrangement. And Mariah was comforted and grieving all at the same time.

The cat licked up the scraps of tuna Mariah spooned into a saucer and then curled up on the padded bench at the breakfast nook beside her new friend, groomed her chops and went to sleep. She didn't want to disturb the cat, so Mariah sat at the breakfast table and read the Lake County News again, liking the flavor of the paper and the culture it reflected without really understanding why it appealed.

She tried working the crossword puzzle, but she just didn't know enough words to succeed, so she turned to the SUDOKU puzzle. In school she had discovered a knack for numbers, and although it took her most of an hour to work out the combinations of numbers in the puzzle, she was pleased with herself when she finished.

An hour after the cat came calling, Bea's pickup turned down the drive and pulled up to the house. The wind had dropped to a breeze and the snow was falling in a more vertical line. There was maybe three inches of the white stuff on the ground.

Mariah waited until she heard the slam of a screen door and when she was satisfied no one would notice, she reluctantly and gently shooed the cat out of the trailer.

The old mama cat hopped down the steps and then just sat there looking back up at the door as if to say, "What is this about?" When she was satisfied the door wasn't going to open again anytime soon, the cat jumped up on a big bale of hay and curled into a ball. She was still there when Bea Johnson's grandchildren, Colleen and Cody, stepped off the bus and let the snow-laden wind push them up the driveway.

A bell tone told Mariah a text message was coming in. Lacey's message asked, Where are you?

Near Lakeview, I think.

What if my Mom came to get you?

She hesitated before sending, No. Watch the papers. If the cops get Manny...Manfred Giles...I'll come home. How's my mom?

Don't know.

Mariah thumbed in, Can you find out?

I'll have to ask my Dad. He's sending Mom and me to Arizona until your mom's friend is caught.

Ask him, please.

Officer Christine Downing's cell rang, and when she answered the call, Lacey's mom said, "Officer Downing?"

"Yes."

"This is Eleanor Largent, Lacey's mother. She just told me she had another text from Mariah. Mariah said that if you catch somebody... let me look...a Manfred Giles...then she'll come home." She paused before adding, "You know, that girl must be terrified of this man."

"Yes, I think she is," Christine said. "She thinks she saw this Giles character murder someone."

"Thinks? As in she didn't really see what she thought she saw?"

Christine took a deep breath, knowing she shouldn't be sharing anything with Eleanor Largent, but also knowing Lacey was her only and somewhat tenuous link to Mariah. "I believe she actually saw her mother's live-in boyfriend beating on another man. And it seems obvious she thought the man had been killed by Giles. That's why she ran. She must have thought she would be next."

"I see, but you are telling me the man who was beaten didn't die?"

"That's right."

"Why don't you tell Mariah that?"

"Okay. I don't think it will make her any safer, but if you give me her number…"

When a text message came in from someone named Christine, Mariah felt a sense of panic and shut her phone off. She had never given her number to Manny, but she didn't trust him. For all she knew, this Christine person was one of his friends. "How in the world did she get my number?" she whispered.

2:00 p.m. ~ Klamath Fall Police Station

THE INTERVIEW WITH THE INEPT GUNMAN they apprehended at the hospital lasted almost an hour. Mathew watched Lionel Hays, the pimple-faced nineteen-year-old warm up to Christine, caught his partner's eye and said, "Go ahead. I'll be right back."

He went to the observation room and watched through the one-way glass as she brought Lionel to a place where it was important that she like him. So he tried to impress here with his cooperation.

At one point she said, "Lionel, you know what you were hired to do was wrong."

Sheepishly he nodded, "Yeah, I knew it was wrong. I been to church before. But I needed a fix and this dude, he offered me a bunch a money and some weed to whack this other dude. Said the guy was gonna die anyway. Just wanted to hurry him along before he could blab about the business."

"So that made it okay to kill him?"

"Yeah, well," Lionel whined, "I mean if he was going to die anyway, what's the harm?"

Christine shot Mathew a glance through the glass that conveyed disgust and a degree of incredulity. She shook her head and said, "Lionel, you know better than that, but it helps that you are coming clean with us. Now, where did you get the gun?"

At the end of the hour, Lionel had identified the photo of a known drug dealer from the KFPD photo files, had signed a confession that he had been hired to shoot the still unconscious Tyson James, and had been rewarded with an "Atta Boy" from Christine.

A uniformed officer led Lionel back to a cell block while Christine conferred with Mathew. "How did you do that?" he asked.

"Do what?"

"Well, earlier you kicked his ass. And then before I can get zeroed in on Lionel, you have him eating out of your hand."

"Yeah, I know. It's just a girl thing."

He shook his head and said, "Bullshit. You are a damned fine interrogator, is what it is."

"Enough, already. That was one disgusting piece of humanity. How in the hell do they get that way? I feel like I need to go home and take a shower."

Detective Harmon shook his head. "Not until we notify the dispatcher to have Lionel's contact picked up. And we need to talk to this Gordon Tusk fellow."

The light was fading from the evening sky before they found Gordon Tusk's driveway. The snow was busy filling in the ruts, but it looked like someone had recently plowed the steep road up to the bench where Tusk's house perched with a view of the Sprague River, a winter view of bare limbs and dead looking willows. A sixty-foot cottonwood stood sentinel over a snow covered gravel bar created by floods and a bend in the small river.

Tusk was at the sink, peeling potatoes and slicing them into chunks ready for the stew pot when he heard the car pull up the hill. The detective had called earlier, so his arrival was expected. Lucifer was sleeping on a worn Navajo blanket along side the cast iron stove.

The slam of car doors woke the big dog and when Harmon knocked on the door, the dog growled, the hair on the back of his neck standing up. Tusk said, "*Sentara.*" The dog just looked up. Gordon laughed and patted the dog on the head. "Sit, you dumb brute. Sit." The dog sat, but was mildly confused. That was twice in the last eighteen hours he'd told to stop doing what he was trained to do.

Tusk opened the door and said, "Come on in."

Detective Harmon stood on the rug inside the door and brushed the snow flakes from his jacket. He showed Tusk his badge and introduced his partner as Detective Downing. She was surprised at her "promotion" but understood the importance of status when working with men…especially Indian men who, for all their bluster about Indian rights, mostly treated their wives like shit. At least in her experience.

Tusk sat coffee cups on an island serving counter, poured fresh coffee, pulled two stools up to the bar, and then asked, "Cream?"

They both declined.

Officer Downing was surprised by the neatness of Tusk's multipurpose living, dining and kitchen area. She was also slightly embarrassed by her subconscious expectations of Indians in general and Klamath and Modoc Indians in particular.

There wasn't one feminine touch to the room, but no woman in Downing's world could have done a better job of decorating. The artwork hanging on the walls, small, expensively framed prints by Bev Doolittle, Judy Larson, Gerald Farm, J.C. Smith, and some others she didn't recognize, was arranged in aesthetically pleasing groups, each group lit by expensive table lamps. The couch and the only recliner were upholstered in thick reddish brown leather.

She thought the coffee table, a slice of a big knotty burl, varnished, perched on four polished juniper limbs was a bit funky. And then she bumped into another of her subconscious biases, that inborn disdain women have of the housekeeping and the house decorating skill of bachelors.

She glanced at Tusk and involuntarily said, "This is nice."

Tusk grinned. "For an Indian?"

She caught herself in time to say, "For a bachelor. I don't know any bachelor who keeps his place as neat as this. Or decorates as well."

Tusk smiled and then laughed. "Well, since I quit boozing and using, I have time for the more sensitive pursuits."

Harmon turned on the stool and looked at the big dog. "That's one hell of an animal. Wow. I see the German shepherd in him. And I'm thinking wolf." He turned back to Tusk. "Right?"

"Good eye," Tusk answered.

Mathew got up off the stool and looked from Tusk to the dog. "You mind?"

Tusk said, "I don't care, but he's liable to take your hand off. And he only understands Spanish commands."

Mathew looked at Tusk and then back at the dog. "*Surgir,*" he said, and patted his knee. The dog looked expectantly at Tusk who said, "Go ahead, dog."

The big animal looked back at Mathew, and when the detective said, in English, "Come on, boy," the dog stood up, and tail wagged across the room. He lowered his head and pushed his shoulder against Mathew's leg. Not his leg really, his hip bone. The dog was that tall.

Christine, who was deathly afraid of dogs, watched with a high degree of anxiety and held her breath. She knew, just knew the dog was going to explode into a snarling demon. "I thought you said he only understood Spanish commands?"

Tusk laughed and said, "I'm trying to teach him Spanish, but he's a slow learner."

Mathew scratched between the dog's ears. "What's your name, boy?"

"I call him Lucifer," Tusk said, a hint of disgust in his voice. "Some watchdog. Now I got two worthless mutts to feed, old Curly and this bum."

Mathew Harmon cocked an eyebrow and said, "I'll take him if you ever decide you don't want him."

"It hasn't come to that yet, But why would you want him?"

"I really like dogs. In my opinion they have an edge over people because most people turn sour as they get older. Dogs, on the other hand go through life, at least most of them do, with their heads up, looking for fun. And I don't care what anyone thinks, they grin most of the time. Ninety-nine percent like people…and the ones that don't have probably been abused by some asshole."

Harmon looked at Officer Downing. "You want to pet him?"

She shivered and said, "No thanks. I'll pass."

The interview lasted through two cups of coffee, but they left with a signed affidavit that confirmed most of what they knew already. What they hadn't known was anything about Manny's Indian Art Import/Export business.

On their drive back, Downing at the wheel, they planned their next move.

"Okay. What do we have?" Harmon asked rhetorically. "A thirteen-year-old runaway. A phone number Manny wants Dora, the mini-mart person, to use if Mariah shows back up. A cell number for Mariah. The note Mariah gave Dora. A statement from Tusk that says Manfred Giles confessed to having done his best to kill Tyson James."

"Which is credible," Downing interjected.

"True. I'm hoping he'll recover so he can testify against Giles."

She tapped the brakes and slowed for a big mule deer doe and two yearlings that decided they needed to cross Highway 97 and get back to the snow-covered stubble of a hayfield on the east side of the road.

"Don't stop," she said with a hint of frustration as they hesitated on the shoulder of the road, and then the deer acted like they heard her and bolted on across the highway. The big doe bounced over the barbed wire fence and the little ones squeezed under the middle strand, sending the thin layer of snow flying from the wire. "Good Job," she said to the deer.

"And we have a 'killer-for-hire' in jail," she continued, "who claims he doesn't know who hired him."

"Do you believe him?"

Downing frowned and screwed her face up. "I don't know. Maybe. I think Giles is trying to tidy up some loose ends but he's also trying to keep his distance. Phone calls, cash drops, but no face-to-face meetings."

"What do you think about finding his import/export business?" Harmon asked.

"Doable."

"And you would start where?"

"I don't know, but actually looking for it would be a good start," she said.

Harmon nodded. "Let's think industrial parks. I want to talk to Sergeant Booker. We know Giles's car hasn't been found. So he's gone to ground. Booker will know where to start and he can put some manpower to work on it."

"People power," she corrected.

"Crap," was all he could say.

Sergeant Booker was sitting on a tall stool at what he thought of as a "yuppy" table in the bar of Applebee's. He watched the door, waiting for Mathew Harmon, whom he thought was a pretty good guy for a detective. He was still in uniform, and his size, his badge and his pistol made the evening patrons of the sports bar nervous. Booker nearly laughed out loud when two young men paid up, put a tip on the bar and scurried out the door.

The slender young black woman tending bar glared at him, but he just smiled back. She finally walked from behind the bar and said, "Grandpa, your uniform makes people nervous. Why don't you go sit in a booth with the regular customers?"

He nodded at the door and asked, "Did you card those two?"

Hands on her hips, she said, "Of course."

"Good ID?"

A smile twitched the corners of her mouth, and she said, "Good solid ID. Sold it to them myself."

"I hope you got a good price then," he said and chuckled.

"Why are you out so late, Grandpa?"

"I'm working the swing shift, now, Ruthie. Just like my granddaughter."

She knew with his seniority he could name his own shift, so she asked, "Why did you change shifts, Grandpa?"

He shrugged and a smile pulled his salt and pepper mustache into a straighter line. "Better clientele after dark. Catch more boogers then."

She shook her head. "You waiting for someone?"

He nodded and then looked beyond her at the TV showing the Lakers playing the Mavs. "You got customers, Ruthie."

She knew her grandfather pulled a swing shift because he had a hard time going home to the empty house he had shared with her grandmother for over thirty years. Outwardly, Grandpa Booker hadn't changed, but when Gramma Booker died from ovarian cancer two years ago, he started finding more and more reasons to stay away from the house. The chief of police ignored the mandatory retirement age for law enforcement officers for two reasons: Booker was the best trainer he had ever known, and had, in fact, trained the chief "lo those many years ago." The chief also rationalized that Booker wasn't a street cop anyway. He was a supervisor.

Booker saw Harmon and Downing push through the door, talk to the hostess and point in his direction. The hostess nodded, menus held against her chest, and nearly bowed to the handsome detective.

Christine shook her head in mild disgust and walked down the carpeted ramp leading to the central area of sports bar. "TV bar," is what she thought of it.

Booker slid down off the stool and held out his hand. "Officer Downing. Nice to see you. And you, too, Mathew. If you can hoist yourselves up on these pissant stools, I'll see if my favorite bartender will bring us some coffee."

Christine looked from Booker to the bartender and back to Booker. "Your daughter?"

Booker chuckled. "You do know how to flatter, don't you, girl? That pretty young woman is my granddaughter. She's enrolled in the nursing program at Oregon Institute of Technology. Smart girl. Too independent for her own good. She'd rather starve than let me help her with tuition." He grinned and added, "She reminds me of me. But that's not why you wanted to meet."

Mathew liked Booker, and in some obscure corner of his mind, feared him as well, at least feared he would do something to earn Sergeant Booker's disapproval. He recognized the influence Booker had on his behavior, resented it to a degree, but also knew it made him a better police officer. He wondered how one man could influence so many people without saying a word.

Booker listened without interruption while they quietly briefed him on what information they had about Manfred Giles. When Harmon related the story Gordon Tusk had given them about Giles having an Indian Art import/export business, Booker said, "Come on, let's take a ride."

Christine asked, "You know the place?"

"Maybe," Booker answered.

6:00 p.m. ~ Westside

BEA JOHNSON TOOK A QUART FREEZER bag of her garden grown green beans from the refrigerator and put the beans in her steamer. While the steamer worked to thaw and lightly cook the beans, she sliced a sweet onion and set the slices to sauté in a heated iron skillet coated with a thin layer of olive oil. She had a green bean casserole in mind, complete with crumbled bacon.

She called down the short hallway between the kitchen and the living room. "Colleen, have you fed the cat?"

Colleen got up off the couch, her eyes never leaving the screen of her cell phone. "On it, Grandma." She finished reading the text from her friend Amber, a girl obsessed with missing kids and "Amber" alerts. In school, "Amber Alert" had become code for "here comes our slightly batty classmate Amber who can't get over the fact the Amber Alert wasn't named after her."

No matter the teasing, Amber kept close watch via the internet on Amber Alerts nationwide. She thought the latest about a missing girl from Klamath Falls was the most interesting. Especially the part which said the missing girl "may be in the vicinity of Lakeview, Oregon." Amber knew the description wasn't much help because she knew several girls who were about five feet tall, blue eyed, and had long brown hair. *Why, heck,* she thought, *that could describe me. Not Colleen, of course, because Colleen has red hair.*

Amber had the inspiration of putting her classmates on the alert, and had spent the last hour texting friends with a condensed version of the Amber Alert and asking them to keep an eye out for anything and anyone unusual. Colleen was her latest text. "We'll find that girl and save her," she asserted in her young girl voice.

Colleen walked to the kitchen and said, "Gramma, is there anything in the news about a missing girl from Klamath Falls?"

Bea nodded in the direction of the newspaper. "I didn't see anything in there this morning. She took her hand from the refrigerator door and looked intently at Colleen. "Why?"

"Oh, you know Amber. She says the missing girl could be in Lakeview. She keeps track of all the Amber alerts. So she just sent me a description of the missing girl and told me to keep on the lookout for anything or anyone unusual. I guess she's texting all of her friends with the same message."

"That's very interesting," Bea said. Then she mentally shrugged and said, "Well, go feed that cat before it gets too dark to see. Sure hate to see the days getting shorter like this."

Colleen stepped out into the garage and took a can of cat food from a free standing wooden cupboard. The small can had a stubborn pull tab that required the use of a pair of pliers, but when the seam had given up the struggle, the girl took a spoon and tapped the side of the can, a light clicking sound that generally brought the old mama cat scurrying through the pet door centered in the garage 'man' door.

"Here kitty, kitty," she called, and spooned the food into the cat's dish. "Here, kitty."

She walked to the side door and stepped outside. "Here, kitty," she called and walked around to the corner of the house to check the back yard. No cat. She walked back around the side of the house in time to see the cat trot out of the hay barn and bounce across the field as though she was trying keep her paws dry.

The cat trotted through the open door and straight to her food dish. "Fluffy," Colleen scolded as she closed the door, "what were you doing in Bob's hay barn? I thought you were afraid of that old Shep dog."

She petted wet fur until the cat started purring, and then Colleen went back into the kitchen.

"Colleen," Bea said, "I'm sure I put some crispy bacon in a sandwich bag this morning and put it in the fridge. It's for our green bean casserole. But it's not there. You and Cody haven't been snacking on my bacon, have you?"

"No, Gramma, I didn't eat the bacon."

"Well…shoot," Bea said. "I wonder what happened to it." She shook her head and sighed, "Must have been a senior moment. I need those carrots washed and scraped."

"Why can't Cody do it?"

"Because I told him to fill the wood box. It's going to get cold tonight and I want a fire in the stove."

Without saying anything, Colleen started cold water running in the sink, and placed the carrots into a large stainless steel bowl to scrub them. Her Gramma thought the Jewish notion of clean kitchens was the right one. "Never eat anything you haven't washed," she preached. "And always wash your hands." It had become second nature to Colleen.

While the big bowl filled with water, she looked out the kitchen window in the direction of Bob Roger's hay barn. The two inch layer of snow helped keep the night at bay, but it probably wouldn't have made any difference. The black fur of the old mama cat was clearly visible as she picked her way through the snow, heading for the hay barn. "What the heck?" she said.

"Gramma, the old mama cat is headed for Bob's pole barn. I wonder if she's had another litter."

Bea, said, "Okay. Why don't you go see. If she's had another litter, I'll be surprised given her age. If she has, you bring the kittens back to the house. It's going to get cold tonight. Oh, and take a flashlight."

Colleen found an old down jacket on a peg in the mud room, slipped into some farmer boots and was out the door in less than sixty seconds. A new batch of kittens was a treat, and she wanted to see them.

She heard the old mama cat meowing just as she walked past the outside row of big bales and into the open maw of the hay barn where the fifth wheel trailer sheltered from the weather. Just as she started to say something to the cat, the trailer door opened and a young girl said, "Oh, kitty. I'm so glad you came back."

Colleen said, "Oh my God…it's you! Your name…what's your name…I should know." And then her memory recovered enough for her to say, "Mariah. You're Mariah!"

"Oh no," Mariah said, and tried to close the door, but Colleen was quick enough to catch the outside handle and strong enough keep her from latching the door. "Wait, wait," Colleen said, "let me in."

Mariah, tears of frustration pooling in her eyes, finally let her grip loosen and pushed the door open. "Damn, damn, damn," she muttered.

"It's not nice to swear," Colleen scolded her as she entered the trailer. The girl she thought might be Mariah sank onto the cushions of the breakfast nook and beat a small fist on the table. "Darned old cat," she said and then pulled the black cat onto her lap, "Ratted me out, didn't you?" She glanced up at Colleen. "How do you know my name?"

"Amber told me. Amber. My friend. She keeps track of Amber alerts. You know, the missing kids alerts. She sent me a text. It describes you and gives your name."

Colleen sat down opposite Mariah and just stared at her in fascination. Here was a missing girl, a runaway probably, and it was real, not something you watched on TV. Colleen couldn't think of anything to say until she saw her cell phone charger, the pink one, plugged into a wall socket.

And then she blurted out, "You ate Gramma's bacon, didn't you?"

Mariah shrugged. "I don't know," she muttered, staring at the cat, not looking directly at Colleen.

Colleen pointed to the counter. "And you've been in our house. That's my cell phone charger. What are you doing out here? Hiding?"

In spite of her resolve, Mariah felt tears pooling in her eyes. She nodded, and then said, "Trying to."

"So you are Mariah, right?"

Mariah nodded, but didn't say anything.

"And that makes it okay to steal my charger and eat our food?"

"I didn't steal it," Mariah said defensively. "I just wanted to borrow it until I had my phone charged up. See?"

She pulled her phone from a rear pants pocket. "I needed to text my friend Lacey."

"What are you running from?"

"From Manny, my mother's boy friend. I saw him kill a man, and he knows it. So he'll try to kill me."

"You can count on our sheriff. He's not afraid of anyone. He'll shoot this Manny guy and keep you safe. Trust me. And his deputies are cool, too. They had a shootout with some terrorists up in Fort Rock. Killed 'em dead."

The inherent distrust of the police drilled into her by her mom and by Manny, made Mariah reluctant to trust the redheaded girl, but she was tired of being afraid, and she truly did want to see her mom again.

"I have something to tell you," Mariah said. And so she told the story of slipping into Colleen's house, of eating a waffle and the bacon and of borrowing a pair of Colleen's undies. "But I left ten dollars. It's in your drawer. I'm not a thief. And I was going to bring the charger back tomorrow when you were in school."

Colleen looked amused. "No school tomorrow. It's Saturday."

In spite of herself, Mariah allowed a smile to creep across her face. "I guess I lost track of the days. So that means I'm not absent from school tomorrow, huh?"

Bea was startled when Mariah followed Colleen from the mud room into the kitchen. "Look what the cat drug up, Gramma."

Bea Johnson turned from the stove, eyed the disheveled girl and asked, "And who might you be, girl?"

"This is Mariah, the one on the Amber alert. Boy oh boy! Wait till Amber finds out. This is so cool."

"No!" Mariah said. "I don't want anyone to know where I am. It might get back to Manny. After I'm back home, you can tell her. But not until. Okay?"

"Boy, do you take the fun out of it, Mariah."

Colleen looked at her Gramma. "And she ate your bacon."

Bea smiled and said, "Aha! The mystery is solved."

"I'm sorry," Mariah said, "but it smelled so good. I just took one piece and then couldn't stop."

"Well, I guess I can understand that. Now, sit over there at the breakfast table. Colleen, you leave us alone for a bit. And ask Amber if she knows who we are to contact. Okay?"

"Now, girl," she said to Mariah, "tell me what happened."

At the end of thirty minutes Bea had the whole story. How Manny had killed a man, how Mariah had hidden, the good luck of the camper being unlocked, how she took food and jackets from the camper, "and four packs of cigarettes, but I've been afraid to smoke in the hay barn, so they're still in the big trailer," and how she watched until the kids caught the school bus and Bea left in the pickup, and how the old mama cat heard her crying and came to give comfort.

"Wow," Bea said softly. "You are a tough young lady. I'm glad you picked our place to light. Although maybe the place picked you. Do you believe in God? You should. Sure as the sun comes up, God brought you here where you are safe. Why else would anyone be rescued by a flea-bitten old mama cat?" And then she chuckled.

"Well, girl. Let's get you fed. Then you can have a shower. I'm going to call Sheriff Blair. He'll know what to do. Don't be afraid. Everything is going to be all right." She had tears in her eyes when she gave Mariah a hug, and that was the final straw for tough little Mariah. She sobbed and let Bea hug and comfort her. It was the first time in a long time an adult had done anything but sneer or yell at her.

Colleen stood in the doorway to kitchen and watched, and learned to love her Gramma all over again. Finally she said softly, "Gramma, the alert just says to call the local police."

7:30 p.m. ~ Lakeview

THE INTERVIEW WITH THE MISSING CORRECTIONAL officer's wife gave Undersheriff Sonny Sixkiller and Officer Michelle Trivoli very little new information. The woman told them she had no idea where the money came from for the expensive bass boat hidden in the garage, or where her husband had gotten the money for his new diesel pickup.
And she had no idea where he might have gone.
Disgust was written on each of their faces as they walked out the front door and out to their vehicles.
"She's lying," Michelle said. "She's lying and she doesn't care where the money comes from as long as it gets her some goodies. Did you see the size of the flat screen on the wall? Two thousand dollars at least."
Sonny nodded. "I think she has a hard fall coming." He looked at Michelle as she started to open the door to her Expedition. "You," he said, "you are getting better at intimidating people. Either that or she is a good actress. The tears looked real at any rate."
Sonny, Michelle, and Bud spent the afternoon looking for the missing girl from Klamath Falls, driving county roads, stopping to talk to people, looking for an older man driving a dark blue or black Dodge standard cab pickup. That it was a 1994 to 2000 year model didn't help. They found several Dodge pickups, and they found several campers on pickups, but nothing that matched.
Bud talked with Lakeview City Chief of Police Augustus Hildebrand and told him what they were looking for. "Hoping for is more like it," he told Gus. "Can you have your guys keep an eye out, do some prowling? We're going run the roads and see what we find. Gus hitched his britches a bit higher, a lost cause given his growing paunch, and said, "I'll ask my officers if they have noticed a camper on a dark Dodge pickup. If the camper is within the city limits, we'll know in the next hour. I read the Amber Alert. Sure hope we can find this little girl"
Bud had called off the search at dark and called Gus. "Not a thing," was the Chief's comment. "It's a little like hunting a ghost."
"Well, thanks for trying, Gus. We all need to keep our eyes open."

Bud had gone home to get some much needed rest. He knew he had missed something, but he also knew that sometimes he would remember any missing links after a good night's sleep. And the Lord knew he needed that.

The cell phone on his bedside table was tangled up in a dream full of gunshots and bombs, but finally his mind sorted reality from the dream and he awoke. In a gravelly voice he said, "This had better be good."

Officer Michelle Trivoli said, "Sorry, boss, but we've found the missing girl."

He was immediately alert. "Where?"

"Bea Johnson out in Westside is feeding her supper as we speak. They have convinced the girl, whose name is Mariah, which makes her our missing girl, that Sheriff Bud Blair, handsome hero and all around good guy will, if necessary, shoot somebody named Manny."

His brain engaged and he said, "Manfred Giles. I saw the BOLO on him. Apparently she saw Giles kill someone. He knows she saw him, so he's after her.

Okay. How should we proceed?"

"I'm not liking this much, but the law requires us to notify the KFPD who will in turn notify Child Welfare, who will in turn place her in temporary foster care."

"Where she'll be so safe she'll run again. By the way, how did she get over here?" he asked.

"Do you know Bob Rogers?"

"Yes, yes I do. And?"

"She hid in the back of his camper. Got into the camper while he was gassing up in Klamath Falls."

"Dang it, that's what I missed. I drive right past his place when I go to the cabin. I've seen his camper dozens of times."

He paused and then said, "I think you can see what I mean. She's resourceful, and if she thinks she isn't safe, she'll run again, and the next time it might not work out so well. Okay. I'll meet you at the station in about fifteen minutes and we'll go meet Mariah. And one more thing, I think we'll take my personal pickup. The girl can sit between us."

"And where might we be taking her?"

"Why, Officer Trivoli, we have our own foster homes, and we know damned well we can protect her over here. I'm thinking she belongs to Lake County at least for a few days. So we let our own child welfare folks know we'll need temporary shelter for our young miss. What's the case worker's name?"

"Deanna Baker."

"Right. Now I remember. I only met her once, but she struck me as smart and capable."

"I think she is," Michelle said.

"I'd better call Gus to let him know we found her, and that she is safe. And then call the judge, although I don't think he's talking to me right now."

Michelle snorted, and said, "Just because you threw him out of your office is no reason for him to get upset."

Bud's personal pickup, a four-door Dodge, had emergency lights hidden in the grill, but the snow storm and the wind, which had backed off enough to let the snow fall at about a forty-five degree angle, didn't encourage speed so flashing lights weren't necessary or even useful.

They eased along the highway to Five Corners, and turned south at the store. Bud said, "You know, I think of Judge Lynch as one of the good guys, and then he pulls that 'don't you think it would be in the interest of the community if you resigned' crap. Where is that coming from?"

"I'm hearing it's coming from the ministers…or at least their wives."

"You've got to be kidding, Michelle. Christ had more guts than any man that ever walked the planet and these guys turn lily-livered? It doesn't make any sense. Gotta be something else going on…something political. I'm thinking somebody wants my job. I've got to talk to Gus. He has a better ear to the ground than I do."

"You mean our esteemed Chief of Police, Augustus Hildebrand, knows more about what's going on that we do?"

Bud nodded grimly and said, "Yes. Yes, he does." He pulled a pocket-sized notebook from his right shirt pocket and handed it to Michelle. "The KFPD phone number is in there someplace. Why don't you call and let them know we are on our way to gather up our wayward child. Tell 'em we're taking her back to Lakeview and turning her over to our Child Welfare case worker for temporary placement.

"If they squawk, tell 'em our storm makes nighttime driving too hazardous." He paused and then added, "I don't mean to lecture. You're up on this stuff better than I am. I just want to stall until we can be sure this girl will be safe."

After the Bill Casey affair, Officer Michelle Trivoli had become nearly obsessed with domestic violence cases. She studied all the cases she could find about women who had been abused by their spouses, but who also refused to leave...sometimes until it was too late and they were killed.

No amount of study had given her the insight she was looking for. But a side benefit was her increasing skill at interviewing children who had been abused. Like her counterpart, Christine Downing in Klamath Falls, she had become her department's go-to woman, the officer chosen to accompany Child Welfare workers to investigate reports of child abuse. She hadn't said anything to Bud yet, but she was seriously thinking about going back to school and working on a Master's in Social Work.

"Okay, Boss. I got it."

Officer Christine Downing's cell phone gave a jingle and a buzz, telling her she had a text message. She tapped the screen and pulled up the message. From the back seat of Booker's Ford Expedition, she nearly shouted. "Great news, guys! The Lake County Sheriff's office found Mariah."

"Good on them!" Booker said. "Now I can quit worrying."

"Terrific news, Christine," Detective Harmon said. The use of her first name wasn't lost on her. Maybe kicking ass is the key, she thought. Harmon was a good, nearly great detective, and somehow it meant a great deal that he supported and accepted her.

"The message asks me to call Officer Michelle Trivoli back," she said as she busily thumbed in a text message to KFPD dispatch. Message received was all she sent.

Booker turned on 6th Street and then turned again down an alley that ran parallel to the railroad tracks and into an industrial park. He half listened to Christine asking someone, presumable Officer Trivoli, if they had the girl in custody.

He said in a low aside to Detective Harmon, "Mathew, I have this vague memory of an import/export shop located someplace in among these light manufacturing buildings. I just can't remember where. So my plan is simple: we drive around and look until we spot something."

Detective Harmon smiled and said, "I'm sure we'll spot something, whatever it is."

"Don't disrespect your elders, Mr. Harmon. It's like your first rattlesnake. When it buzzes and you see it, you know it's not a bull snake and you're looking at the real thing."

Christine shut her phone down. "Okay. They haven't picked her up yet, but Officer Trivoli said they were only about ten minutes from the house. She wasn't long on details so I don't know how they found her. But she said they were working with their Child Welfare caseworker to find emergency shelter. I suggested they bring her over tonight. She is after all from Klamath County, but I think they are going to try and stall us on that. Trivoli didn't say anything direct, but she did say they were having one heck of a snow storm and didn't want to risk the roads at night."

Harmon nodded and then said, "I think that's okay until we get Giles off the street. I don't know what the rules are, but I'll bet their judge can talk to our judge and let Lake County keep her safe for a while.

"Giles can't stay hidden forever, and I know the type. He's a junky and junkies can't sit still very long. He'll bolt and we'll nab him. Right, Sergeant Booker?"

Sergeant Booker didn't say anything, just turned left into a complex of fairly new green, single story light industrial buildings. "Keep your eyes open. You watch the left side, Officer Downing, and you, Mathew, look right."

"What are we looking for again?" Downing asked.

"Import/Export," he said.

7:45 p.m. ~ Best Western Motel, Lakeview

AMANDA KNEW SHE SHOULD CALL ASAC Dennis Moore back and tell him the storm had driven her to shelter in the small town of Lakeview. Instead she dialed a number from memory and hit the call button on her cell phone. It rang three times before a familiar voice said, "Yes?"

"John?" she asked.

"Ah! Amanda. I'll tell you the same thing I told Dennis: The answer is No and that's final. I'm done."

"So you know about NCIS planning an operation to snag the Ortega Cartel?"

"No, he didn't talk about an operation. He just said he wanted me back on the counter-terrorism team."

She hesitated a couple of seconds and then said, "And you aren't going?"

"No. Look. I'm married, I'm buying a small ranch...well, hay farm anyway, and I'm out of the game. I'm happy you didn't get killed. My wife Larae filled me in on what happened. It might be a little morbid, but we had to laugh when the bomb squad found a second detonator. What the sheriff said to Larae and her partner Roger Hildebrand was he was grateful they didn't use words like 'dumb shit' or 'stupid' when they were explaining how he was nearly sucker punched."

"I was there. We all got lucky. Bud's cop friend from Portland had some flash bangs in his car, so he and Gino set them off down by the boat ramp. Made the killer think the bomb had gone off." She hesitated and then added, "Congratulations, John. I really mean it."

"Thanks. Larae is a terrific person. I'm lucky she chose me. I think it was that or shoot me. Glad she decided not to shoot." He laughed and then added, "As a matter of fact, we're having dinner at the Christmas Valley Lodge with your advance team, a retired DEA agent who has lots of contacts in Sonora. He's telling me he can locate the other Ortega, brother Juan, for us. Pinpoint his location. Wally wants us to bomb him to hell. Says Ortega is worse than Omar Khadafy ever was, so if it was okay to try and kill that terrorist, it shouldn't bother us to kill Ortega."

"Sounds like he's a little bloodthirsty."

John reached across the dining room table and lightly tapped Wally on his right shoulder. "Nah...he's just pissed because the Ortega Cartel keeps trying to kill his friends. Hold on. I'll let you talk to him."

"Agent Spears, I'm Wally Pidgeon, DEA, retired. I hear from my friend Gar, aka John Bernard, your agency is planning to go after Ortega. I want to be part of the advance team. I have contacts that should be very helpful."

"I don't have authority to hire you...or to pay you for that matter," she said.

"No problem. This is pro bono. Let me give you a cell number. I'll be in Guaymas in three days. Call me mid-morning. I'll be out fishing." He read off a phone number and asked, "You got that?" She read it back and Wally said, "Here, I'll give you back to Gar."

When John Bernard was back on the phone, she asked, "Is he for real?"

John laughed and said, "Speaking as Gar, I'd say he might just be the answer to finding your target. He's the genuine article."

"Ask him if we can meet."

"Where are you, Amanda?"

"I'm in Lakeview. This storm put more snow on the ground than I've ever driven on. So I'm kegged up here until the storm blows over."

She heard him talking to Wally and then his strong voice said, "He's not going to wait. If you are in the Redmond Airport, Roberts Field, he says, by 0700 tomorrow morning, he'll have a cup of coffee with you and listen to what you have to say. Otherwise, he'll talk to you in Guaymas."

"How far is it up there?"

"From Lakeview, I'd say about 200 plus. That's miles, not kilometers."

"Well, crap. How's he getting to the airport?"

"I'm driving him up there in the morning in my pickup. We'll leave here about five o'clock."

"Okay. I have a four wheel drive, a 4-Runner. I'll be in Christmas Valley as soon as I can, but I'm really slow on these roads. Book me a room at the motel."

"Can do. Call when you get in. We might still be here."

She gritted her teeth and repacked her carryall. The night manager of the Best Western looked surprised that she was leaving so soon, and politely refused to refund her money. She decided to just let it go and tossed her carryall in the back of her SUV, slammed the door and started the engine. A cursory look at the gauges convinced her she had enough gas to go another three hundred miles. She punched an icon symbol on the dashboard and a tiny microchip confirmed she had three hundred and twenty-seven miles of fuel remaining. She asked OnStar for mileage to Christmas Valley and saw 117 on the screen. She took a deep breath, turned on her headlights, turned on the wipers, front and back, and backed out of her parking slot. She turned north on 395 and edged cautiously out on the highway, hands frozen by white knuckles to the steering wheel.

She was still creeping along at about thirty-five miles an hour until a pickup doing about fifty-five or sixty passed her just north of Chandler State Park. In her headlights she could see the powder dry snow swirling and billowing in the back draft of the pickup.

"Okay," she muttered through gritted teeth and pushed her speed up to forty-five. By the time she reached Paisley she was feeling more and more confident. That lasted until she felt her tires break traction on the highway bridge over the Chewacan just at the north edge of town. Her speed dropped back to a sedate thirty-five miles per hour.

"To heck with it," she said aloud. "I'll get there when I get there." She popped in a CD and cranked the volume up on a Verdi opera, and started feeling better. Her cautious speed was justified when eight or nine big mule deer jumped the fence between Summer Lake and the highway and bounced across the road into a big field on the other side. "There, now. If I'd been doing fifty-five, I might have hit one of those."

Her vehicle clock read 10:30 when she pulled into the parking lot of the Christmas Valley Lodge.

7:45 p.m. ~ *Business Park, Klamath Falls*

SERGEANT BOOKER EASED THE BIG FORD Expedition through the complex of light industrial buildings and shop areas with built in offices, noting with a grim acceptance the number of "For Lease" signs on empty spaces. Like most boom and bust cycles, the last cycle had led late entries into the building business. The consequence was a spurt of over-building, followed by the "bust" part of the cycle. New offices and shop areas went begging.

"There's something," Harmon said. The windows were dark, and the carved relief blocked most of the window. But the light across the driveway from an open overhead door where someone was working late hours gave enough light for Detective Harmon to see the words, "Indian Art, Import/Export."

"Too easy," Officer Downing said.

"Yes, I'd say so, unless you think I'm just lucky and not possessed of a finely tuned mind," Sergeant Booker said. And then he stopped the vehicle and gave his orders, "Downing, go talk to the guy in that shop, the one with the open door. Find out if he's seen anybody coming or going from our suspect's little shop.

"You, Mr. Harmon, set up in front of the next doorway and wait. I'm going to circle the block and see if there is a rear door. If there is, I'll block that and you two go calling."

"No search warrant?" Harmon asked.

They could see Booker's smile and then he said, "I'll just accidentally hit the siren and turn on the lights. That should spook him if he's in there. He'll try to boogey, and that means an open door and an easy arrest."

"What about another car to help us cover the front?" Mathew asked.

"You willing to share the glory?"

"You bet. I'd rather catch him than play hero. Then our little girl can come home and live safely."

"Until he gets out again," Downing said sarcastically.

"She'll be grown and most probably gone by then," Booker said, "but I'll call for another car as soon as I cover the back. You two get busy."

Five minutes of standing in the snow let the chill work its way through Harmon's boots. He unholstered his pistol and held it down to his side. He glanced across the driveway and watched Christine taking notes. *Guess the guy sees things*, he thought.

A faint "Thank you" drifted across the paved thoroughfare, and then Downing sloshed her way across the drive and up to Harmon. "That guy, Tom Franks," she whispered, "says there are all kinds of creeps coming and going from our import shop." She caught the reflected glare of emergency lights coming down the alley next to the railroad tracks and then two KFPD cruisers pulled into the drive. Mathew held up his open badge wallet and waved the cars on up and then directed the first officer to drive around the building and give back up to Booker. He told the other officer to block the front overhead door in the import/export shop.

"Okay," he told the second officer, a near rookie named Benjamin Dwyer, "Call Booker and tell him we are in place. And then I would get the hell out of the car and just beyond the big window. You make too good a target if you just sit there."

Officer Dwyer just grinned, pulled his shotgun free from the Velcro strap and put a KFPD baseball cap on the head rest on the driver's side of the cruiser.

Dwyer called Booker via radio, "We're in place, Sergeant."

"Who is this?" Booker asked?

"Dwyer, sir."

"Okay, Dwyer, wait sixty seconds from right now, and then hit the siren and we'll light that place up. Got that?"

"Got it, sir. Sixty seconds and counting."

When Booker's siren screamed into the night, Dwyer hit the siren, racked the slide on the shotgun and chambered a ten-gauge round loaded with double ought buckshot. He and Downing took position just to the right of the office window. Harmon stationed himself behind the cruiser where he could watch the office door.

Manny was feeling pretty smart. Getting Lionel to snuff Tyson James was, in his opinion, pure genius. Lionel didn't know who had hired him, so there wasn't any tie back to Manny. Maybe when that Dora broad called and told him she had Mariah locked up someplace, he'd pay Lionel to do that job, too. Then, it was smooth sailing. He could keep running his business, get old Barbara back and have some fun. He knew he'd have to apologize for hitting her to get her to let him move back in, but that had always worked before, so it would work this time.

He took another deep drag from a roll-your-own filled with heavy duty marijuana, laid back on his cot and turned his eye to the tiny TV. The program was another *NCIS* rerun. He always watched that to make sure he was up on police procedure and forensics. The fact that it really didn't work that way in the real world was lost on him. *NCIS* was almost over and *WWE RAW*, his other favorite show, was about to kick off.

He was just taking a second, long, slow drag, and feeling no pain when a siren went off right outside his back door. He jerked upright, stunned. He thought no one knew about this place...except Tusker maybe...and Tusker wouldn't rat him out.

In truth Gordon Tusk really hadn't ratted him out. He had only mentioned to Harmon and Downing his suspicion about Manny's import/export business, not its location.

Manny threw the joint across the concrete floor, sat up and slid his shoes over so he could get his feet shod and the laces tied. "Maybe it's something else going on," he said through gritted teeth, and then he realized there was a second siren out front.

He hurried to the Mazda, slid under the steering wheel and started the engine. The remote control for the power door was clipped to the visor. He hit the button and watched as the door rose into the overhead rack. When the door was about four feet off the ground, all he could see were headlights and "sear-your-eyeballs" million candle power spot lights. He stopped the door and reversed the direction of travel.

His adrenaline was pumping and his hands were shaking. In spite of the chilly temperature in the shop, a trickle of sweat started down the side of his face. He was breathing heavily and he was scared.

"Now what?" he said aloud, and turned they motor off. "I know I'm not going down for no murder rap." He walked to an unused workbench and pulled open a drawer. A 9mm Beretta and a spare clip were wrapped in a towel at the back of the drawer.

"Gonna get killed is what's gonna happen," he groaned. But he worked the slide, chambered a round and headed for the office. When he peeked out the front window, all he could see were flashing blue, red, and white lights, and another "burn-your-eyes" spotlight. But he thought he could make out the silhouette of a man sitting the cruiser. *Just one*, he thought. *I can get by just one guy.*

He jerked the door open and started shooting. In spite of his shaking hands, he actually managed to punch two holes in the windshield. Voices were shouting, "Drop the weapon! Hands in the air!"

He pulled back into the office and shut the door just as Officer Dwyer, shotgun held waist high, fired three quick rounds through the metal sheeting of the building. The steel studs used in the construction of the building absorbed some of the heavy buckshot, but enough rounds snarled into the room to knock Manny off of his feet and end any hope he would ever have for a sex life again.

He dropped the pistol and grabbed his crotch and started yelling, "Help me! Oh God help me! You shot me! Oh God." And then the yelling trailed off into groans and sobs.

Harmon ran to the shop door and found it was still locked. "Dwyer," he said pointing at the lock, "shoot that son-of-a-bitch." The blast blew the door open. Harmon stood outside the door frame and felt for a light switch, bumped it with his left hand and then flicked it on.

Manny was lying in a growing pool of blood, the crotch of his trousers torn and bloody. Downing walked over and kicked the gun out of reach and said, "I think we're gonna need an ambulance."

Through tears Manny looked up at her pleading and angry all at the same time. "You shot my balls," he gritted.

Downing shook her head, "Nope. Not me, but I'm okay with it."

"Okay?" Manny said. "You're a cruel bitch."

"Not as cruel as someone who planned to kill a young girl."

"You gonna help me?" he asked the three officers.

Harmon furrowed his brow like he was thinking it over. Then he brightened and said, "No."

He looked at Dwyer and Downing. "Clear the shop and then go tell Sergeant Booker what we have here and call for an ambulance. Okay?"

The two officers found the light switch for the main shop area and turned the rows of overhead lights on. They checked the bathroom and were satisfied no one else was on the premises.

Dwyer hit his lapel mike and reported to Booker what had just transpired. When Booker gave him the okay, he hit the power button that raised the big overhead door in the rear, and Booker and the second officer, a tall guy named Bill Sharps, came through the door, guns drawn.

Downing took two blankets off Manny's cot, rolled and stuffed one under his head, and used the second one to cover him.

Dwyer came back into the room with the big first-aid kit carried in all KFPD units. He popped it open, slipped on blue latex gloves and pulled the blanket back. "Well," he said as he started cutting Manny's pants away from the wounds. "What's your name?"

"Manny."

"Okay Manny, let see what we have here. Ooh. That looks nasty, Manny," Dwyer said cheerfully, "looks like you won't be using that thing for awhile."

Booker, Downing and Harmon looked on in slight amazement at the ministrations of Dwyer. He caught their look and laughed, "Navy Corpsman, once. They train you well. But," he shrugged, "law enforcement has more sex appeal. You know…the uniform, foxy chicks…a real gun. But I'm a cop because mainly I just hate drug dealers. This is the first one I've ever gotten to shoot." Manny winced as a wraparound bandage on his leg was pulled extra tight.

Manny said, "Is that why you shot me? Cause I do drugs?"

Dwyer's hands never miss a beat while he answered. "Let's see if I can explain this. Oh yeah, this dude comes barging out the front door banging away at my car, and trying to kill my hat. That's two things you shouldn't have done. So I got wondering if double ought buck would punch through the aluminum sheeting. Now we know. I wasn't trying to kill you, just knock you down," he ended with a smile. Dwyer patted Manny's leg and then stood up. "You can back to holding your crotch."

"Am I going to live?"

"Unfortunately. I don't know what's going to become of us, but this state just doesn't execute the right people anymore."

Downing shook her head and grinned at Harmon who just sighed and shrugged.

Dwyer turned his siren off, killed the spotlight, but left the emergency lights flashing, glaring off the snow onto the rows of light industrial shops and offices windows. He used a glove to sweep the shards of glass off the driver's seat, slid in and backed the car out of the way just as an ambulance pulled up to the open door of Manny's office.

Booker's lapel mike beeped and he walked out into the snow to take the call. When he came back in, he said, "Max is on the way."

Harmon frowned and Downing groaned. "What?" Booker asked, "You don't like the Chief?"

"What is she doing out on this one?" Harmon asked.

"I suspect," Booker said, "she has taken a special interest in our runaway."

"But Mariah is in protection," Downing objected. "Surely she knows that."

Booker pointed to Manny's import/export front door. "She might be interested in knowing where those three holes came from," he said dryly. "Nice group, Mathew. The DA is gonna love that."

The EMTs started an IV drip, lifted a groaning, cussing Manfred Giles onto a gurney and loaded him in the ambulance. Booker ordered Officer Sharp, whose unit still had all its windows intact, to follow the ambulance and guard Giles until better security could be arranged.

While they waited for Maxine Detweiler, Chief of Police for KFPD, the first woman to ever hold that rank in the history of the Klamath Falls Police Department, they worked the scene, took photos of the big holes Dwyer's ten-gauge had blown through the metal sheeting in below the window, bagged the bloody blanket in the hatch of Manny's Mazda, labeled and loaded a locked safe into the back of Booker's Expedition, cut the packing tape seals on several boxes and identified two basic drugs, marijuana and Ecstasy, but one box was hiding a small amount of cocaine.

"For his personal use, you think?" Downing said.

Chief Detweiler wasn't alone when she arrived. District Attorney Darren Winslow was in the passenger seat. He was known as a rabid anti-gun campaigner. While police officers didn't really like him, they tolerated him because he was just as hard as the law would allow on criminals who used guns.

He just had one bad habit. He always stuck his nose in their business when a police weapon was discharged. The review process publicly identified the officer by name and then reported the officer as "on administrative leave pending an investigation." For some citizens that was tantamount to a guilty verdict. District Attorney Winslow took twice as long to conduct an investigation as it took for departments in other cities. It deprived the Chief and her Lieutenant of valuable officers. But the Chief was also a politician who served at the pleasure of the Mayor who told her to play ball with the DA. So she did without ever betraying any displeasure—publicly at any rate.

The Chief told Dwyer to drive his car back to the station and turn in his pistol, his badge and the shotgun pending review. The ever cheerful Dwyer said, "Yes ma'am," and did as he was instructed.

Max next turned her attention to Harmon and Downing. "All right," she said, "Whose weapon punched those holes in the door?"

Downing and Harmon glanced at each other and then said in unison, "Manfred Giles." Downing added, "He was spraying lead all over the place. I think he shot the door when he was backing out of sight. Isn't that right Detective Harmon?"

"I believe that's what might have happened."

Booker was standing behind the chief of police and the DA shaking his head. Chief Max looked at the three holes in the door, not three inches apart and chest high, and then at the mangled door latch. She nodded, "Yes. That's what it looks like, and that's what it better be in the report you two write. Understood?"

"Yes ma'am," they said, nearly in unison again.

When the DA started to protest that the obvious angle of the holes didn't support the story, Chief Max stared at him. Her brilliant blue eyes and red hair could have come straight from a Viking forefather. She knew Harmon had likely fired the rounds, but she was sick and tired of the long review process run by the DA, and she needed her officers on the job. DA Darren Winslow finally ran down and stopped just short of an idiot's stutter. He felt foolish and deflated.

"Sergeant Booker," The Chief said, "please make sure all the evidence is tagged and bagged. I'll want an inventory by morning. I called the lab and they will have a team here to dust for fingerprints. We might find the prints of people who are not supposed to be where drugs are manufactured or sold. And have a wrecker take his car to the impound lot. What else do you have?"

Detective Harmon was torn between admiration for her loyalty and his resentment that she was taking over his case and his crime scene, even though he knew Booker was really the one in charge. But he kept his face and voice neutral.

"Thirteen sealed cartons, containing mainly marijuana, but some Ecstasy and what looks to be cocaine. We didn't open all of the cartons. We also have one pistol, the one he used to shoot at us, and which we have tagged and bagged. And a locked safe we plan to take back to the shop where we can open it. We also have half a dozen cell phones."

Officer Christine Downing looked at the DA and said, "And a bloody blanket from the back of his car. We think it will probably match the blood of Tyson James who is still in Sky Lakes in a coma. Shouldn't be too hard to prove Giles tried to kill James."

Mollified by that news, the DA smiled and said, "All right, then!"

It was nearly 10:30 p.m. before Detective Harmon and Officer Downing printed off their reports and turned them into their watch commander. Booker was sitting in his office in a worn captains chair drinking coffee and reading the Herald and News when they emerged from their offices. He spotted them through his office window and put his paper down. He put his cap back on and stepped into the hallway.

"Why don't we all have a cup of coffee at Applebee's?" It was mildly said, but they each knew it was more of an order than a request.

"Sure," Mathew said. "Back to the beginning."

Booker laughed and slapped Mathew's shoulder with a meaty hand. "This is the beginning, Mathew my boy," and walked down the hallway.

"What in the world does that mean?" Christine said aloud to herself as she followed the two big men down the hallway and out the front door.

Applebee's was packed, mainly with OIT students celebrating as college kids celebrate everywhere. In this case, it was Friday night and the end of another week of classes.

Booker's granddaughter Ruthie was busy at the bar, filling the orders of a dozen bar customers, most of whom were watching a sports commentator analyze the NBA game just completed, an overtime win by the Lakers. The producer of the show was running highlights, including one long distance three pointer by Kobe.

When they were seated, in a booth this time, but still in the bar, Harmon pointed at a TV and said, "That's what my dad would call looking up a dead horse's ass."

Booker chuckled. "Never thought of it that way, but it's not a bad description. I like it."

Downing yawned and in mild protest asked, "Why are we here? It's been a long day, and I need some sleep."

Booker smiled and said, "Just give me a minute." He rose and stepped to the U-shaped bar. He crowded in between two kids who didn't look old enough to be in college let along drinking in a bar. One of them turned and started to say something when Booker squeezed between them. The bigger one choked off a swear word and just stared at the big policeman. "Booker," he said.

"Howdy," Booker said. "Your sponsor tells me you missed Wednesday's meeting. You aren't back on the sauce, are you, Tommy?"

Tommy collected his thoughts and lifted his glass. "Just Pepsi, Mr. Booker."

"Okay then, Tommy. Don't you disappoint your sponsor...and don't you disappoint me. I want to hear you went to meeting. We have deal, right?"

"Yessir."

Booker slapped him on the back hard enough to make Tommy spill a little of his Pepsi. "Good. You have a nice night. Try to study a little this weekend. Okay?"

When he was seated, he looked almost embarrassed. "Sorry. Tommy's one of my projects. I arrested him twice for DUI. When he sobered up after the second time I had arrested him, one of my AA buddies paid him a visit, and I talked the judge into a suspended if he gave up the booze."

"And if he doesn't?" Christine asked.

"Six months in the county lockup. Now, I wanted a cup of coffee and I wanted to ask you two how Mr. Dwyer handled himself. He's still on probation. You first, Mr. Harmon."

Ruthie came over and set a cup of coffee and a little pitcher of cream in front of her grandfather. She smiled and asked Harmon and Downing if they wanted anything. They both shook their heads.

"Thanks, girl," Booker said.

"Now then, Mr. Harmon."

"Well, he was cool under fire. He didn't shoot to kill Giles, just wound him, which he did. Giles will live and the DA will get himself a high profile case to prosecute."

"So you would pass Dwyer through his probationary period?"

"I haven't even seen the guy before, but based on this incident, I think I would. Why not?"

"You didn't think his comment about Giles being the first drug dealer he ever had a chance to shoot was out of line? Or bloodthirsty?"

"Sergeant Booker," Christine scolded, "He was just making noise, trying to keep Giles calm. He did a marvelous job as a first responder. I'll admit he was pretty cheerful about it, though."

"Will you give him a pass?" Booker asked.

"Yes. Without reservation."

"Good on both of you, because you will be asked."

Harmon and Downing looked at each other, wondering if they hadn't just passed some kind of "Booker" test.

"Okay," Booker said, "I'll take you back to your cars." He waved at his granddaughter, who was busy mixing drinks and filling beer mugs. "Night darling."

As they walked outside, Harmon asked, "Sergeant Booker, why didn't we do this at the station?"

"Because if I did this in the station it would be official, and I'm not ready for 'official' right now. And because I wanted to check and see if any of my special projects were at Applebee's tonight."

Christine stopped in front of Booker and asked, "Are you in AA, Mr. Booker?"

He laughed. "It's not nice to ask, but, yes. I've been going to AA meetings for over thirty years. I still don't know if I'm a drunk or not, but I do know I had a hard time staying sober when I was younger. An old guy told me to sober up or buy a casket, and then invited me to AA. I think he may have saved my life. In a way, I'm trying to pay him back."

7:55 p.m. ~ Bea Johnson's home in Westside

BUD PULLED HIS VEHICLE ONTO THE parking pad in front of Bea's garage and stepped out into the snow storm. Michelle came around the front of the vehicle and they tromped through about three inches of snow up the sidewalk and to the front door.

He pulled his Stetson off and slapped it against his leg to knock away the dusting of snow on the hat brim. Before he could ring the door bell, the door flew open and a redheaded girl a little over five feet tall stood in the doorway. A tall lanky boy stood behind her. She was wide eyed, and Michelle could tell she was excited. She just stared for a long five seconds.

"May we come in?" Bud asked.

"Oh. Sure." She stepped back and motioned them in. "I'm Colleen. I'm the one who found her. My friend Amber tracks Amber alerts and told me all about this girl who was missing from Klamath Falls and then the cat went out to Bob's hay barn and I followed cause I thought she might have a batch a kittens and that's when I found Mariah. And I told Mariah our sheriff would protect her. I mean if you can take care of terrorists, you can protect Mariah, can't you?"

Her big brother Cody said, "Take a breath, Sis."

The words "our sheriff" weren't lost on Bud. He smiled and felt like tousling Colleen's hair, which of course he didn't do. But "our sheriff" was a lot nicer than what the "get out of Dodge" people had been saying.

Bea came out of the kitchen and down the short hall to the entry. She was drying her hands on a kitchen towel. She held out her hand and said, "I'm Bea Johnson. I know you, Sheriff Blair, and you must be Deputy Trivoli. Mariah is in the shower getting cleaned up. I'm so glad we found her. Do you want some coffee while we wait?"

She led them to the kitchen and to a round maple breakfast table with four spoke backed chairs. Colleen and Cody crowded into the kitchen right behind them.

A fresh red-and-white checked table cloth was laid out with cups, saucers, sugar and cream.

Michelle said, "That would be nice, thank you. Deanna Baker, a caseworker for Child Welfare will be here in a few minutes."

"Child Welfare? What do they do?" Colleen asked.

Bud looked at Michelle and gave her a nearly imperceptible nod.

"Well," she said, "Child Welfare assigns a case worker who works with families that are having trouble and gets them the help they need to stay together."

"You mean," Colleen interrupted, "like Mariah's mother could go to rehab so they could be a family again."

Michelle smiled. "Something like that. But in the meantime, Mariah will need a place to live, someplace safe."

"Like right here," Bea said. "She can stay with us."

Michelle glanced at Cody, a nice looking young man, square shoulders, his grandmother's brilliant blue eyes, and a smile that hinted at the soul of a rascal. "That decision will up to the caseworker."

The sound of a car driving up to the house and the sweep of car lights on the kitchen window announced the arrival of Deanna Baker, caseworker for Child Welfare. Bea answered the door and was pleased by Deanna's appearance and manners. She was young, dressed in designer jeans, snow boots, and a hooded white jacket over a cable knit sweater. Perhaps her most attractive feature was her smile. When Deanna smiled her whole face lit up.

Bea, Michelle, Deanna and Bud were sitting at Bea's table drinking coffee when Mariah came into the kitchen. Her tiny figure was swamped by a pair of Colleen's blue jeans and a dark blue sweater. Her hair was combed out and still damp, and she was so thin Bud felt his heart breaking in pity.

Based on the information he was getting, Bud had built a mental picture of a self-reliant, tough kid, which Mariah was. But the reality of seeing this almost tiny young girl, was nearly too much to handle. He wanted to find and punish the people who had neglected her, especially the jerk who had sent her running into the night.

Bud got out of his chair and said, "Miss Mariah, I'm Sheriff Blair. Boy, am I glad to see you." He held out his hand and she offered a hand that was swallowed by his big paw. "Why don't you take this chair," he suggested.

She was tentative and nervous, but the Sheriff's kindness and his solid no nonsense presence soon had her telling them about watching Manny use a two by four to beat on a man. "I told Manny to stop, and then he called me a bitch and told me he would take care of me later. So I ran."

"What do you think me meant?" Michelle asked.

"I know what he meant," she said. "He meant he would kill me."

"And that's why you got in the camper. Right?" Bud asked.

"Yes."

"Why didn't you go to the police?" Michelle asked.

"Because, they would have just taken me home." She stopped talking for a long few seconds and looked at Bud and then Michelle. "How's my mom? Lacey sent me a text that Mom was in the hospital."

Bud pulled a cell phone from his jacket pocket, and said, "I'll find out." He stepped out onto the front porch and punched the speed dial number for the KFPD. When he said he wanted to talk to Detective Harmon, a pleasant sounding woman said, "Hold please."

He pulled his collar up around his ears and waited, watching the light show in the big security yard light mounted on a phone pole, the snow flakes gusting, swirling, dodging, and dancing in the pale light.

A voice came through the phone, "Harmon."

"Detective Harmon, this is Sheriff Blair from Lake County."

"I understand you have Mariah in protection. I'm sure glad you found her, Sheriff."

"Me, too. We're trying to figure out where she's going to stay tonight. She's a tough little lady, but she wants to know how her mom is doing."

"I really don't know," Harmon said. "We just had a dust up with Manfred Giles and took him into custody. He was wounded in an exchange of gunfire, and was still in surgery thirty minutes ago. But I'm told he'll live."

"Anybody else get hurt?" Bud asked.

"No."

"Well, I'm glad to hear that. Now look, it's snowing like crazy over here, so I don't want to risk the roads until this storm blows over. But if Giles is in jail, we could bring her back to Klamath tomorrow."

"Where has she been hiding?"

"Out in the area we call Westside, an area, believe it or not, west of Lakeview. Farm country. The old man who owns the camper also has a big fifth wheel trailer in a hay barn. She broke into the trailer and hid there."

"How did she get caught?"

"An old mama cat went calling on the trailer, and another young lady followed the cat. Easy as that."

"Okay. Let's talk in the morning. I think it would be okay to tell Mariah that her mother is resting and should get better soon. That's the official line. The unofficial line is that she may have suffered a stroke from a meth overdose, but you don't have to tell Mariah that."

"I won't mention it. She has enough trouble for now. Thanks. Until morning, then."

When he walked back into the kitchen, Deanna Baker, the young, attractive caseworker, was saying to Bea Johnson, "Mariah is very vulnerable right now, and Cody is obviously a compassionate and caring young man, however..."

"Ah, I understand," Bea interrupted. "Just a minute."

Bea walked to the phone and called Bob Rogers. They all listened to Bea's side of the conversation, and Bud heard her say "thanks" as she hung up. "Okay," she announced, "Cody is going to stay with Bob tonight. Bob was really surprised to hear about Mariah stowing away in his camper and then hiding out in his fifth wheel. Anyway, that solves the boy-girl problem for tonight."

Bud looked at Deanna Baker with an unspoken question on his face.

Deanna nodded. "That will work for tonight, and it gives me a chance to figure out where we go from here. I'll talk to the Judge in the morning."

"One more thing," Bud said and looked directly at Colleen. "No one is to know she is staying here."

Colleen's ears turned red and she gulped and squeaked.

Bud shook his head and said gently, "Been texting, have you?"

Colleen gulped again and said, "Only to Amber."

Colleen's Gramma shook her head. "Talk to Amber and tell her she can't give out the location. We understand, but people like this Manny fellow don't play games."

On the way back to town, Bud asked Michelle, "What do you think of Deanna Baker?"

"Good at her job, I'd say."

Bud was concentrating on driving and didn't respond until they reached Five Corners. "Wish we had a more secure spot for her. I don't trust that little pistol Colleen to keep the excitement to herself."

In spite of herself, Michelle grinned at the picture of the saucy red head opening the door and plunging in with her story of how she found Mariah because of an old mama cat. "I think they'll be all right until we can move Mariah to a safer place."

Two snow speckled tumbleweeds blew into the headlights and bounced across the road to keg up against a pile of tumbleweed kin folks. Bud nearly swerved to miss them, but caught himself in time. Swerving on slick roads was definitely not recommended.

10:35 p.m. ~ Christmas Valley Lodge

WHEN SHE WHEELED INTO THE PARKING lot of the Christmas Valley Lodge, Amanda could see a battered looking pickup and a white 4X4 four door pickup with a County Sheriff shield on the doors. There weren't any lights on in the front of the restaurant, but as she got out, she saw John Bernard open the front door and wave her in.

A stiff snow laden breeze pushed Amanda past the low growing ornamental shrubs lining the walk to the Lodge and into an A-framed sheltered foyer. John locked the door behind her and said, "Took you long enough."

She stamped the snow from her boots on the fiber foot mat and said, "I don't drive snow. I was doing all right until I was coming out of that little town, Paisley I think it was, and my tires started spinning on the bridge. That really slowed me down. And then a bunch of deer ran out into the road in front of me."

"Did you see the Black Angus cows?" he asked.

"What black cows?" But when she caught the sly smile he gave her, she smacked him on the shoulder and said, "Not funny, John."

Four people were sitting at a round table in the bar drinking fresh coffee and chatting when John and Amanda walked in. Wally stood up, all sixty-six inches of him, and walked over to Amanda. She was struggling out of her jacket, and he said, "Here, let me help you with that."

He handed the jacket back to her. She stared skeptically at the nearly bald man, and finally said, "You must be Willy."

"Wally," he corrected her. He clicked his heels together and gave a slight bow. "Walter Pidgeon at your service. Let me introduce you to my friends. This beautiful young officer is Deputy Larae Holcomb-Bernard, Lake County Sheriff's Office." He nodded at Roger who reached across to shake hands with Amanda. "This is Deputy Roger Hildebrand, also of the Lake County Sheriff's Office. And this is my good friend, Billie Thompson, owner of the Lodge."

"Sit," he concluded pointing to an empty chair at the table.

Amanda pulled the chair out, hung her damp coat over the back and sat down. Billie went behind the bar and poured coffee into a heated mug. The steaming coffee smelled simply delicious. Amanda took a sip and looked over the rim of her cup at Larae. *Honey blond hair, trim figure, brown eyes. She looks remarkably like John's sister. No wonder he was attracted to her. I wonder if he would have been attracted so strongly if his sister hadn't been raped and murdered.*

Amanda experienced a raw twinge of jealousy and then mentally dismissed it as irrelevant. "Well, Mr. Pidgeon. What do you propose? John's call said you were going to be my advance team. What does that mean? And how many people know about it?" She looked pointedly at Billie Thompson.

"I haven't shared anything specific. I think just the few of us should know what I'm planning. It would be safer for everyone else if it was our little secret."

Billie sniffed and said, "Well, in that case Wally, you owe me ten dollars for the pot of coffee and twenty dollars for my lost sleep."

"Billie, darling, I love you with my heart and soul, but I won't be here to protect you. The best I can do is keep you out of the loop."

Billie said, "Okay, Wally, but you better tell me when you get back just what in the heck you've been up to. Understood?"

Wally nodded and said, "Promise."

They all listened until the door between the living quarters and the restaurant slammed shut.

"Pissed off, I think," Wally grinned.

"Okay, Wally," Amanda said, "You asked for this meeting. What do you want from us?"

"You have assets and equipment I don't have. What I do have is an old, old friend in the American Community in Guaymas. He's retired DEA, but he keeps his old intelligence channels open. He tells me he can pinpoint Juan Ortega's location. That's the starting point.

"John tells me NCIS is planning an operation. So…I pinpoint Ortega, you take him out."

"And how would we do that?"

Wally pulled a map out of his black carryall, and opened it up. Spread out on the table, it was a map of Northwest Mexico. "Here," he said pointing to the map, "is Guaymas. The American Community is right around the point from Guaymas. My friend actually launches his boats right through the small surf and into the Gulf of California. Also known as the Sea of Cortez.

"Here is Alamos. My friend says that's the key to finding Ortega. He has a small hacienda there. So do a number of Hollywood types. Ortega likes to rub shoulders with these movie people. Winter is upon us; ergo, the big egos head to Alamos for some mild winter sun. My friend knows a man, a Mexican citizen, who works in one of the nicer cantinas. Ortega comes in, with his body guards, of course, and when he does, the man plants a bug in someone's pocket. Doesn't matter whose because they are all going to the same place.

"That gives you his location. You kill him, and we have no more problems with cartel assholes trying to kill my friends. End of story."

"Who is this cantina worker you're talking about?" John asked.

"Another old friend. All I'm going to do down there is go fishing." Wally said.

John shook his head. "Pretty loose, Wally. You won't have any backup."

"Wrong. Another of my old friends is a retired Mexican Army Major who worked hand and glove with DEA in the past. I've already talked to him. He also lives in the American Community. So, if things turn sour, he'll be there to watch my back."

John said, "Okay. We need to set up a system of contact, but I'm thinking we can fill in the blanks as we go."

"We?" Larae asked?

"I mean, uh, NCIS. I'm not going, am I, Amanda?"

"No. But Wally, I want to send someone with you as part of the advance team. He's blooded, never backs down in a gun fight, and he's soon to be retired."

Wally looked skeptical, but said, "Who?"

"Gino Maretti, a senior detective for the Bremerton City Police Department."

"Wasn't he down here during that fracas with Cowboy's gang?"

"One and the same. He was also with us at Sheriff Blair's cabin last night when one of Ortega's thugs tried to blow us all up. How did you know about Gino?"

Wally smiled and looked at Larae, "My Sweet Mama, the best bartender an undercover cop could be, she briefed me on it...about the bad guys blowing themselves up...everything. She might have shared too much, but then when a person is all banged up and drugged up, and hooked up to an IV, lying in a hospital bed, she might share more than she intended.

"And I have a terrific memory...except, of course, on those days when my forgetter is working over time." He paused and then said, "Ok. Marretti is in. But I'm not waiting for him. He'll have to make his own way to Guaymas. Here's a phone number he can use to call when he gets there. And here's a brochure for my friend's charter fishing service. He has a plane he uses to ferry people from San Felipe to Guaymas. Float plane. Might be the way to go. My friend's clients never have their luggage inspected. Understood?"

Amanda nodded, and Wally said, "Okay, then. How am I going to know Maretti when he gets there?"

Amanda started to laugh and then just couldn't stop laughing. She finally managed to choke out, "He's Italian," before she burst into uncontrollable laughter again. They just sat and watched her and wondered if she wasn't having a psychotic break.

She finally got her laughing under control and said. "Sorry. I don't know what got into me. Maybe it's just that this whole thing is so bizarre. Jésus, whose name is pronounced something like 'Hayzeus', tries to blow me up. But he bungles it. I decide to hide at Bud's cabin. Dennis Moore, the ASAC, calls to let me know my resignation was never processed, and then orders me back to Silverdale to help plan an operation against Juan Ortega.

"And then this gentleman, forgive me Mr. Pidgeon, but you don't look like you can take care of yourself, let alone go undercover in Mexico, this gentleman decides to be the advance party all by himself.

"The drive up here from Lakeview was nerve wracking, my tires spin, I can barely see the road for all the damned snow flakes in the headlights, and I nearly hit some deer.

"When you asked how you would know Gino, I guess my mind slipped a cog and I thought the question was hilarious. I'm thinking 'He's Italian!' Cracked me up."

Wally managed a tight little smile and then said, "Okay. He's Italian. Is he a tall Italian, a skinny Italian, black hair, gray hair, one armed, what? How am I going to know him?"

Amanda took a deep breath, got her emotions under control and said, "He's around five feet eight inches tall, a little paunchy. The last time I saw him his left arm was in a cast. Don't know when that's coming off. He has a gravelly voice, sort of like yours, Wally. His hair is blue-black and wavy. And he always wears highly polished penny loafers. He eats like a horse and cusses like a truck driver. And I'll tell him to wear a Seattle Mariners baseball cap. Okay?"

"That'll do. Give me his number. I'll send him my picture."

Larae started yawning and Roger said, "I'm not sure I even heard what I heard tonight, but I think I like it. Wish I was going along. You know, Gar here…I mean John…and I could be your team. He's never said anything, but I know he's special forces.

"I was once a Navy Seal." He patted his belly, and said, "And a lot thinner. But once a Seal always a Seal. Anyway, when I was in an oil rich, sandy son-of-a-bitch of a country whose name I cannot share with y'all, we managed several times to convince some local sheik that his rival was out to kill him, so he would try kill the other guy first. Great little wars they had among themselves, and they never suspected we were turning them against each other. I wonder if something like that couldn't be done this time as well."

Amanda was interested and Larae was mouthing the word "no" to John and gripping his forearm.

"One time," Roger continued, "we had a nifty little UAV armed with a couple of small rockets tipped with tiny, blow-your-ass-away war heads. We called this local bandit up and told him his arch rival was out to get him. Then we blew up a vehicle with our rockets, and watched while the bad guys scrambled for cover. Two days later, the rival war lord is killed by an assassin. Does that give you any ideas?"

John said, "I like it."

Larae said sharply, "John, you told me you were out…for good."

"Well," he said lamely, "this isn't really 'in' per se. No dirty work, just put a twist in some cartel shorts."

He looked at Larae and said quietly, "I just have to do this. Just one more time."

One hour and another pot of coffee later, they had a plan that appealed to each of them.

Wally yawned and said, "I like it. Low risk, high pay off."

Amanda nodded and said, "John and I will fly to SeaTac in the morning and present it to Dennis and SAC Thompson. In the meantime, get your credentials all polished up and get your asses to Guaymas. Travel separately. You have my secure number, and I'll send a scrambler with Maretti. Who needs money?"

They each shook their heads.

Day Two

Day Two

8:15 a.m. ~ Sky Lakes Medical Center, Klamath Falls

MANFRED GILES LAY HANDCUFFED TO A bed in a locked security room normally used for psychiatric patients. At the moment, he was sleeping. A bored unarmed security guard, wearing the uniform of a contract security company, was sitting on a high stool at the nurse's station keeping watch on Giles through a narrow, shatterproof window, and playing games on an iPad. An older nurse with short graying hair sat on a padded stool writing in a chart held captive by a metal notebook.

Neither looked up when Detective Harmon and Officer Downing walked down the hallway. "Good morning," Harmon said.

"Yeah?" the security guard replied without looking up from his screen.

Downing was immediately angry. "Listen," she leaned over and whispered in his ear, "we've come to kill your patient. Is that all right?"

The dunderhead finally looked up, eyes big. He didn't say anything until Downing showed him her badge and said, "What's the use of having security if you're asleep."

"I'm here to just keep the patients from hurting staff or themselves," he said defensively. "I don't do gun work."

The man pulled the phone clipped to his belt and held it up. "If there is serious trouble, we run like hell and call our supervisor."

"Oh good," she said sarcastically, "that will really help."

The nurse chimed in, "Only sworn peace officers can carry guns in a hospital."

Harmon produced his badge and said, pointing at Manny's room, "We need to talk to your patient."

"He's really out of it, and his attorney was here earlier. He told us no one other than medical staff was to talk to Mr. Giles."

Christine Downing and Mathew Harmon looked at each other and shrugged. "Thanks for your help," Christine said sarcastically.

They were out of earshot before Harmon said, "Lawyered up? All ready? How does that happen? We need to move him to the infirmary at the jail. Make the attorney come to us."

Harmon pulled his cell phone from a shirt pocket and thumbed in Detective Jones's number. When Jones came on the line, Harmon said, "Boss. Need your help. We need to move this Giles asshole to the jail's infirmary. I think that's probably something that will take you or the Chief to make happen. Oh…and one other thing. He's already lawyered up."

Harmon paused, and then Downing heard him say, "I don't know how anyone even knew he was in custody. Which is another good reason to move him. He's in a locked room, but it's only locked from the inside…to keep patients in…not to keep people out."

The gray-haired nurse caught up to them before they started moving again. "He says he wants to talk to you. Something about not feeling safe where he is."

"How did he know we were here?" Downing asked.

"I think he saw you through the window. Somehow he knew you were police."

Downing could hear Jones talking, just not what he was saying, and then Harmon said, "Hold a second, Boss." He looked at Downing who said, "Giles want to talk to us."

Harmon nodded and spoke into the phone. "It looks like Giles wants to talk to us after all. I'll keep you posted," and turned the phone off.

Giles was punching the button on the morphine pump over and over again when they opened the door and walked in.

"I want a deal," he said. "I'll plead to possession. That's it. You can't prove anything beyond that. You can't prove any of the junk in the warehouse was mine. But you gotta move me to someplace where I'll be safe. I think Hollywood is going to come after me." His words were slightly slurred, and they weren't sure he even knew what he was saying.

Downing pulled a small, high fidelity tape recorder from a belly pack and turned it on. Harmon crowded in on one side, towering over Giles, and Downing crowded in on the other. She held the tape recorder up where he could see it. "Do you understand that you don't have to talk to us without an attorney present?"

"Yes, but he don't know what he's doing. So ask away."

Harmon said, "First, we have to read you your rights." And so he did, intoning the rights of defendants arrested by law enforcement officers as prescribed by the Miranda laws.

Manny tried to shut him up by saying, "You don't have to do that." But Harmon read the whole of the Miranda, concluding with, "Do you understand?"

"Yeah, yeah. I understand," Giles said. He held up the control for the morphine pump, looked at the light under the button and said, "Damn thing isn't working, and I hurt like hell. Why'd you guys shoot me?"

Harmon said, "I guess because you were shooting at us. Don't you remember?"

At the end of ten minutes, Manfred Giles drifted off to sleep before they had asked all of the questions they wanted him to answer. But he had told them about some guy whose call sign was Hollywood, and that Hollywood was the regional boss who controlled the illegal drug trade in the Klamath Basin. According to Giles, Hollywood brooked no failure, and Giles was afraid he would be the next dealer to disappear.

They also knew Giles was deathly afraid of what Mariah might testify to. Just as he was fading out he smiled and mumbled, "Not to worry. I can get her, even from jail."

Downing shut the tape recorder off and said, "What a disgusting piece of crap."

Harmon didn't answer. Instead he tapped on the door and the security guard let them out.

She put the tape recorder back in a belly pack and said, "You know we can't use any of this. He was so drugged up he couldn't even stay awake."

Harmon nodded, and pushed the door open. He waited until they were out of ear shot and then said, "That's right, we can't. But we have a little more information than we had before. Did you understand what he said before he zonked out?"

"I'm sure he was referring to Mariah," she said.

Harmon nodded. "I've got to call Sheriff Blair this morning. I'm thinking Mariah would be safer in Lakeview than she would be here."

"Leave her there? I'm afraid that's up to the judge. I wonder if we can find any relatives?"

"When we get back to the office, why don't you use your patented charm and your Child Welfare contacts to get the ball rolling. Try to convince them she should stay in Lake County for now."

10:30 a.m. ~ Alaska Airlines,
somewhere over Northern California

WALLY HAD DECIDED A LONG TIME ago that he really didn't mind flying. But he admitted, he was more than a little paranoid about takeoffs and landings. Once air born and in level flight, he was content to watch the scenery and identify landmarks to keep track of the plane's progress.

This morning, he had a window seat on the left side of the plane in first class. The night's storm had blown on out of Northern California, leaving a fresh blanket of snow on the Sierra Nevada Mountains and scrubbing all but a few thin cirrus clouds out of a crisp blue sky. They were scheduled to land in Sacramento in about forty minutes, be on the ground for forty-five minutes and then resume flight to Los Angeles.

He had a book to keep him company, but at the moment he was staring down at the massive shoulders and rough peak of Mt. Shasta. "Beautiful," he said aloud without realizing it.

His seat mate, a stout matronly looking woman, leaned across and peered at the white coated mountain. She sniffed and said, "I'd hate to land there," and turned back to her Kindle reader.

Wally didn't respond. He identified Shasta Lake, or what he thought must be Shasta Lake, and then heard the engines change pitch slightly and felt the plane begin a gradual change in elevation as the pilot started the long descent into Sacramento, California.

Twenty minutes later the flaps whined and cranked into place and the plane hopped like it had hit a speed bump. The pilot increased the power of the engines and tilted the plane to the starboard side to begin a gentle sweep around Sacramento to line up on the airport. And Wally's fingers tightened on the arm rest.

The stewardess gave the passengers their instructions "prior to landing," and there was a stir as tray tables were latched into place and seat backs brought to the upright position. Wally was gratified in a perverse way to see a trickle of sweat start down the temple of an older man seated two rows ahead on the right side of the plane. *I guess I'm not the only one who finds air travel to be just slightly barbaric. Helpless, that's what we are. Helpless. Reminds me of funerals. All you can do is just sit and take it.*

The pilot set the plane on the runway much too hard in Wally's opinion, and he feared the reverse thrust and the brakes wouldn't be enough to keep the plane from plunging off the end of the runway. But in spite of Wally's trepidations, the plane slowed rapidly and then turned onto a taxiway and toward the terminal.

The external look of terminals didn't make Wally feel any better about flying. The tarmac was always oil soaked, and black tire strips made him wonder how any tire could take the mammoth weight of the big planes. Finally the pilot eased the plane to a stop at a numbered gate, shut the engines down and said over the intercom, "Welcome to Sacramento, and thanks for flying Alaska."

Wally chose to stay in his seat while, by his count, about half the passengers disembarked. None looked suspicious to him. So he picked up his book, a Tony Hillerman novel about a murder on the Navajo Indian Reservation. The dead man's shoes had been placed on the wrong feet.

He was enjoying one of his favorite Hillerman characters, Joe Leaphorn, when his cell phone buzzed. "Yes?"

"Wally Pidgeon?"

"Who wants to know?"

"Gino Maretti, your new fishing partner."

"Ah, Mr. Maretti. Good. Here's what you do. Fly to San Diego. Then take the commuter flight to El Centro. Take a cab to the Mexicali border crossing. Our fishing guide will meet you on the American side of the border. Do what he says."

"How will I know him?"

Wally laughed and said, "Look for the biggest damned Mexican you ever saw. His name is David and he'll have on a Charger's jacket. He never misses a Chargers home game. But don't get him started on Phillip Rivers."

Maretti laughed. "Okay. I can talk Seahawks instead."

"Wear your Seahawks cap. And load up on bottled water. David will drive you to San Felipe and then fly you to Guaymas. He's has a first class Beaver float plane." He paused, "You got all that?"

"Yeah, I got it."

"Where are you now?"

"On the ground in San Francisco. I'll be in San Diego in about an hour."

"You're fast."

"Got some bills I want our friends to pay."

"Well, wait for me then in the terminal at El Centro. We'll cab it together."

Gino said, "How will I know you?"

"Look for a skinny old fart carrying a fly rod case and wearing a khaki fishing vest. I'm not nearly as tall as I used to be, but I still stand five six in my socks."

"See you there," Gino said and clicked off.

10:30 a.m. ~ Quartz Mountain, west of Lake View

SHERIFF BUD BLAIR AND UNDERSHERIFF SONNY Sixkiller spent the morning working a wreck on the Lakeview side of Quartz

Mountain on Highway 140. It wasn't much of a wreck. Just a jackknifed truck and trailer, but a woman driving a Subaru Forester left the road to avoid the sliding Freightliner and smacked a small pine tree with enough force to deploy her airbag. The truck slid into the ditch behind the Subaru and completely plugged the road.

After checking on the woman who was complaining of chest and neck pains, the truck driver called 911 and asked for an ambulance and also a tow truck to help him get his truck back on the road. The Lake County Emergency Services Center dispatched the ambulance and two units from the Lake County Sheriff's Department. Only three people were available for patrol in South Lake County, and since Michelle was in Westside talking to Mariah, that left Bud and Sonny to work the wreck.

The traffic on the highway between Klamath Falls and Lakeview had managed to pack the night's snow into a smooth, slick surface. The storm had blown on out of Lake and Klamath counties, so the sun was out and the snow on the pavement was beginning to melt, but not in the shady stretches. What Mother Nature left was melted snow water seeping across the road on top of packed snow. Bud figured the truck was carrying too much speed when it topped the hill and when the driver tried to slow his speed, the brakes locked and the truck jackknifed. He sent Sonny and his long legs up the road beyond the truck to stop traffic. The young woman who wrecked her car called relatives in Lakeview who said they would send a wrecker out and would meet her at the hospital.

The EMTs placed a neck brace on the woman and then helped her walk to the ambulance. Bud asked paramedics to wait a minute and introduced himself. The injured young woman told him her name, Becky Eagen, age twenty-five, a resident of Klamath Falls. Becky said, "I waited until the storm blew over to go home. Trying to be safe," she grimaced. "Just before I saw the truck coming down the hill…sort of sideways…I was listening to that wonderful news about the missing girl."

"What wonderful news would that be?" Bud said and waited with some trepidation for her answer. "The radio said you found that missing girl alive and well. That's just wonderful." She stopped and looked out the rear door of the ambulance. "My poor car. I bought it so I would have a safe vehicle to make the drive over here."

Bud got her address from her driver's license, handed the license back to the young woman and told the EMTs she was ready to roll.

He watched the ambulance head down the highway, studded tires clacking on the bare stretches of pavement. He pulled his cell phone from his shirt pocket and called Michelle's cell number.

"I heard," she said before Bud could even say hello. "I heard an interview between the station and Colleen Johnson's friend, Amber. She was so proud to think she and her friends had found Mariah before we did."

"What do you think?"

"I'm just going to keep her with me until the two counties decided where she should stay. Right now I think she should stay with me."

"When we finish here, I'll call you back."

"Any injuries?"

"A woman who left the highway to avoid a jackknifed truck sliding down the road at her smacked a tree. She was complaining of neck and chest pain which might have been caused by the air bag. The ambulance has her headed to the hospital in Lakeview." The truck driver was walking gingerly down the slick pavement toward Bud, so he said, "I'll call you back later."

Bud took a statement from the truck driver and then took lots of photos with his digital camera, including the Subaru tracks in the snow, the front end of the car and what he could see of the skinned bark on the little pine tree.

A big wrecker from Lakeview was there about thirty minutes later. The tow truck driver looked the scene over, turned the wrecker around, and went to work. He set blocks under the rear tires on the semi trailer, powered down the hydraulic jacks on the back of the tow truck, and ran a cable to the frame of the jackknifed truck.

Bud watched in fascination as the big drum on the tow truck tightened the cable and then slid the truck sideways and slowly straightened the truck and trailer combination out. The truck driver pulled the blocks from behind the rear wheels on the trailer and the rig was ready to roll again. Bud waited until the tow truck had backed down the road and into a drive way and turned around, heading back down the hill towards Lakeview. The truck eased on down the hill and then Sonny started letting traffic through again.

Sonny came slipping and sliding down the side of the road and said, "Hey, Boss. I think that does it. We aren't going to wait for the wrecker for the Subaru, are we?"

"No. It's off the road so it's not much of a hazard. I think the woman's family is sending a wrecker out for it. We need to get back to town. The woman who wrecked the Subaru told me about some wonderful news on the radio." He stopped and waited.

Sonny frowned, his green eyes locked on Bud's. "Okay, I'll bite. What wonderful news?"

"By now," Bud said in disgust, "every radio and TV station in Oregon, Idaho and northern California knows we found Mariah... safe and sound."

"Crap," Sonny said. "How did that get out?"

"Do you remember me telling you about Amber?"

"She didn't, did she?" Sonny said incredulously. "She was told not to let anybody else know!"

"I think she already had before we warned her."

Sonny shook his head. "Cat's out of the bag now. Is Michelle with her?"

"Yeah. I'm going to have Michelle bring Mariah back to the station until Child Welfare, both Klamath County and ours figures out what to do for her. We can protect her at the station."

"Guess we better get back to town, then," Sonny said.

11:00 a.m. ~ SeaTac Airport

AMANDA AND JOHN BERNARD WATCHED AS bags rode the powered beltway through a narrow window to be dumped and bumped unceremoniously by other bags on the circling carousel. Travelers crowded the carousel, pulling bags from the queue and then heading toward the double doors that led to bus and taxi stands.

Amanda grabbed her lone bag and turned to find tall Dennis Moore standing in her way. "Let me take that," he said and smiled. In spite of herself, Amanda smiled back, forgetting for a split second she was truly angry at NCIS Silverdale, Washington. *Damn, but he's good looking, all six feet-four-inches of him. All that wavy dark hair, good teeth, broad shoulders, and that self-assured, half amused look he always has. I could forget I'm mad at him.*

She stiffened and said, "I can carry my own bag, thank you."

"Still mad at Thompson, I see."

"What makes you think I'm not mad at you, Dennis?"

"Well, other than the fact I ordered you back to work, I can't think of a single reason."

John Bernard, large pack sack on one shoulder walked over and said, "Lover's quarrel?"

"Don't even think it," Amanda said.

Dennis frowned. "What don't you understand about 'resigned'?" he asked John.

"Private contractor is what I am. Why don't we go someplace and talk about it."

They walked down the concourse until they found a coffee bar. Steaming cup of Seattle's Best in hand they squeezed into a corner table with tall stools. John didn't wait for Dennis to open the conversation.

"We have an advance team headed for Mexico, ostensibly to do some fishing with a guide named David Pena. Peña says Ortega has a small, heavily guarded hacienda on the edge of a town called Alamos. He likes it there because of three things: one, there's only one road into Alamos; two, a number of Hollywood types own, like the old song says, 'adobe haciendas' in Alamos; and three, he likes rubbing shoulders with famous people. I'm guessing, they may like him for the free coke he is rumored to hand out like candy to the right people. Easy target, I think." He handed Dennis a folded sheet of paper. "Here's the equipment I'll need.

"Our plan is to use an Archer UAV, fly it off a fishing boat from the Sea of Cortez, recon his place, which our inside man will identify. My new partner and I, a former Navy Seal, will put a target laser on the hacienda.

"When we are in place, our advance party, one old man who grew up speaking Spanish, will call Juan Ortega on his 'unlisted' number, which David Peña somehow knows, and pretend to be from the Reynosa Cartel. He will tell Ortega to stop killing Americans because it is bad for business, and if he doesn't then it means war.

"By the way, Peña is a retired DEA agent with dual American-Mexican citizenship. He lives in the American Community in Guaymas and really is a sports fishing guide. Perfect cover.

"So what we need from you, Special Agent Moore, is a UAV, satellite photos of the area in and around Alamos, and the promise of helicopter extraction if things go to shit. Can you do that?"

Dennis was grinning. "This should be fun. I'll get you the UAV, I'll get you a backup team, about two dozen marines on standby in San Diego ready to ride to the rescue, and I'll have a civilian yacht, a big one-hundred-twenty-five footer anchored in Guaymas harbor in two days. The Navy uses it to spy on people. It's faster than it looks, and has some heavy-duty armament on board. So, you do your recon, and the civilian yacht will take the UAV down the coast until it's as close to Alamos as it can get and still be wet."

John looked at Amanda. "You already briefed him?"

"Yes."

"I thought you were mad at him."

"I am, but we still need him if we are going to pull this off."

"No 'we' in this, Amanda," Dennis said, "Ortega knows what you look like. You can't stay lucky forever, so until Juan Ortega is taken care of, you stay home. And that's an order. You can watch and sweat right along with me and SAC Thompson. Got it?"

She didn't answer, just glared at him.

Dennis glanced at John and asked, "Where's your partner?"

"He should be in El Centro by this evening. I'm thinking you could lay on a jet and let me catch up on my sleep. The Navy flies and I rest."

"How you going to get the UAV across the border?"

"David Peña has bribed the crossing guards on the Mexican side of the border. He has clients coming and going year round, so they never look in a 'client's' luggage. We disguise our UAV to look like a big, protected fishing rod carrier, and we simply walk it across the border. Next step is to risk life and limb in an old Beaver float plane which will fly us from San Felipe to Guaymas. Everybody hooks up at Peña's house, we say nothing about our plans until we are offshore…fishing."

"Personally, I'm taking a fly rod for bonito. They're the next best thing to bone fish."

Dennis took a sip of coffee and asked, "Do you need anybody else?"

"Yeah," John said, "I need someone to fly the UAV."

"Dudley," Amanda said. "He loves computer gadgets."

"No," John said, "I have a lot of respect for Dudley's skills, but I want someone who flies a UAV for breakfast, lunch, and dinner."

"I'll get someone on board the yacht who can handle that job."

"What's the name of this yacht?" John asked.

"The *Nemo*, out of Port Angeles."

"Captain's name?"

"Silas."

John shook his head. "You've got to be kidding."

As they finished their coffee, ASAC Dennis Moore said, "The Boss laid on his private limo for us. We'll drop you at home, Amanda, and then put John in a plane for El Centro. The Boss really likes this operation, by the way."

"That's scary," John said. "I hope he knows plans go to shit as soon as the fire starts."

11:30 a.m. ~ Lake County Sheriff's Office

MICHELLE WAS LOOKING GRIM WHEN SHE and Mariah walked into the station. Mariah hadn't objected to leaving Bea's house, especially when Michelle told her Amber had talked to the local radio station. "Your friend ratted me out," Mariah accused Colleen. "You have no idea what that means. Now you and your family are as much at risk as I am."

She finally looked at Bea and said, "Thank you, Mrs. Johnson. I think you are a really nice person, but I have to go now."

And then she turned on Colleen and said, "Your friend Amber is a busybody who should learn to mind her own business. Now Manny knows where I am and he'll send someone after me."

"Really?" Colleen said, her voice cracking with excitement.

"It's not funny," Mariah said in exasperation. "You don't have any way to understand these people. There isn't anything they won't do to other people. They don't even need a reason."

She walked out the front door of Bea's house without saying goodbye to Colleen or looking back. Bea wiped a stray tear and then held out her hand to Michelle. "Officer Trivoli, you take care of that little girl because obviously we can't."

Michelle could hear Bea speaking in a loud voice as Cody closed the front door behind her.

Mariah was quiet during the drive from Bea Johnson's house to the station. They were driving past the snow-covered golf course when Mariah said, "It must be nice to live a normal life. You know, play golf without wondering if somebody is going to shoot you." A tear of self pity crept down one cheek, and she scrubbed it angrily away with the sleeve of her freshly laundered hooded sweatshirt.

"I think it must be," Michelle agreed. "I'm not sure I live a normal life either. The young men I've met are all afraid of me or hate cops or just can't see me as a person. So…I live alone a lot.

"But sometimes I get to help people and that makes it a lot nicer."

"People like me, you mean?"

"Especially you, Mariah."

Michelle parked her vehicle in front of the office and started for the front door, but Mariah hung back. "Can I have a quick smoke before we go in?"

Startled, Michelle barked, "No. Of course not. You are too young to smoke."

"I do anyway. Babs never cared."

"I care. I care about anything that isn't good for you." Michelle paused and then asked, "Can you quit?"

Mariah looked uncomfortable and then nodded.

"Okay, then. You are now smoke free."

"It's hard," Mariah said, "but okay. I'll try to quit, but I'm not making any promises."

Michelle smiled and touched Mariah's shoulder. "I have faith in you."

Once inside the station, Michelle introduced Mariah to Karen Highsmith and then took Mariah down the hall to a small office. She set Mariah up with pen and paper and the command to write down everything and anything she remembered about Manny, when he started living with Mariah and her mom, any names she could remember of the dealers Manny supplied. In short…everything.

Karen Highsmith, Bud's unofficial administrative assistant and his official Technical Deputy in charge of the jail, brought Mariah a fresh, soft oatmeal raisin cookie and a glass of chocolate milk.

Mariah said, "Thank you," politely which is all it took to win Karen over completely.

"She's such a tiny thing," Karen whispered to Michelle. "Makes you want to kill that son-of-a-bitch, doesn't it."

Michelle was slightly startled. Not by the words so much as by who was saying them. Karen, in spite of all her years in a business that bred cynicism and used a long series of swear words for punctuation, had never, in Michelle's memory, uttered a single swear word, not even anything as strong as "damn."

"That would be against the law, Karen," Michelle said, "but I can't imagine it would bother me much if someone offed the guy."

Bud and Sonny walked in together, Molly padding along behind them. Michelle could tell by the way Bud slammed the front door that he was furious.

"Is our girl here?" he asked.

"In my office," Michelle answered, "writing an essay about her life as the child of a drug addicted, crackhead mother and a nasty live-in boyfriend."

Sonny nodded and said, "Good idea. It might be helpful for her to get it all out into the open, sort of a way to talk about it. If she were military, we might think PTSD, and she sure as hell has been living in a war zone."

Michelle nodded and said, "She's tough. You should have heard her chewing out Colleen Johnson because Colleen's friend Amber didn't have enough sense to keep quiet about Mariah. I wouldn't want her mad at me."

Karen Highsmith waited until Bud slipped into his office before bringing him a cup of coffee. Molly turned around three times on the cedar-chip pad and settled with her chin on her paws, black eyes blinking and switching back and forth from Karen to Bud. Bud set his tan Stetson on a filing cabinet and said, "Thanks. I'll go check on Mariah." Molly scrambled to her feet and looked expectantly at Bud. When he didn't give her a "stay" command, she followed him down the hallway.

Two pages of precise cursive writing were turned upside down on Michelle's desk, and a look of determined concentration wrinkled Mariah's brow. A half eaten cookie in her left hand, she was rereading the last few sentences on page three.

Bud set his cup on the desk, dragged up a wooden visitor's chair and sat down across from Mariah. She looked up and he pointed to the two sheets she had turned upside down. "May I?"

She shrugged, but didn't say anything. "I'll take that as a yes," he said and turned the pages over. She watched his face intently while he slowly and carefully read what she had written.

Molly startled her by laying her black head on Mariah's leg and wagging her tail gently, looking up at Mariah with soft brown eyes, inviting Mariah's hand to stroke her head, scratch her ears, or rub her neck. "What's your name?" Mariah asked and rubbed Molly's neck.

Bud looked up from his reading and smiled. "Her name is Molly, and she likes girls. A lot."

He finished reading the pages and then took a sip of coffee before he said, "Hard work, isn't it?"

She nodded. "I'm not very good at writing."

"I disagree. What you have so far is clear and compelling... at least to this reader. So keep going, and I'll ask Karen keep the cookies and the chocolate milk coming."

"Sheriff," she said and then hesitated. "I...uh...I want to see my mother."

Bud nodded and then said, "We'll have to make a call, but if I can arrange it, how about today?"

"Oh good! I'd like that a lot." She looked up at him, her clear blue eyes poking holes in his soul. She shook her head slightly. "I guess I let her down."

Bud was startled. "How in the world did you decide that?"

Mariah dropped her eyes to the pages on the desk. "If I had been home, maybe I could have kept her from doing so much meth."

He wrinkled his forehead in concentration and finally said, "Okay...I'll grant you that much, but you must have had a good reason for not being there. Like maybe staying away from Manny. Right?"

She looked tortured, but she finally, almost imperceptibly nodded. In a voice so low he could barely hear her, she said, "He kept grabbing me when Mom wasn't looking, trying to kiss me... and other things. I hate him! I hope he dies!"

"I'm not sure that will happen anytime soon, but I'm pretty sure he'll spend a lot of years in jail. Will that do?"

She shrugged and said, "I guess so," without a lot of conviction in her voice.

Bud nodded and said, "Okay, then. Keep writing. I'm really hoping you don't forget to write down what you just told me. Understand?"

She straightened up and looked directly at him. "Yes" she said emphatically, "Child abuse is a crime. Right?"

"Yep. If we can nail him for child abuse, we can add some years to his sentence." He grinned when he noticed Molly sitting on her haunches looking at the half eaten cookie in Mariah's hand. A small drool was starting drip down one side of her jaw.

"Molly, come with me."

12:30 p.m. ~ Lake County Sheriff's Office

OFFICER DOWNING TOOK BUD'S CALL, AND when he asked how Mariah's mom was doing, Downing told him the hospital had just confirmed that Barbara Caldwell was awake and responding to her doctor and the nurses.

"They said a stroke is common for meth overdose. So as a precaution she was treated for stroke almost immediately. They think they managed to reverse most of the damage."

"Most," he echoed.

"Right. She has some brain damage. Her speech is slurred and she forgets some of the words she wants to use. She doesn't have much control over her left arm, and she can't walk...yet. But, given her youth, with the help of speech therapy and physical therapy there is every reason to be hopeful she'll fully recover."

"I love scientific medical terminology, especially words like most and hopefully." Bud said. "Look, I practically promised Mariah she could see her mother today, but I'm wondering if that's such a good idea now."

"I think it would give Barbara a boost, and maybe ease Mariah's mind that her mom is well taken care of."

"Okay. We'll talk it over, and if we get an okay from Child Welfare, I'll have Deputy Trivoli take her over there for a brief visit. And then we'll bring her back here. What do you think?"

"Giles is being moved to the infirmary in our jail, so I can't imagine he would be any threat."

Bud opened the security door leading to the courthouse hallways and down to the court room. He knocked on Judge Lynch's door and pushed it open.

"Judge," he said, "I'm here to apologize, and to ask for a favor."

Lynch stood up and reached across the desk, offering Bud his hand. "Hell, Bud, I'm the one to apologize. Sometimes I think I like this job too much. Just let those old biddies talk me into a moment of insanity. I'm plumb humiliated. Total lapse of character is all. You name it and if I can do it, consider it done."

Bud grinned and said, "How do two old campaigners like you and me get so crossed up?"

"I don't know," Lynch said, "but let's put it behind us okay?"

"What I need is Child Welfare to request the court...that's you in this case...to appoint Michelle Trivoli as Mariah Caldwell's temporary guardian. Can you do it?"

Lynch picked up his phone and dialed an extension.

"Deanna? Could you come to my office? Sheriff Blair and I want to talk to you about Mariah."

Michelle drove carefully and ignored the scenery. She was more concerned with icy spots on the pavement than with the beauty of white snow, blue skies, and rusty-barked Ponderosa lining the road in its climb up the east side of the Quartz Mountain pass.

She was only half listening to Mariah, when it finally sank in that Mariah wanted to know if the sheriff was married, how old he was, where he lived, and did he have any family.

Michelle hid a smile. Mariah wasn't the first female in Lake County to have a crush on Bud Blair, but she was certainly the youngest that Michelle knew of. It set her to thinking of her own feelings about Bud. He was her boss, so she worked hard to deflect any feelings of affection that strayed into her relationship with Bud. But she had to admit her maternal instincts were running full flood when she thought Bill Casey shot her sheriff.

She had clearly intended to kill Casey, but all of her "killing" shots smacked the pine tree he was standing behind. "But for a tree..." she intoned, thinking of the old saying, "But for a nail, a shoe was lost. But for a shoe, a horse was lost. But for a horse, the battle was lost."

Her version wasn't exactly parallel, but she figured any wife beater like Bill Casey deserved to be shot, and she had certainly lost the opportunity. *And if you are going to shoot someone, why not do it right? I wonder what kind of cop that makes me?*

Her silent musing was interrupted by Mariah. "How did he get that scar in his left eyebrow?"

Michelle laughed and said, "I don't think I ever heard him mention it. Why don't you ask him the next time you see him."

Mariah asked, "What does temporary guardian mean?"

"I think it means I'm to look out for you, feed you, keep you safe and make sure you don't sass me too much." She gave Mariah a smile.

"I think I like that."

By the time they drove into the little town of Bly, Michelle's stomach was growling. "Are you hungry?" she asked Mariah.

Mariah gave her an impish, sidelong smile and said, "Is this the 'feed me' part of being my guardian?"

Michelle grinned and said, "It could be."

"Well, in that case, I could eat," Mariah said.

"Let's stop at the deli. They bake their own bread, and they make great sandwiches. Their pastry isn't bad either."

Fifteen minutes later they pulled back onto the highway armed with two tuna salad sandwiches on warm, fresh-baked whole wheat bread, Michelle's sixteen ounce coffee laced with French Vanilla syrup and lots of cream, a bottle of orange juice for Mariah, and a white bakery bag with two cream-filled donuts.

The sun had worked its magic on the pavement in the open fields between Bly and the Sprague River section of Highway 140, erasing the snow and turning puddles to steam, so Michelle kicked the speed up to sixty and listened to Mariah talk about her friend Lacey, and her favorite teacher at Henley Middle School, Miss Brown.

When Michelle asked her if she had a favorite subject in school, Mariah promptly answered, "Math. Math explains everything."

"How about reading?"

"I like to read fantasy books. I read *The Lion the Witch and the Wardrobe*. That was good."

Michelle nudged her to keep her talking. "What was good about it?"

"I think I liked it because the girls are brave. And because the good people win. Wouldn't it be neat to walk into your closet and into a different world?"

"Aren't girls supposed to watch from the sidelines while the boys do the rough stuff?"

Mariah shook her head. "No," she mumbled around a bite of sandwich. "We have to take care of ourselves; otherwise boys tell us what to do."

Mariah devoured the sandwich, drank the orange juice and wolfed down the cream filled donut with avarice akin to desperation. And Michelle wondered if Mariah had been eating on a regular basis. When Michelle offered Mariah the second donut, Mariah said, "Thanks." She rolled the bakery sack down around the donut and said, "I'll save it for later."

Once started, Mariah talked non-stop for the next forty miles, and it was apparent to Michelle that this tiny girl really had no one to talk to after Barbara Caldwell slid into the fog of drug addiction. Mariah had Lacey, of course, but some things were too painful and too personal to talk about with anyone. That she trusted Michelle enough to talk about those painful, personal experiences, wasn't lost on Michelle. Her heart ached for Mariah, and in some profound way Michelle was humbled by her trust.

"Does your mom ever talk about your father?"

Mariah shook her head. "He died in a car wreck when we lived in Dunsmuir."

"When was that?"

"I think I was five. Mom had to go to work after that."

Michelle made a mental note to contact the Dunsmuir police to see if the story was true.

As they drove the last couple of miles into Klamath Falls, Mariah stopped talking and just stared out the window. Michelle stole a glance at Mariah, at her silky brown hair, shiny and combed out today, pulled back from her temples by two red berets Michelle had given her. A tiny piece of icing clung to her chin, somehow adding to a picture of innocence.

Michelle shook her head slightly and turned back to the road. *She looks like a clean cut, normal thirteen-year-old girl. Looking at her, you'd never guess her mother was a meth addict, or that her mother's drug dealing live-in boyfriend is a killer, by inclination if not in fact. What kind of a mother brings a slime ball like that into a house with a young girl? Only an addict would do that, or a drunk. Somebody should shoot Manny **and** the mother.*

2:00 p.m. ~ Lakeview

BUD DROVE MOLLY TO THE HOUSE and dropped her off at his single-story rambler out on the highway north of town. He scooped dry food from the big bag in the metal locker on his back porch, gave her fresh water, and locked her in the fenced back yard. When she turned her back on him and did her nesting spin before lying down on her blanket in the corner of the covered porch, he knew she was irritated at being left behind.

He laughed and said, "Molly, you are as temperamental as any human female I know."

He liked the drive back down the highway to town; something in the setting appealed to him, the little town tucked in against the lower west slopes of the Warner Mountains, the land sloping gently south to the upper marshes of Goose Lake, a sizable body of water that shrank in the dry seasons and expanded to flood fields and drown fences in the wet ones.

The highway carried him past the old Civilian Conservation Corps-style buildings of the 1930s in the compound of the Lakeview Ranger Station, USDA Forest Service; Hunter's Hot Springs, sitting west of the highway, the warm-water pools covered with mallards, widgeon, buffleheads, cinnamon teal, coot (commonly known as mud hens), and a few Canada geese among the more common species. One of Bud's best photos of a cinnamon teal had been shot on the ponds.

Even though the geyser that once spouted in and over one of the ponds rarely made an appearance these days, Bud still carried his camera and hoped for a good shot of the geyser in action. It was no rival for Old Faithful in Yellowstone, but it was a local landmark.

Closer to town, he could see off on the right the log deck feeding the Lakeview Lumber Company saw mill, and then the old cemetery before he rounded a slight curve in the road and drove into town. He liked the town, the old cottonwoods, willows and other broadleaf trees, bare now, but giving comfort and shade in the heat of summer to yards which had matured years before. He pulled onto the main street where Highway 140 joined Highway 395. The Lake County Emergency Services Center sat on a corner near the junction, and he reflected on how much nicer his life had been when he and Nancy Sixkiller were still courting, and not ex-fiancées.

The driver of a blue Ford SuperCab pickup traveling in the opposite direction waved and honked at Bud. Bud waved back. "Titus...whozzit? Dang, it all. What's his last name? Too short on sleep and too long awake, I guess." He knew his mind would keep on working until he remembered so he just let it go.

A small covey of quail skittered across the main street, probably heading, Bud guessed, for a yard where they could find a daily handout of bird seed.

He turned left at the courthouse and pulled into a parking spot around back by a door with the legend Lake County Sheriff on the glass.

The long night, the business with the bomb, and short sleep made it difficult to focus, so he just sat at his desk pushing papers, literally moving one pile to a corner of his desk, restacking, shuffling, and moving the pile to a different spot on a desk that was gradually attracting enough forms, letters, files and miscellany to bury any open spaces. He turned on his computer and looked at wanted "posters" on his monitor, and signed time sheets without reading them, trying and failing to concentrate on the job of running a county sheriff's department.

Karen briefed him about the operation of the jail with information about average occupancy, average length of stay, current income and current expenses. She also told him the names of the two current occupants of Bud's six-bed jail, a couple of local drunks incarcerated for assault—on each other and on another drunk at the Pastime. She told him Harney County was bringing them two more "guests" for a period of forty-five days. "I would like you or Sonny to be here when they arrive. Harney County says they are not happy campers."

Bud nodded. "What time?"

She checked the clock on Bud's wall and said, "The deputies bringing them down called in a few minutes ago. They were ten miles south of Wagontire. I'd guess another ninety minutes."

"I'll be here." He knew without asking why the Harney County prisoners were unhappy. Prisoners counted county jail incarceration as hard time.

It looked to Bud like the jail was almost paying for itself since Karen had started renting jail space.

Sonny dropped in to let him know the Arson Task Force was being temporarily reactivated with a meeting scheduled for Monday in Bend. He was headed today, Saturday, to Bend to interview a suspect in last summer's arson fires, one of which burned thirteen homes in a suburban area near Bend. Bud shook his head and said, "I'm wondering why someone in Bend can't interview your suspect."

Sonny's squinted at Bud, green eyes showing a hint of exasperation that Bud would challenge his decision. "Of course they can. But they don't know my guy is a suspect yet, and if someone goes barging in and hammering on the guy, he'll clam up. Right now he's having fun, because he doesn't know I'm on to him. He actually thinks he's helping me track down somebody else. The guy works as a temporary summer fire fighter, but he's got a degree in chemistry. That in itself is suspicious.

"So I'm going to ask him to help me figure out how to set a fire without leaving any clues as to the ignition source. If I appeal to his ego, and if he tells me how our arsonist has been setting fires, I'll know where to look for the physical evidence that will tie him to last summer's fires." Sonny paused. "Or clear him, I suppose."

"Well...I guess I can only say, Go get 'em Sonny. Put him 'em away."

Sonny grinned and said, "Oh, I will, Boss. I certainly will. I should be back on Tuesday, the Lord willing and the creeks don't rise."

"Drive safely, Sonny."

Bud stared at the Lake County map pinned to the cork board panels behind his desk and shook his head. Even with the addition of Officer Larae Holcomb in the North County area, he still only had four full-time deputies to patrol 8,300 square miles. The population density was about one person per square mile, almost. As Bud often told visitors, Lake County runs long on cattle, timber, and high lonesome.

"Well," he muttered, "Michelle will be back this afternoon, and putting Cowboy out of the drug business and into prison has calmed things down in the Fort Rock-Christmas Valley area. So maybe we can skate through this weekend without any major problems."

"Karen, get in here," he called out the open door.

A few second later Karen Highsmith was standing in his doorway. "You mistake me for Molly?" Her tone wasn't friendly.

Bud looked disgusted. "No. I need you to get Lonnie Beltram in here, in uniform and with all his gear. Now. I'm putting him to work for a couple of weeks."

"When are you going to put him on full time?"

Bud looked at Karen, one hand on her hip, her chin out, challenging.

"Think I'm taking advantage of him, do you?" he asked.

"Yes, you are, Boss. You just seem to be stringing him along."

"Judas, Karen! You know our budget as well as I do. It's pucker tight, and I'm about to go over budget as it is. But I need his help today. When I can, and don't you say a word to him about it, I'll bring Lonnie on as a permanent full-time officer. Okay? Better?"

"Okay, Boss." She looked at his bloodshot eyes and his disheveled appearance, and said, "Now about the coffee, I'll go make some."

Bud was still stewing about Karen's jibe when his cell phone rang. "Sheriff Blair," he answered.

"Hey, Boss," Roger said, "I just wanted to let you know I'm taking a few days off. Got a chance to catch some fish in the Sea of Cortez."

Bud shook his head and said, "Can't spare you right now, Roger. Michelle is busy, and Sonny is headed to Bend for an Arson Task Force meeting. So I need you here."

"Well, I'm not really asking, Bud. I'm already gone, so this is a courtesy call."

"Where are you?"

"Let me look. I can't tell for sure. Lots of ocean down there, but I think I'm about thirty minutes out of San Diego."

"What the hell are you doing in San Diego?"

"Don't you ever read your email, Boss? I don't want to talk about it over the phone. Go look it up. If you still don't want me gone, you'll just have to fire me, because this is the fishing trip of a lifetime. I don't want to miss it."

"What fishing trip?"

"Read your email, Boss."

"Okay...hold on." Bud put the cell phone down and pulled up his in-box. He scanned for Roger's message and opened it up. It was vague, but Bud understood enough to know that Roger Hildebrand and Larae's new husband John, first known to the Lake County Sheriff's department as "Gar," were part of the advance team for an NCIS operation to take out Juan Ortega.

Bud picked his phone and said, "I think I will fire you, Deputy Hildebrand, just on general principles. I wish you had said something. I like this kind of fishing."

"I know how you feel. And we thought about it, but both you and your buddy Spears are too well known. Liable to get mobbed by fishing enthusiasts. I hate to tell you this, but you would only be a liability."

"What the hell makes you say that?"

"Boss, think about it. Your picture has been all over the world. I'll bet they would recognize you in Nepal. In Mexico, for sure. So the best thing you can do is hold down the fort." Roger paused and then added, "By the way, your old Bremerton buddy is going fishing with us."

Bud couldn't even say good luck before Roger killed the call. Bud tried dialing back and got a message that took him straight to voice mail. As she neared his door with a fresh mug of steaming coffee, Karen heard him grumble something about "damned independent deputies."

She set the mug down on a ceramic coaster that occupied a corner of the wooden desk, a corner scarred by a history of interlocking coffee rings burned into the varnish by hot mugs.

He nodded his thanks, lifted the mug and nearly scalded his mouth. "Hot," he said and put the mug down. She started to turn away, her short curly brown hair reflecting a gleam of light from the hallway, until Bud said, "Did you know about Roger's fishing trip?"

She nodded. "Yes. Remember? You told me to check your email when you're out. I check it several times a day, because I know you don't like using the computer very much."

"Then why didn't you mention it?"

"The fishing trip or reading your email?"

"The trip, of course!" he nearly shouted.

She shrugged. "I just assumed Roger had already cleared it with you. I guess he had not. Right?"

"Right. He didn't." He spun his chair to look at the map of the county, and asked, "When is Beltram coming in?"

"He said he would try to be here in an hour. He's living on the old Didier place up Cox Creek. He fixed up the old cabin so he can keep an eye on the calves he and his father bought last spring."

"An enterprising fellow, our Deputy Beltram." Bud looked at Karen and suddenly grinned, "You are a patient woman, Karen. I think the short night is catching up with me. I might just go home and take a nap when Lonnie gets here."

"That might be a good idea, Boss, before you make any new enemies. Oh, and speaking of enemies, the FBI wants Jésus held for another day. " She turned and walked back down the hallway to answer her ringing phone.

Bud liked Lonnie well enough, but Lonnie's hunger to be in law enforcement nagged at Bud a bit. Naked ambition was something Bud had learned to distrust during his years as a detective for the Portland Police Bureau.

Still, Bud had to admit, the few times Lonnie had worked as a Lake County Deputy Sheriff, he had done a good job. Members of the volunteer-mounted posse, important people in times of lost hunter searches, liked him, and he had worked up some good training exercises for the other three volunteer officers on the Lake County Sheriff Department rolls.

A local man who paid his own way through the police academy in Monmouth, Beltram apparently commanded the respect of his peers and of his elders.

Bud shrugged and thought, *You can worry a thing to death and change it not at all.*

2:45 p.m. ~ Mariah's house, Klamath Falls

OFFICER MICHELLE TRIVOLI, LAKE COUNTY SHERIFF'S Department, was surprised when Mariah asked to stop by the house she shared with her mom, Barbara Caldwell, and her mom's live-in boyfriend, the recently jailed Manfred Giles.

"I want to change clothes before I see Mom," Mariah said by way of explanation.

Michelle pulled into a motel parking lot and killed the engine. "I'll have to get permission from the KFPD first," she said to Mariah. "It's a crime scene, and I'm not sure they'll let us in."

When Mariah frowned, Michelle said, "If they won't, we'll stop someplace and you can pick out a new outfit. How would that be?"

"Is that another one of those 'temporary guardian' things?"

"Well...sure, but it's also a woman-to-woman kind of thing." Michelle wrinkled he nose and said in a confidential voice. "It's not something a man would understand."

For the first time in a long time Mariah actually giggled, and Michelle's tension eased a bit. *I want to keep her. I don't want her to go back to that other life. Yeah, but don't get too attached, because she already has a mom.*

A pleasant-sounding receptionist answered on the first ring, and Michelle asked to speak to Officer Downing.

"She's not in at the moment. Would you like to speak with her partner, Detective Harmon?"

"Sure."

Mariah had the volume on the vehicle radio turned down and was punching the Seek button, looking for a particular FM station when Detective Mathew Harmon came on the line.

"Harmon," he said.

"Hello. This is Officer Trivoli from the Lake County Sheriff's office. I need to ask a favor."

"Sure. Ask away."

"Mariah wants to go by her house and pick up some clothes and other things. So...is that still locked down as a crime scene?"

"Huh. Well…yes and no. We have an officer watching the place to see who comes knocking on the door, drug buyers, dealers, that type. But I suppose a quick in-and-out wouldn't hurt too much. I'm thinking about calling the surveillance off anyway. Now might be as good a time as any. Tell you what, I'll meet you there in ten minutes. Don't go in without me."

Michelle pulled her Lake County Sheriff vehicle, a white Ford Expedition with a prisoner cage in back, across the street from Mariah's house and waited for Harmon. They had been waiting for about two minutes when a woman who looked to be in her early thirties used a knuckle to rap on the passenger side window.

Mariah's face lit up and she tried to power the window down. She looked at Michelle and said, "She's my friend Rowena. I babysit for her sometimes." Embarrassed at being caught unaware, Michelle studied the woman for a good five or ten seconds before powering the window down.

The woman gave Mariah an awkward hug through the window, tears pooling in her eyes, and "Thank God you're safe. We've been so worried about you."

"I'm okay," Mariah said and looked at Michelle. "Rowena, this is Michelle, my temporary guardian. She's taking me to see Mom."

The woman gave Michelle a small wave and said, "Hi. I'm Rowena Norris. Mariah babysits my brats sometimes while I run to the store."

"Officer Trivoli," Michelle said.

"We heard on the radio this morning that Mariah had been found…alive…and my husband and I just sat and cried. We were so worried. But when the officer who has been watching the house left a few minutes ago, I knew it must be over. Thank the Lord."

"Yes," Michelle echoed, "thank the Lord."

Detective Mathew Harmon pulled his black Crown Victoria up to the curb in front of Mariah's house. He frowned when he saw the front door was still ajar, the door frame splintered from his heavy-footed entry. He pulled a cell phone from a jacket pocket and called Handy Andy's Honey Do's.

Michelle watched as he nodded. She lip read his "Thank You," and watched with some trepidation as this handsome, well-groomed young man walked over to her car. She instinctively brushed her bangs back from her forehead, a gesture that wasn't missed by either Rowena or Mariah. Rowena looked at Mariah and winked.

Michelle opened the door, stepped out, and was surprised when she saw him hesitate for just a split second with something like awe on his face. It didn't last, and she wondered if she had seen anything at all in his face.

"Detective Harmon," he said and held out his hand. She noted with some surprise, although she couldn't have said why she was surprised, that his hand was calloused. She did know that he held her hand in a gentle grasp for at least two seconds longer than necessary.

She finally gathered her wits enough to say, "Officer Trivoli... Michelle...Lake County."

He grinned and said, "Very nice to meet you. He and leaned down see through the open driver's door and said, "You must be Mariah."

Mariah blushed, too shy to speak, and just nodded.

"And Mrs. Norris. Nice to see you again."

Rowena walked around the Expedition and held out her hand. "I'm so glad you found Mariah and kept her safe. Did you get that slime ball boyfriend?"

Michelle glanced at Mathew and gave him an imperceptible nod, a shared gesture neither one of them would ever fully understand. They just instinctively communicated.

"Yes. He's in custody," Harmon said, and Michelle knew there was a lot more to the story than that.

"Good. We need to get his kind off the streets. Frankly, we need an island someplace to keep scum like that away from the rest of humanity. Let 'em prey on each other."

Harmon laughed. "Sounds like a plan." He looked at Mariah and said, "Shall we do it?"

Michelle and Mariah waited by the Expedition while Harmon made a quick sweep of the house and then came back out on the front porch and waved them over.

The two officers wrinkled their noses but didn't comment on the smell of stale tobacco smoke and stinky garbage in a can under the kitchen sink.

"You go change," Michelle said to Mariah. "I want to talk to Detective Harmon. Okay?"

Mariah grinned and said, "Okay." She started to walk down the short hallway to her bedroom and then turned and said in a stern child's voice, betrayed only by a giggle, "Behave yourselves."

They glanced at each other, looked away, and then broke into smiles, followed by quiet laughter.

"Quite a girl," Harmon said. "She's the only responsible person living here."

A rap on the door brought them out of whatever introspection they each were engaged in. A redheaded man about Harmon's age pushed the door gently open and peeked around the corner. "Knock, knock. Anybody home?"

Michelle's hand moved toward her pistol, but Harmon put his hand on her wrist. "It's my buddy Handy Andy.

"Hey, Andy. Come on in."

"Hi, Matt." Andy pointed to the splintered door jamb. "Is that what you want fixed?"

"Yep. That's it. I also want you to put a passage lock on the back bedroom door after we leave. If you have two keys, I'll take one now."

"You got it."

Michelle's look asked for an explanation.

"He's here to fix the door, replace the door latch, and give us new keys. When Mariah's mother comes home, I'll give her the keys."

"Who's paying for that?"

Harmon looked slightly embarrassed. "Well, I kicked in the door, so I guess I am."

"Not the city?"

"No. Too much paper work. This is quicker and easier."

"Why? It's just a drug house, isn't it?"

"No. You should see Mariah's room. Neat as a pin. Pictures of her and her mother from an earlier time. Books all lined up. Curtains, matching bed spread. The bed was made. It's her refuge. If they move back here, I want her to at least have a door she can lock."

Michelle studied his brown eyes until he became uncomfortable. Finally she nodded. "I want her to have chance for a better life, too."

At twenty minutes, Mariah was quicker to get ready than most girls her age. But then she was motivated by the promise of seeing her mother. She emerged in new blue jeans, clean tennis shoes and a red sweater. She was carrying two day packs stuffed with personal items and clothing, and holding her clock radio under one arm.

"I'm ready," she announced.

Harmon invented the excuse of checking on Tyson James to follow Michelle's Ford Expedition to the hospital.

"He likes you, you know," Mariah said impishly.

"No. He doesn't even know me," Michelle said, wondering why she was even having this conversation with a thirteen-year-old girl.

"And you like him. I can tell."

5:30 p.m. ~ Highway 140 east of Klamath Falls

ABOUT THE ONLY GOOD THING MICHELLE could think of from the trip to visit Barbara Caldwell was the promise from Detective Harmon to keep her posted on Barbara's progress.

Her mother didn't even appear to recognize Mariah when the nurse woke Barbara up. But Mariah took her mother's hand and said, "Babs, you've gotta get well." Barbara squeezed back and then fell asleep again without saying one single word.

Mariah refused to look at Michelle or Mathew. Instead she just turned and walked out of the room. When Michelle caught up to her she was headed to the parking lot where their vehicle was parked.

Michelle tried to give her a hug, but Mariah squirmed free and said, "Let's go."

During most of the drive back to Lakeview, Mariah sat half turned away from Michelle staring out the vehicle window at the landscape, even after sunset, not saying anything, arms tucked around her chest, the hood on her sweatshirt pulled half over her face.

Michelle made no move to intrude on Mariah's privacy, but she guessed Mariah's thoughts must be running something along the lines of, "What becomes of me now?"

When a big mule deer came up out of the willows in the Sprague River bottom between Beatty and Bly and onto the highway, its hooves scrabbling for traction on the pavement, Michelle swore and instinctively slowed and swerved to miss the deer. "Boy, that was close," she said. She knew it was a bad idea to swerve, "But instinct sometimes just take over," she muttered aloud.

Mariah said, "Missed him."

Michelle grinned and said, "Her, actually. A doe."

"Can I ask you something?"

"Anything at all."

"Do you think Mom knew who I was?"

Michelle thought about it for a few seconds, and then said, "I hope so. Did you think not?"

"The only thing she did was squeeze my hand."

"Good. That's a lot, Mariah."

"Will she get well?"

Michelle took a deep breath and let it out slowly before saying, "The doctors think so, and that's what you and I will plan on. Okay?"

Mariah nodded, straightened up and faced forward. She pulled the bakery bag from the center console and took a bite of cream filled donut. "Can we stop at the deli again?" she mumbled around the bite.

5:30 p.m. ~ *El Centro Airport, California*

THE THREE MEN WAITING BEHIND THE six-foot cyclone fence that separated vehicle parking from taxiway, made an odd assortment. There was nothing that would alert any watcher. They simply looked like mismatched tourists bound for Mexico to do some fishing.

Walter Pidgeon was wearing a light gray, soft brimmed khaki hat, and a dark gray fishing vest over a blue denim long sleeved shirt. He was holding a rod carrier. He looked the part, which was good because he was still on the Ortega hit list.

Slightly taller and a good dealer stouter, Gino Maretti was wearing a Seahawks wind breaker and Seahawks baseball cap. He had managed somehow to slip the sleeve of the windbreaker over the cast on his left arm, a cast that kept him from bending his elbow.

He was wearing brown khaki pants and scuffed, brown Wellington boots. A small .25-caliber pistol rode shotgun in his right boot, and a short-bladed Gerber dagger rode companion in his left one. He had used a small, locked metal pistol box and his Bremerton City Police badge to check them through to El Centro with his luggage.

He had taken Wally at his word they would not be inspected by the Mexican police at the border crossing, and once his luggage had come sliding down the carousel, he carried his two small bags to the restroom, where, in the privacy of a closed stall he seated the pistol and dagger into his boot holsters.

Wide-bodied Roger Hildebrand wore a faded Honkers baseball hat, a cowhide vest over a light brown cotton shirt, blue jeans, and scuffed cowboy boots. He looked Western, which is what he was. It just wasn't all that he was. He carried no weapons except his big fists. John had promised to provide what they would need.

They were almost overdressed for the pleasant seventy-degree temperature. "Ah," Wally said, "winter in Southern California."

Roger grinned and said, "What? You don't like zero temperatures and the snow in Christmas Valley?"

Wally nodded and said, "I'm okay with snow, but Christmas Valley winters run a bit long sometimes."

A small blue and white jet rolled to a stop just outside the gate. The pilot shut the power off, and the engines spiraled down and faded from hearing. Wally looked at Roger and asked, "What type of plane is that?"

Roger shook his head, "VIP transport for sure. Maybe a Global 5000, but I'm a bit behind the times, so I wouldn't swear to anything."

The cabin door opened and dropped down, the built-in steps ready for use.

First out was a young woman dressed in the blue uniform of a Marine Staff Sergeant. She stood at the bottom of the steps and held out her hand to steady the descent of John Bernard. He carried a knapsack in one hand and a battered black rod carrier in the other.

During the two-hour wait after John's phone call to give them his ETA, Wally, Gino, and Roger had spent time in the little airport lounge. They sipped drinks...coffee for Roger and Wally and some red wine for Gino...and shared what they knew of John Bernard, which was little enough. They knew he had been special ops for an NCIS counter terrorism unit. They knew of his exploits in foiling the drug-and-people smuggling operation run out of Cowboy's ranch near Fort Rock, a running gun battle during which John had killed one terrorist and captured three others, including a former NCIS operative, a man called Crazy Charlie. What they didn't know is that Crazy Charlie and John Bernard had once been very close friends.

But they hadn't quite figured out John's status. Either he was retired NCIS, or he wasn't quite retired. Or he was retired and reinstated. Or he was freelance and under contract. Or...

"Probably doesn't matter," Roger said quietly at one point in their discussion. "What matters is that he knows how to run a fishing trip like this one."

The Master Sergeant opened a cargo door and set a five-foot black canvas cylinder on the tarmac, and then a shorter black canvas bag that appeared to be heavier. Both bag and cylinder were plastered with worn labels and fishing stickers...swordfish, salmon, bass, trout...that appeared to have been there since the bags were new. There was nothing to suggest it wasn't just fishing gear.

An armed security guard unlocked the gate and waited while the Master Sergeant helped John carry his gear through the gate. "Hang on a minute," he said to the guard. "I've got one more bag."

It was also black canvas, and from the looks of it a lot heavier than any of the other bags.

John set it down outside the fence and thanked the Master Sergeant for her help. Then he grinned and shook hands with his three companions. Gino grinned back and said, "What the hell took you so long?"

John shrugged. "We had to pick up a two-star in San Francisco and then drop him and his entourage in San Diego. And," he added as he patted the nearest bag, "even a priority flash can't make our bean counters move very quickly. You do understand that the military has been counting bullets since the War of 1812."

They all laughed. Gino said, "Never been in the military, but our admin people are the same. You lose it, you buy it."

John nodded agreement. "I wouldn't want to pay for this baby... probably couldn't anyway."

An airport shuttle took them from El Centro to the Mexicali border crossing. Roger, who had never been east of San Diego in his one brief transit through the naval base, was amazed at the huge farm fields growing what looked to him like carrots and cabbage... lots of carrots and cabbage.

Their Hispanic driver glanced in his mirror and saw Roger looking at the fields, some filled with workers and machines harvesting carrots.

"We are very proud of our farms here," he said. "We grow vegetables all year round...or nearly so. We are the carrot capital of the world. Believe it or not, Death Valley isn't the only place in California below sea level. We are also below sea level. It moderates the climate, I think," the driver said.

The drive took a little less than twenty five minutes, and the driver pulled into a parking lot about a hundred yards from the border. He stopped next to a white Dodge Sprinter with California plates. Big blue letters declared the van to be from the Sea of Cortez Guide Service. A big Mexican was sitting in the driver's seat with the door open. He was talking on a cell phone. "There's Señor Peña, I think," the driver said.

Wally hopped out almost before the shuttle rolled to a stop. "Hola! You big ugly son-of-a-bitch," he said. David Peña stepped out of the van and ignored Wally's hand. He simply wrapped his big arms around the small man and lifted him completely off his feet. In nearly flawless English, Peña said, "My old friend. What a treat. I never thought to see you again in this life. I think this will be a good fishing trip."

"I think so, too, but you have to put me down first."

They off-loaded their gear and sent the shuttle driver on his way, encouraged by a fifty-dollar tip handed to him by Wally.

When the shuttle was out of sight, Wally introduced John, Gino, and Roger, using only first names. Roger was big by most standards, but standing beside David Peña's six-feet-seven inches, he looked ordinary. He saw Roger sizing him up and laughed. "I played defensive tackle for the Chargers until a guy named Lulay took out my knee. But it was okay; I carefully hoarded the big bucks the Chargers paid me. And I had a degree in business from USC. Like who doesn't? And the rest, as they say, is history."

He pointed at John and Roger and said, "You two...special forces, I'm thinking. You got the look." He grinned and pointed to Gino. "And you are a cop, I'd guess. Same look without the edge."

Wally smiled and slapped Peña's heavy shoulder. "You be careful, David. The last people who came after Gino didn't like it much."

"Like your dustup with Ortega's thugs?"

"Something like that. Same results."

"Well, let's load up. This weather is supposed to give us a blow. I want to beat the storm to Guaymas."

The border crossing was perfunctory. Peña pulled to a stop next to an armed Mexican officer who smiled and joked with Peña like an old friend. David slid out of the van and walked to the rear door. He popped it open and smiled when the officer found two fifty dollar bills folded on one of John's black canvas bags. He palmed the bills, and Peña nodded and handed the happy officer Wally's rod carrier. "Ah," the man said, as he slid Wally's expensive spinning pole out, "Nice."

"You should come fishing some time," Peña said.

"I'd like that, I think."

The officer slid the pole back in the rod carrier, screwed the cap down and put it back in the Sprinter. He closed the door and said, "Have a good fishing trip, *amigos*."

Wally rode up front so he and Peña could talk and catch up on old times. John and Roger caught the tail end of a story about drinking Margaritas on the veranda of the old Ruby Hotel. "So we are having a good time," Wally was saying, "and I get to looking at my glass. There's about a half-inch of silt in the bottom. I ask him, where did you get the ice? And he says, 'From the fish house.'"

Both Pena and Wally laughed and Pena added, "And I'll bet they got the Mexican two-step."

"For three days."

The drive to San Felipe took nearly three hours. A storm front to the west treated them to a spectacular desert sunset, rose and purple clouds and shades in between, and then faded as the sun slipped below the horizon. It was full dark before they got to San Felipe.

Pena said, "We have reservations at San Felipe's finest Bed and Breakfast. It's run by an old friend of mine. It's a nice, walled hacienda with security systems. Wait until you see it. And wait until you see her."

"What happened to the storm?" John asked.

"Scheduled, God willing, to stay away until noon or so. We'll be out of here and fishing in Guaymas before then."

Peña pulled off the main highway a mile from the town of San Felipe and drove about three hundred yards east on a dusty track through a patch of Sonoran desert complete with ocotillo, prickly pear, and mesquite.

A short stretch of paved lane led from the desert track to a gated hacienda. Peña pulled up to an intercom mounted on an adobe column and leaned out to punch the button. The intercom cracked and a pleasant female voice said, in English, "About time, David. Come on in." The gates swung inward and Peña pulled the Sprinter into an inner courtyard with a bricked circular drive, a water fountain, and, lit by yard lights, a cascade of glorious red bougainvillea flowers spilling over the walls.

"Nice, David. Very nice," Wally said. "I live with alfalfa fields, rabbit brush and sage. I suddenly find I've been missing the bougainvillea. And the mild winters."

"But you've been staying alive, Wally. That's something." David Peña said.

A porter dressed in black pants, white shirt and a short red jacket, came skipping down the wide steps from the veranda. He opened the side door for his guests and said, "*Buenos noches*, Senor Peña. And you also, *amigos*. Welcome to Hacienda De La Rosa. We hope you have a pleasant stay."

Peña smiled and said, "*Gracias*, Roberto. I'm sure we will. Would you have our luggage brought in?"

"*Si*."

A tall, red-headed woman wearing a short sleeved white blouse and white slacks, walked barefoot across the cool tiles of the lobby floor. She looked to be in her late twenties or early thirties. Wally thought she was simply stunning.

She smile and said, "Welcome, my friends. David tells me you have come to hunt the big shark."

The Americans glanced at Peña as if to say, "What's going on?" The big man bowed his head slightly and said, "Allow me to introduce Madeline Peña, my wife. She is also an agent for an organization I can't mention, because if I did, she would have to kill all of us." He laughed at the old, old joke, but Wally and his friends did not.

She punched David lightly on the arm, and then pulled on his ear until he bent his head low enough for a kiss on the cheek.

"Well...she said, turning to her guests, "Supper will be served in about thirty minutes, so if you want to unpack, I'll make sure everything is ready."

They all watched until she walked through an open archway and out of sight. *She doesn't walk*, Wally thought, *she glides*.

Wally turned and looked at his old friend. "Where did you find her?"

"You mean to ask why she hooked up with an old reprobate like me?"

"Yes, that, too," Wally chuckled.

After a traditional Mexican dinner, complete with lots of tortillas, frijoles, jalapeños, grilled shrimp fresh from the Sea of Cortez, sizzling steaks, and hot "kill-your-taste-buds" salsa, a rich coffee was served. Two servants cleared the table and Peña asked, "The meal was okay?"

They all laughed and nodded. "A killer meal," Wally said. "Ate damned near enough to do me in."

7:30 p.m. ~ *Michelle's house, Lakeview*

MARIAH STOKED UP ON JOJO'S AND a corn dog at the deli in Bly, drank a root beer, and belched as she and Michelle got back in the Expedition.

"Oops. Excuse me."

Michelle laughed and said, "In some countries it's considered polite to belch, and impolite if you don't."

Mariah giggled and said, "But we're still in America."

"It's okay, though."

By the time they started the climb to the Quartz Mountain summit, Mariah's chin was on her chest and she was asleep.

"Worn out, I'd guess," Michelle said quietly to herself. She slid a disc into the player and listened to a Helen Reddy CD, the volume just barely audible, a level she hoped would encourage Michelle to stay asleep. She yawned and shook her head to clear the fatigue setting in.

Forty-five minutes later, Michelle pulled the Expedition into her garage and shut the engine down. The stillness and the hum of the garage door opener was enough to penetrate Mariah's dream filled sleep.

She sat up, rubbed her eyes and asked, "Are we there?"

"Yep. This is it. I have a guest room I think you're going to like."

"Sorry I fell asleep."

"Don't be sorry, Mariah. I'm tired, too. Let's get your things into the house."

Mariah trailed Michelle through a brightly decorated kitchen and down a short hallway. Michelle opened the door on the right and said, "This room is yours, and the bathroom is straight ahead. You get the first shower."

She flipped the lights on and lit a small bedroom with frilly white curtains. A twin bed with a white wrought iron headboard, and a soft rose colored matching bedspread and pillowcase sat in one corner. A touch lamp with a rose decorated, glass lampshade sat on a white and gold bedside table, and a matching dresser set off a pale pink carpet. It was all "girl."

Mariah said, "Oh. It's so pretty."

"And because I'm a police woman, you expected camo?"

Mariah blushed and stammered, "Well…not really, but…I guess I didn't know what to expect."

Michelle smiled and said, "It's all right. I have lots of alone time, so I decorate. Anyway, you get unpacked. Feel free to use the dresser and the closet for your things. I'll have a snack ready when you finish your shower."

An hour later the two of them were sitting on the couch, wrapped in blankets, their wet heads close together, eating popcorn and watching a smaltzy old black-and-white romantic comedy starring Cary Grant. Mariah felt secure, and Michelle felt like a big sister.

Or is that a maternal stirring? Right. Every mother has a pistol hiding between the sofa cushions.

Her cell phone buzzed and she grumped. "Not now," she said out loud. But she picked it up. The screen told her it was a private number. She hesitated and then answered the call. "Yes?"

Mathew Harmon said, "Hello. This is Mathew Harmon. I wanted to make sure you made it home okay."

She started to ask would he check up if she were a man, and then stopped. She glanced at Mariah who was grinning. Obviously Mariah could hear his voice coming through the speaker.

Aloud Michelle said, "Yes, we did. Thanks for asking. Mariah and I are watching an old Cary Grant movie and eating popcorn. What are you doing?"

"The wind on Klamath Lake has been kicking up, so I had to go check on my boat. Make sure it was tied down. Check the heater to see if it is still worked. Run the bilge pumps. That kind of thing. For a big lake, Klamath is kinda shallow. Makes for big waves sometimes."

"Oh," Michelle said, "What kind of boat do you have?"

"Sail boat. Not too big. In the summer I live on board, but the winter weather makes it pretty small. No deck time and no sailing. I move back into my house come bad weather."

Michelle found herself saying, "I've never been sailing."

"Oh? Well, we can fix that…if you'd like…as soon as the weather gets decent."

"Sounds like fun. You let me know when and I'll be over."

"Deal." They both paused, suddenly at a loss for words, each wondering where this sudden mutual attraction was coming from. Or where it was going.

"Well," he said and cleared his throat, "Glad to hear you made it safe and sound. We'll talk tomorrow."

"Thanks for calling. Tomorrow then."

"Good night," he said.

"Yes, you too," she said and ended the call.

Mariah, who managed to contain her giggles until the call ended, cracked up when Michelle closed the phone. "Michelle has a boyfriend, a boyfriend," she managed to chant through her giggles.

Michelle tickled Mariah in the ribs and said. "I do not." *But I'd like to.*

7:30 p.m. ~ *Lake County Sheriff's Office*

BUD STOPPED FOR A TO-GO HAMBURGER and fries from the Polar Bear ice cream shop. He was restless, but not quite sure why. Instead of going home, he drove back to the office and with a wave to Winona, the night matron walked to his office to eat his supper.

He chewed on a French fry and reread the bulletin lying on his desk. The correctional officer who was in cahoots with Jésus Mendoza, the cartel assassin who had tried to kill Special Agent Amanda Spears with a bomb, had been found dead near Winnemucca, Nevada. He had been shot. There were no other details.

"I have a bad feeling about this," he said to himself.

He called Warner Creek Correctional Facility and asked for the night supervisor. When the receptionist wanted to know who he was, he barked, "Henry Blair, Sheriff of Lake County."

"Walt Glass," a man answered. Without preamble Bud told the night supervisor, "Your missing CO is dead. Looks like somebody shot him. Check with the Winnemucca Police Department if you want details, because that's all I know.

"What I do know is the same people who shot your officer will probably try to kill Jésus Mendoza. So…can you send some armed officers here to pick him up? Maybe you can take better care of him out there than I can in here."

"Damn. That's bad news about our guy, don't you think?"

"No. He got greedy." Bud hesitated and then asked, "So, can you do it?"

Bud heard the man sigh and then say, "We'll have a car there in fifteen minutes."

"Give me the names of the people you're sending." He listened and then scribbled Rodney Hardin and Kent Marks on a note pad.

He hung up without saying goodbye, and grumped at his own short temper. He rose and walked down the hall to the booking desk.

Chunky Winona Peel, the fifty-five-year-old wife of the town's only mortician, worked Saturday and Sunday night at the jail. She joked about the job being her "pin money." But the "Good Ol' Girl" network said it was because her tightwad husband was too cheap to give her an allowance. And he was rumored to be rich.

When Winona saw the sheriff she said, "I gotta go." She held up her cell phone and said, "Just catching up with the girls."

"That's all right, Winona, I want you to pack up and go home. Now."

"Why?"

"I don't think it's going to be safe for you here tonight. I'll cover for you."

"I need the money, Bud."

"I'll pay you for the shift. All right?"

She brightened and started putting snacks and drinks back in a small pink soft-sided cooler. "Thank you." She grabbed her coat from the back of a chair, scurried around the counter and headed for the door. Hand on the latch she turned back and said over her right shoulder, "I checked on our guests about thirty minutes ago. They were squabbling about which TV program to watch, so I told them to shut up or I'd turn it off. That did the trick. I turn everything off at 10:00."

When the pneumatic arm closed the door and the lock clicked, Bud rubbed his hand together and said, "Now, to work." He opened the office door and looked up and down the street. When he saw nothing suspicious, he stepped across the sidewalk to his pickup, hit the door lock and opened the door. The Velcro strap on the center bracket holding his loaded 10-gauge shotgun gave up the fight with a protesting rip.

He grabbed a box of double ought buckshot from the center console, and dismissed the nagging thought that any trouble would already be over before he had time to reload the shotgun.

"But it doesn't hurt to be prepared," he told himself, citing a variation of the Boy Scout motto, an echo of BB's recitation a day earlier. Once back inside, he dimmed the office lights. An outside yard light stood guard over the entrance, a beacon and a warning to those wanting to find the Lake County Sheriff's office. The half glass of the door reflected enough light back toward the street to make it difficult to see into the office without standing directly in front of the door.

The counter gave Bud both a narrow view of the street and a barrier in case of trouble. He leaned the shotgun against a visitor's chair, made sure his pistol was where it was supposed to be and pulled his cell phone from his shirt pocket.

Beltram answered on the second ring. "Hello?"

"Lonnie, this is Bud. I need you to do something for me."

His next call went to Augustus Hildebrand, Chief of Police for the city of Lakeview. When he told Gus about the dead correctional officer, the one who had run when Jésus Mendoza was caught, Gus said, "Yep. Tying up loose ends, aren't they. And you figure they'll come after Jésus?"

"It fits their MO. They have to."

"Okay. Let's set a trap and catch the bastards. Beltram can stake out Bullard Street, make sure they can't escape up the Canyon, and I'll have two cars ready to block both ends of the street in front of your office. I suppose you'll be the bait."

"No. Jésus is the bait. I'm the jaws of the trap. I'm sending him to Warner Creek."

"Did you send Winona home?"

"Yes. You know, Gus, I have two Harney County prisoners in jail. I'm wondering if we shouldn't move them out of here, too. Maybe Warner Creek can watch them for a few hours."

Gus was silent for a few seconds and said, "I'll call the Pucker Brush Pen and tell them I'm dropping your guys off. I'll be out in front in about five minutes. Have 'em ready to take a ride."

Bud unlocked the cell block. A skinny young man with about a five-day growth of reddish blond beard occupied the first cell. Bud told him to get his shoes on, he was going for a ride. The man just glared at him until Bud said, "I think we're going to have some damned nasty people coming here tonight to kill anyone and everyone in this jail. So either get a move on, or I'll let you be a target." He rattled the door on the next cell. The second man already had his shoes on. "Get me out of here," he said.

Both Harney County prisoners were in handcuffs, waiting in the booking area when Gus pulled his black and white Crown Vic up to the door. The two prisoners slid willingly into the back of Gus's vehicle. He slammed the rear door, slid under the steering wheel, and sped away, heading north.

Ten minutes later, two armed officers wearing the uniform of the Department of Corrections knocked on the front door.

Hand on his pistol, Bud looked them over and opened the door. "I need to see some ID."

Each produced photo ID issued by the Department of Corrections. One read Rodney Hardin, and one said Kent Marks.

"Good." He pushed a shackled and handcuffed Jésus Mendoza toward the door. "Get this piece of garbage out of here. And I sure as hell hope he's alive when the FBI comes to pick him up. People connected to the Ortegas keep winding up dead."

Officer Hardin, a hint of resentment in his voice, said, "We'll keep him alive."

He watched the Warner Creek van disappear up the street and then sent a text message to Dutch Vanderlin, Special Agent in Charge, Portland FBI.

Jésus Mendoza is back in the Warner Creek Correctional Facility. I wasn't sure I could protect him here.

A message came back almost immediately.
What's the trouble?

Bud typed an answer.
I think the cartel will send some people to kill him. Got a little surprise for them if they do.

Dutch asked, You got any backup?

Four other officers and a 10 gauge shotgun. What more could a man ask for?

Dutch waited a full thirty seconds before he sent a reply.
How bout a half dozen men from our SWAT team and a Black Hawk?

Bud thought about it for all of five seconds. Suddenly he didn't feel quite so alone or quite so vulnerable.

Give me an ETA and I'll have a van waiting at the airport.

Dutch was as good as his word. In twenty minutes Bud had a text message that read,

Two hours. And they can pick up Jésus while they're down there.

Next Bud called Lake County Emergency Services and asked them to find State Trooper Charlie Prince. "Ask him to call my cell, please."

Charlie called almost immediately. "What's up, Bud?"

When Bud explained his dilemma, Charlie said, "I'm rolling your way now. Where do you want me?"

"I think I could use some backup here in the office."

"Damn, Bud, you sure throw a lot of parties. See you in ten."

Bud placed one more call to the Warner Creek Correctional Facility. Mr. Glass, night supervisor and all around good guy, was happy to have a van waiting at the Lakeview airport for an FBI Swat team. In truth it was the only excitement he could point to in the last year.

Bud put the phone back in the cradle and wondered what else he should do to get ready for any bad guys that might come calling.

Charlie knocked on the door. When Charlie was inside, Bud explained what preparations he had made, and then asked, "Charlie let's think about this. How will they come at us? Blow the door and storm the place?"

Charlie shook his head and said, "Not likely. Probably pose as police officers come to take Jésus into custody."

"I agree. So, we let them in and trap them inside. Nothing like the big hole of a 10 gauge to bring a little shock and awe."

"Right."

"Okay," Bud nodded, "you stay in the hallway and out of their line of sight until I close the door behind them. I'll use the door as a shield until they're inside."

"You are just going to let them in?"

"Yep. Easier to confine in here, and no innocent citizens get hurt."

Charlie shrugged and said, "Okay."

Bud hung his personal portable radio on his equipment belt, clipped the mike to his lapel, and plugged an ear bud into the radio. He pushed the talk button and said, "Control, this is County One."

"This is Control, County One. Go ahead."

"We are running a coordinated training exercise tonight that involves the Lakeview City Police Department, the FBI, and the

Oregon State Police. Code name, Nighthawk. Please advise all officers to go to TAC Channel One now."

"Will do."

Bud watched Charlie turn his personal portable to the TAC channel, and tuck an earbud in his left ear. They both heard the Emergency Services Center dispatcher saying, "All units. This is Control advising all units to switch to TAC Channel One now. Again, all units switch to TAC." Bud liked the temporary dispatcher, but he missed the sound of Nancy Sixkiller's voice on the radio.

Bud waited fifteen seconds and pushed his mike button. "Gus? You on the air?"

"I am. I'm about five minutes from town, but cars Two and Three are in place." Bud heard double clicks from both cars and smiled. *They love it*, he thought.

10:30 p.m. ~ Lakeview

The Warner Creek van dropped the six-member FBI SWAT team at the sheriff's office. They were dressed for the cold in black winter gear and wearing Kevlar vests, Kevlar thigh and shin pads, Kevlar-covered helmets, and carrying an assortment of assault rifles, hand guns, and night vision goggles.

They looked to Bud exactly like their reputation. Taut, disciplined, and ready for almost anything.

Bud introduced himself and Trooper Charlie Prince. The SWAT team members looked up at Trooper Prince, and to a man they all wondered where he had played basketball. But no one asked.

FBI Special Agent Bernie Hornsby introduced himself as the team leader. Hornsby was a dark-haired, medium-sized man who somehow reminded Bud of John Bernard. Same hard eyes. Hornsby introduced the five members of his squad as Todd, Jim, Justin, Bob, and Jake. "Just think of them as SWAT Two through Six. I'm SWAT One."

Bud nodded, "Good. We have four officers outside, Chief of Police Augustus Hildebrand is coming in from the Warner Creek Correctional Facility; Deputy Beltram is parked up Bullard; and two others in patrol cars we'll call City Two and City Three are positioned to block the street on either end of this block." He glanced at his radio. "We're all on TAC Channel One." He handed Hornsby a piece of notepaper. "Here's the frequency. Set yours to that."

Hornsby nodded and then asked, "Do you have any intel that say's they'll come tonight?"

Bud shook his head. "No, I don't. But it makes sense. They have to before Jésus Mendoza makes a deal and decides to tell us things they don't want us to know. He's not talking, but the drug thugs won't know that for sure. So...they have to come tonight."

"Dutch must have a lot of faith in you. This is costing the FBI a shitload of money."

Bud grinned and nodded. "Dutch and I worked a major crimes task force a dozen or so years back. And we had some dealings not too long ago."

The blond-headed agent, Todd, asked, "Portland Police Bureau? Detective. Right?"

Bud nodded. "Seems like a long time ago."

"So give us the layout," Hornsby said.

They all crowded around as Bud used a flip chart to sketch the block the courthouse occupied, the street grid, the access ladder to the flat roof on top of the courthouse, the doorway to the apartments across Bullard from the courthouse, and the location of the three cars with Gus in reserve.

"How do you think they'll come?" Hornsby asked.

Bud said, "Trooper Prince and I talked about this. We think the likeliest scenario is that they will look like policemen...maybe even FBI...come to pick up a prisoner."

Hornsby turned to his team and said, "I want Swat Two and Three on the roof, Two on the southeast corner, Three on the northeast corner.

"I want Four and Five in the darkened doorway on the side street...Bullard? Is that right, Sheriff?"

"Yes."

"Okay. I want Six with me. If the shrubbery is thick enough, we can set up shop right around the corner."

Bud nodded. "You need anything?"

Five laughed and said, "A warm tent." He, too, reminded Bud somehow of John Bernard. In fact, they all did. There was some subtle difference in the way they moved, a confidence and an edge. Not an "attitude" exactly, but something parallel, quieter, and maybe a bit more dangerous.

Bud unlocked the inner door to the hallways of the courthouse and led Two and Three up a stairway to the second floor. He used a master key to open a janitor's closet and pointed to the ladder. "The hatch is never locked. Not sure that's a good idea, but that's the way it is for now."

He offered his hand to each of the men and said, "Good luck. Take no unnecessary risks, please."

Their handshakes were firm and Three said, "Good luck, Sheriff."

Five minutes later Bud heard each member of the FBI team check in, and the waiting began.

12:15 a.m. ~ Lake County Courthouse

BUD TOOK A FRESH CUP OF coffee behind the counter and yawned. He had slept very little the night Jésus had planted the bomb. And while he had gotten some sleep the second night, fatigue was setting in with a vengeance.

"I sure hope I'm right about this," he mumbled through a yawn.

A set of vehicle lights lit the street outside the office door and then a dark Suburban pulled in against the curb, passenger side next to the sidewalk.

Nosed right in against my pickup.

He clicked his mike and said quietly, "Get ready. I think they have arrived."

Charlie Prince poked his head around the corner and gave Bud a thumbs up.

Two large men wearing dark suits, white shirts and ties, got out of the vehicle, and walked to the front door. They were clearly lit by the night light over the door. They knocked and waited. Bud didn't move until they knocked again and one said in a loud voice, "FBI. We've come to take Jésus Mendoza to a federal facility."

Impulsively, Bud mussed his hair, and said, "All right. Don't get your knickers in a knot. I'm coming." He held his pistol at his side and turned so they couldn't see it.

He didn't immediately open the door, but he did ask in a loud voice, "Who are you?"

One of the men pushed a badge wallet against the window and said, "FBI. We've come for Jésus Mendoza."

"No one told me about it."

"Listen, you dumb shit. Washington sent us."

"Oh. Okay. No need to get abusive."

Bud pretended to fumble with the lock and finally opened the door. "Why so damned late?"

"Wreck held us up."

Bud shut the door and said, "You got papers for me?"

"Sure," one of them said and reached his hand inside his jacket, only to find the barrel of Bud's pistol pointed at the end of his nose.

Charlie Prince stepped around the corner and into the booking area. He held the shotgun on the big middle of both men. It looked like a cannon to each of them. "Get your hands in the air. You are under arrest," he said.

"You have no idea what you are doing," the first man blurted out, but both men looked at the shotgun and raised their hands. The aggressive one continued to bluster, "Interfering with a federal officer is a felony."

Bud keyed his mike. "Block the street. The driver is still behind the wheel."

"You can't do this to us! We're federal officers."

"Bull," Bud said. "You're cartel enforcers, and you are under arrest." He walked behind the men and handcuffed each of them.

The driver of the Suburban could see enough to know that his companions were in trouble, but a two-second debate convinced him it was time to boogey. He reversed and started to back up just as City Two pulled in behind him.

SWAT Three shot his right rear tire, leaving him with a flat that just wouldn't climb the curb. He put the Suburban in drive and tried to ram Bud's pickup just as another bullet fired by SWAT Two ripped through his right front tire, and a three-round burst from Three silenced the engine.

And suddenly there was a police officer dressed in black at his window pointing a big ugly pistol at his head. He put his hands on the steering wheel just like the nice officer told him to. The fact that the officer's hands were shaking had a lot to do with the fake FBI driver's decision to call it quits.

After the three cartel enforcers had been given their Miranda rights, strip searched, dressed in orange jump suits and flip flops, and locked in individual cells, the SWAT Team and Bud's friends and officers celebrated in Bud's small conference room.

Bud accepted their congratulations and placed a bottle of Courvoisier Cognac and plastic glasses in the center of the conference table. "Gentlemen, a small libation to celebrate our success. And without gunfire, I might add."

"Not true," Hornsby grinned as he splashed an ounce of cognac in a glass. He sipped the drink and added, "We fired a total of five rounds, all suppressed, so there is hope the community didn't notice the ruckus."

Special Agent Hornsby's phone chimed and he held the screen up to read a text. "Aha. We have a winner. Facial recognition says two of them are on the FBI watch list. Which means, friend Blair, we will be taking all three of them back to Portland with us. Along with Jésus, of course."

Gus started clapping and all of the officers joined in to give Hornsby a round of applause.

Morning found Bud asleep in his own bed dreaming dreams he wouldn't remember when he awoke.

The black Suburban which turned out to be registered to a known drug dealer in Reno, Nevada, had been confiscated by the Lakeview City Police and towed to the County's maintenance yard.

Charlie Prince skipped sleep in favor of writing his report and letting his lieutenant know he was no longer the lead investigator on the Dog Lake Bomb case. That, in fact, he no longer had a suspect in custody and the uppity FBI had taken all suspects away to an undisclosed location. Charlie wasn't unhappy, but he knew better than to say so to his superiors.

6:30 a.m. ~ Hacienda De La Rosa

WALLY FOUND GINO ON THE UPPER veranda sipping coffee and watching the sun come up over the Sea of Cortez, the water blue-black in the early light. The shoreline dunes had yet to don their searing daytime gold.

Gino said, "My sense of direction is fouled up. The sea is supposed to be in the west."

Wally chuckled and poured coffee from a big carafe centered on a round patio table. "We'll get you squared away when we get to Guaymas. The Sea of Cortez will be back in the west. Have you seen Roger and John?"

Gino pointed toward the sea where a pair of distant figures were jogging along the beach. "Taking a morning run."

He held his left arm up, the cast visible because of his short-sleeved Hawaiian shirt. "Wanted me to go along, but I couldn't see the point as long as I'm lugging this cast around." He paused. "You don't suppose we could find a doctor and get this damned thing cut off, do you? I should have had it done in Bremerton, but I couldn't take the time."

Wally started to say "maybe" when Peña's deep voice startled them. For a big man he moved very quietly. "*Si*. I'll have a doctor here within the hour."

David poured himself a cup of coffee and set it on the glazed red tiles that armored the top of the thick adobe wall of the veranda. "We use an American doctor. He lost his license for drug use, but he's still a very good doctor. And he thinks he owes us because Madeline helped him get a Mexican license, and then set him up in a clinic near the marina. After he kicked his habit, of course. The locals love him because he generally forgets to charge."

An hour later, after a light breakfast of fresh strawberries, coffee, and cinnamon rolls, compliments of Madeline's imported American chef, she shooed them out the door with a kiss on the cheek for Peña and Wally. "You have a three-to-four hour window before the storm blows in." She looked at Peña and said, "Call me when you get there."

Gino, sans elbow cast, feeling balanced again for the first time in six weeks, shook her hand and said, *"Gracias.* You don't have a sister, do you?"

Madeline laughed and said, "Yes, but she's too mean for any man to live with."

John and Roger each shook her hand and said, "Thank you." They both knew the risk Madeline was taking on their behalf. "If you ever need help," John said, "call." And he meant it.

Roberto drove the van this time with Peña riding shotgun in the passenger seat. The trip to the Marina took less than fifteen minutes. Given the early hour, there was very little traffic on the streets of San Felipe.

Roberto parked in front of a locked gate that guarded an inclined ramp leading to the dock and the boat slips in the marina. A gleaming white Beaver, an airplane last produced in 1967, sat in a slip just inside the outer breakwater.

Peña watched Roger and John eyeing the ancient plane and laughed. "Don't worry. This isn't your ordinary Beaver. This is a Kenmore Beaver from Kenmore, Washington, with new everything. New engine——not rebuilt——brand new. New avionics, new skin, new paint, new tanks, new floats, new interior, you name it. I don't have fifty hours on the engine yet. Cost me more than I care to think about. But it's tougher than Madeline's sister."

They all chuckled at that. Roberto ran to a row of "bag" tubs used by yacht owners to roll bags and provisions to their boats and wheeled two of them over. "We can load your gear in these, *amigos.*"

The trip to Guaymas took an easy ninety minutes with time out for a low-level pass over a pod of grey whales breeding in the warm waters of the Sea of Cortez.

"I watch these same whales from the clifftops along the northwest coast of Washington," Gino shouted over the roar of the big engine. "It's one of my favorite spring trips. Better than watching the Mariners, even. Whales don't lose close games."

Peña pointed to the west. They could see the storm front coming in from the Pacific, but it wasn't close enough to cause any turbulence. "We'll be tied down and snug before it gets here."

Peña set the plane smoothly on the water in Guaymas harbor and taxied to a ramp. He killed the power and a handler backed a small tractor to the top of the ramp while a second handler wearing heavy leather gloves unspooled cable from a drum. They felt a slight jerk as the drum took all the slack out of the cable, and the float plane was smoothly winched to the top of the ramp.

A second Dodge Sprinter advertising the Sea of Cortez Guide Service turned in a circle and stopped beside the Beaver.

John walked around the plane and eyeballed the boats in the harbor. He wasn't sure he had ever seen such decrepit-looking fishing boats, old nets moldering away in the sun, rusty unpainted hulls, one small fishing boat kept afloat only by the lines tying it to the dock. An involuntary, "Damn," escaped before he could help it.

Peña saw him looking at the harbor and said, "It's all in the eyes of the beholder. Eighty percent of our population works at the fishing and shrimping business. But...many cannot stay out of the cantinas.

"Besides, there isn't the urgency to work that you find in the temperate or northern climates. There you have to hurry to get your planting and harvesting done. But here seasonal changes are so marginal that tomorrow will do as well as today."

"I see a couple of boats in good repair, but the rest look like nobody gives a damn," John said.

"Those two? The blue ones?"

"Yeah."

"Those are mine. Shrimpers. I pay two skippers to keep a small crew busy. Helps feed eight families." And then Peña laughed. "I suppose I have so much freedom here because I'm the best thing Guaymas has going for it. These lazy peons don't manufacture anything, so if it wasn't for fishing and tourists and Peña, they would all starve."

A two-foot by four-foot brass plaque set in an adobe wall declared the big house behind it the Sea of Cortez Guide Service. Along with the rest of the American settlement, it was hidden behind a rocky hill that overlooked the town to the south, the American settlement to the north, and the Sea of Cortez to the west.

Peña's rear wall backed up to a short stretch of golden beach lined with a half dozen twenty-foot jet sleds pulled up onto the sand. Each mounted a fifty-horsepower Honda outboard.

Peña's driver pushed the button on the remote clipped to the visor and the heavy iron gate swung slowly open. Inside the walls, the courtyard mirrored Hacienda De La Rosa, complete with a water fountain in the center of a brick-paved circular driveway. And Wally's bougainvillea again, streaming over the walls, a comfort of crimson blooms.

A tall nine-or-ten-year-old barefoot boy bounced down the steps of the open veranda. His dark tan made it hard to determine his origins, but a hint of reddish auburn highlights in his shaggy hair hinted at a touch of European genes.

"*Hola, Papa!*" he shouted and ran to the passenger door. Peña stepped out and swept the boy off the ground and held him out at arms length.

"You been a good boy, Eddie?" He asked sternly.

"*Si*. I'm always a good boy. That's why it's so damned dull around here."

Pena put him down and said, "I told you not to swear. You'll embarrass me in front of my friends."

Wally, Gino, Roger, and John exited the Sprinter through the sliding side door and stretched. Wally stared at Peña in amazement, and Peña laughed.

"Eddie, let me introduce my old and dear friend, Walter Pidgeon. You may call him Mr. Pidgeon."

Peña pushed the boy forward and said, "Mind your manners, Eddie."

Eddie stuck out his hand and said, "Nice to meet you, Mr. Pidgeon. I'm staying with Dad for a few days. I actually go to school in El Centro, and I'm actually an American." He eyeballed Wally's fishing vest and floppy Khaki hat and asked, "You want to go fishing? Dad got me a new boat."

Peña laughed and tousled Eddie's hair. "Not today, Eddie. We got a storm coming in, so you stay off the water. Okay?"

"Oh, all right."

A servant came down the steps, a fit-looking man wearing a white, coarse cotton shirt, untucked. It came down over his hips. John and Roger were both willing to bet he was carrying a handgun.

David Peña said to Eddie, "Help Pedro get the gentlemen's gear unloaded and into their rooms."

"*Si, Papa.*"

Pena's sister matched David's family genes. She was an elegant six-foot-one without a hint of gray in her short, black hair. David introduced her as Tia Maria, "A little family joke," he explained. She smiled when she was introduced and then led her visitors out onto an open veranda where a big breakfast waited for her American guests—lots of orange juice, sizzling platters heaped with grilled shrimp, rice and beans, scrambled *huevos*, hand made corn tortillas, a soft pastry twist dripping with icing, and rich coffee.

Two servants, both male, both looking very fit and muscular, and wearing untucked shirts that hid their belt lines, cleared the table, and Tia Maria hauled Eddie out of the room, "To do his homework," she explained. When the room was empty except for Peña and the Americans, Wally said, "I would like to pay for our stay with you, David."

"No. I don't do this for money. Real fishermen I charge, but you Americans are helping me with my work. No. No money. I do this for Eddie and all the other Eddie's in this world. The cartels must die."

John and Roger nodded in agreement. "Yes," John said, "We agree, but we really do want to catch some fish while we're down here, and we really do intend to pay for the guide service. And it's not coming out of Uncle's deep pockets."

Peña nodded. "Okay. Maybe in the evening if the storm has blown itself out." To mark his words, a stiff breeze smelling like rain funneled under the roof of the open veranda."

Day Three

Day Three

8:30 a.m. ~ Lakeview

THE FAINT ODOR OF COOKED BACON filtered into the guest room, and Mariah's dreams shifted from ghost images to a near conscious level. A soft rap on the door and Michelle saying, "Breakfast," did the rest.

Mariah brushed her teeth, slipped into her gym sweats and pattered down the hallway to the kitchen.

Michelle beamed at Mariah and set two plates with toast, bacon, hash browns and scrambled eggs on the little round table in the breakfast nook.

"Morning, Sunshine."

Mariah fell to with a ravenous appetite. "Mmm...good," she managed to squeeze out around a mouth stuffed with bacon and toast.

Michelle watched in amazement, convinced once again that Mariah had not been eating on a regular basis.

Breakfast over, Mariah helped clear the table and load the dishwasher. Michelle asked, "What do you want to do today?"

Mariah nearly startled her when she said, "Do you ever go to church?"

"Sometimes, but I work a lot of Sundays, so it's not a regular thing for me. Why? Do you want to go to church this morning?"

Mariah nodded and said, "Yes."

Michelle glanced at the clock. "Okay. If we hurry we can be there in time for the 10:00 o'clock service. Is the Presbyterian church okay?"

Mariah nodded. "Yes. I brought my Bible. Mom and me used to go to Sunday School." He face fell, and she added, "Until Manny came along."

Michelle nodded understanding and then asked, "Why do you like going to church?"

Mariah brightened and said with just the hint of a smile on her lips, "Because no one shouts at you except the preacher, and he's paid to do that."

Michelle burst out laughing. "Well, in this case the minister is a woman, and she doesn't shout, but she does point her finger a lot… either to the heavens when she talks about God or to the congregation when she talks about sin."

With a growing realization, Michelle decided she liked this business of being a surrogate parent. *I wonder if a single female can be a foster parent?*

And then she acknowledged that her preoccupation with spousal abuse had nearly become an obsession, and her obsession had already started her down a new path.

Mariah interrupted her train of thought. "I wonder if the sheriff would like to go with us?"

8:30 a.m. ~ Bud's house

BUD WASN'T EXACTLY WHAT ONE WOULD call refreshed, but he woke after a solid seven and half hours of uninterrupted sleep feeling like he was going to live after all.

He put the coffee maker to work, pulled on old paint-spattered blue jeans, the pair he dubbed "mud" pants, and a sweatshirt, and opened the back door. Molly barked and then jumped up and tried to lick his face.

"Get down, old gal," he said mildly and pushed her down and then gave her a pat on the head. He opened the old metal locker that sat sentinel on the back porch, used a tin can to scoop food into her dish, knocked a thin skim of ice out of her water bowl and then refilled it from the tap at the corner of the house. Molly sat looking at the food dish, saliva forming along one side of her mouth until Bud said, "Go for it." She chomped down on a mouthful of dry food and gave her best hound dog imitation by trying to eat the whole bowl in one pass. He chuckled and shut the door on the locker.

The morning was crisp, and a thin coat of snow was the only evidence of the storm. The main highway was steaming as the sun coming up over the Warner Mountains promised to work its blue sky magic on the snow and on the human spirit, at least on Bud's spirit. Except in the shady spots, most of the snow would be gone by afternoon. He mentally reminded himself to make sure all the vehicles were switched to the studded tires waiting for winter in the warehouse.

His cell phone rang as he poured his first cup of coffee. It was Beltram wanting to know if he was coming in this morning. Bud felt a slight twinge of guilt for leaving Beltram in charge of an empty jail, but there just wasn't anyone else, and Bud's tank had run dry.

"Is Karen Highsmith there?"

Bud heard Beltram stifle a yawn and say, "Yes."

"Well, in that case, why don't you go on home and get some rest. I'll cover South County, and you can pull a swing shift. All right?"

"Okay, Boss. I'll be back in at 1800 hours."

"Do that. And thanks for the good work last night."

"I didn't do anything except block Bullard Canyon. The SWAT team was all over that vehicle before I ever got into action. Boy... they were good."

"I'll let the FBI know that. They take a lot of hits, but I wouldn't want them after me. Especially not one of their SWAT teams. Now go get some rest. I'm gonna need you to cover things tonight. And get rid of that hair on your upper lip."

Bud's phone rang almost as soon as he hung up. "This is Bud," he answered.

"Bud, this is Larae. I'm hearing you had some excitement last night."

When he didn't say anything, she added, "You want to brief me?"

He thought about the highly effective grapevine running through the county. In a fit of pique he once told Asa Connor, owner and editor of the *Lakeview News* that he couldn't see how Asa's paper stayed in business when the grapevine told everybody about anything and everything, important or not.

He had told Asa that the busybodies even knew things that had yet to happen and even about things that might never happen.

Asa had chuckled and compared the phenomenon to a fart in a wind storm. Just because it hadn't happened yet, didn't mean it wouldn't. "So just to be safe," he added, "stay upwind."

"Bud? You there?"

"Good morning, Larae. Just getting Molly fed and my coffee going, but I was going to call you in a bit. You heard about our excitement, huh? I won't ask how or where."

"The long and the short of it is the Ortega Cartel sent three men, big men I might add, to take Jésus Mendoza off our hands. But we were ready. The FBI flew a SWAT team down here. Chief Hildebrand and his officers, with the help of Deputy Beltram blocked the street after the bad guys parked in front of the station. I let two of them into the station, the ones posing as FBI agents, and Charlie Prince and I arrested them.

"Actually, I think Charlie's shotgun had a lot to do with their surrender. I don't know what happened outside, but the SWAT team apprehended the driver. And they took Jésus and his would-be assassins back to Portland with them last night.

"Also, we are now the proud possessors of this big beautiful 'drug' Suburban. I'm trying to think of a legal way to add it to our fleet. Put it up there in North County with you and Roger. Put two vehicles up there. What do you think?"

"I think I'm sick of all this is what I think. We need to put an end to the Ortegas."

"I think NCIS is working on that."

"No...my husband is working on that. Along with a sixty-something-year-old retired pipsqueak of a DEA agent no bigger than a teenage girl, and a fat, out of shape ex-Seal. That's not a team to inspire confidence."

"Not to mention," Bud interjected wryly, "a pudgy Bremerton detective with a bad arm."

"That's exactly what I mean," she said in an exasperated tone. "Why would NCIS even go along with this?"

"How credible would a story about some banged-up old farts sound if the Mexicans protested we were messing around in their country?"

She sounded deflated when she said, "Deniability."

"Almost as clichéd as 'National Security.'"

"Can't you call it off, Bud?"

"I know Roger has put on some pounds, but did you ever see him shoot?"

"No," she said, "at least not unless he was shooting to qualify with his pistol."

"I have. He's incredible. I watched him shoot a cougar between the eyes at two hundred and fifty yards. All he said was anybody in his unit could make that shot. It doesn't take much imagination to believe John is as good.

"As for Gino, he's tough and capable of taking on the bad guys. He proved that when he killed those terrorists in Bremerton. Think about it. There he was with a terrible wound to his left elbow and he's still pumping rounds and taking down the bad guys...after he shielded Ruby Goldstein and got her to a safer place.

"I don't know much about Wally, however, so I can't give any reassurances there."

She sighed and said, "Based on what Wally told Roger and me, he worked undercover in Mexico for over a year and survived at least one attack by the Ortegas. I don't know, Bud. Maybe you're right. Maybe they can take care of themselves. All I know is John said he was out, and here he is back at it again."

"Not much I can do about that," he said lamely.

"If you hear anything, please let me know."

"I will. And you keep your eyes open. I don't like you being alone up there."

She said, "Thanks, Bud. I'll be fine. I'm used to working alone."

Bud could hear the frustration in her voice, and it occurred to him he hadn't really spent much time with Officer Holcomb-Bernard. During an undercover stint as a bartender at the Christmas Valley Lodge, her warm personality, good looks, short ash blond hair, and soft brown eyes had completely won over the generally standoffish population of North Lake County. It probably helped that she traded tank tops for a long sleeved blouse that hid the Cobra tattoo etched on her left arm, a souvenir from an undercover assignment as a biker.

He shut his phone down and said aloud, "I've got to get up there and spend some time with her."

8:45 a.m. ~ *Sea of Cortez*

JOHN BERNARD WATCHED FROM THE BOW of the open twenty-foot sled as David Peña's 8-weight fly rod sent a light plastic skirted jig shooting out in a long graceful arc to settle on the blue surface of the water. Peña let the jig sink for a count of five and began a retrieve with an experienced "jerk-wait-jerk" rhythm.

The storm had ended sometime before daybreak, leaving a flat blue sea and air swept clean by a brief but driving rain. It was like the world was remade, new all over again. John loved it, and although not very "churchy," he secretly thought of it as God's renewal project. New day, new possibilities.

John hated to admit it, but his arm was tired from working the hard charging bonito with his own fly rod. He had grinned for the camera after the last fish, holding the wriggling bonito by the tail before slipping it back in the water.

Peña grinned as he lowered the camera. "Nice fish, John. I think you've done this before." He looked as Roger sent a jig sailing out a good one-hundred-feet with a spinning reel. "You better get busy, Roger," he said, "or we'll be eating stringy beef for dinner."

Roger gave him a single-digit salute and then set the hook on another bonito, gave a little whoop and a "fish on," and settled in for some fun.

John nodded to Peña and said, "Twice. I've done this twice. Love it, I do, but I think I'll let Roger catch the supper fish." He held up his cell phone. "Gotta call to make." He turned his back on the two men, each of whom was focused on the tornado on the end of Roger's line.

Larae answered on the second ring. "Morning, John," she said. "Where are you?"

"I'm on the beautiful Sea of Cortez, resting my arms and watching Roger fight a nice fish."

"Resting your arms? What does that mean?"

"Well, my sweet, it means I caught a ton of fish this morning, all hard fighting fish, and my arms are tired."

"Really?"

"Truly. What's going on in Christmas Valley?"

"Hmmm. Let me see. I slept alone last night, I, with emphasis on *I* fed the calves this morning, and it's colder than a well digger's butt in January even though the sun is out. Other than that everything is just peachy."

He tried to hide the smile in his voice when he replied, "I miss you, too."

"And," she continued, "the Lake County Sheriff's department is shorthanded…again."

"I know where Roger is, but where are the rest of you?" A yell skipped across the Sea of Cortez from another of Peña's sleds. John and Roger watched Gino's rod bend as he fought what was obviously a big fish. When a dorsal fin split the surface, the skipper of the other Peña sled reached for a rifle.

David Pena pointed and said, "A shark."

John realized that he had lost the thread of the conversation he was trying to have with his new wife.

"What?" he asked.

The exasperation in her voice was clear when she answered. "I said, Sonny is in Bend on an arson task force assignment, you have Roger with you and Michelle is guarding a young runaway who witnessed a murder in Klamath Falls. Her name is Mariah. An Amber Alert went out and she was found. I think the story is a little more complicated than that, but I don't have all of the details. Bud and Michelle picked her up. And now Michelle has temporary custody until a hearing can be arranged."

"No mother?"

"Yes and no. Michelle told me the mother had a meth-induced stroke. Her recovery is still in doubt."

"And if the mother doesn't recover?"

"Then Mariah will become a ward of the State of Oregon and most likely placed in foster care. I guess there are no other relatives."

"Terrific. Well, now. I guess we'll have to see if we can put a dent in the drug traffic for Mariah's sake and for all the other Mariahs in the world."

"When do you go fishing for a really big one?"

He said, "Tomorrow, I hope. Look, I just wanted to let you know I love you, I miss you, and I'm glad you remembered to feed the calves. If all goes well, I'll see you in two or three days."

"One more thing. Bud and an FBI SWAT team took down three Ortega slugs last night. I wonder if that won't put them on high alert."

"Hmmm. I'd like to hear that story sometime, but not over the phone."

"If you get hurt..." And she killed the call. His cell was pulling in dead air. *Pissed, she is. I guess I can't blame her, but I have to do this.*

He turned back to the fight. Peña was leaning over the side of the boat, holding a big net, saying, "He's not ready, *amigo*. Just keep the pressure on and he'll come." The big fish started stripping line again and Roger grunted with the effort of keeping the rod tip high. "And," Peña added, "when you get him near the boat, get his head up. When I net him, drop your rod tip."

A second cell phone chimed from inside the black carryall resting under the small bow deck of the boat. John unzipped the bag and fumbled the phone from an inside pocket. This was not your ordinary cell phone. This one unscrambled messages bounced off a U.S. Military Satellite in synchronous orbit over the border between the U.S. and Mexico.

John instinctively dropped his voice a decibel or two when he answered. "JB, here."

"Hey, how's the fishing?"

"Who is this?"

"A friend. Your partner needs to keep his rod tip up or he's going to lose that big fish."

"Dennis, are you watching us?"

"Yes. As our radio reporter says, This is your Eye in The Sky with the morning traffic report."

"You're in a good mood."

"The *Nemo* should drop anchor about 1700 hours, or for the civilians out there, 5:00 p.m."

"Screw you, Dennis. I am a civilian."

"Not true. You've been recalled by your friendly Marine Commandant to active service, for...let me see what it says...quote, the duration, end quote. So for now you belong to NCIS."

John's voice rose several decibels in reaction to what Assistant SAC Dennis Moore was telling him. "You can't do that!"

"Can and did...but just for this one operation. Moves you from the spook ranks to military operative. Makes it easier to run any rescue operation. A Marine-to-Marine kind of thing."

"What about my partners?"

"Of course they will be rescued if necessary because they are American citizens who just happen to be with you. Stay tuned, same time, same place tomorrow. Oh, and by the way, a Master Archer is on board the *Nemo*. We're told he has recent archery experience in the mountains of an allied Muslim country. Gotta run."

And once again John was listening to dead air. He turned in time to see Roger hoisting a bonito by the tail and grinning for the camera, his floppy safari hat pushed back on his head, the blue Sea of Cortez for background.

9:00 a.m. ~ Sky Lakes Medical Center, Klamath Falls

DETECTIVE MATHEW HARMON HAD A HARD time focusing on the phone call from his partner Officer Christine Downing. His thoughts were on Michelle Trivoli. In his mind he could hear her mellow voice, see her brushing her bangs back from her forehead, see her eyes peering into his soul. It was like he hadn't known anything was missing in his world until he met her. It made for restless sleep and a groggy morning.

"Tyson James regained consciousness," he heard Downing say on the phone. "I think we should get over there as soon as possible."

He heard himself saying, "Sure. Give me thirty minutes. I haven't even had my coffee yet."

"Fine. Want me to pick you up?"

"That would be great."

He barefooted to the kitchen to hit the start button on his coffee maker and then headed down the hall to his bathroom. Ten minutes later, after he had shaved in the shower, a trick learned in the Coast Guard, he was toweling off.

He set a fresh-from-the-laundry bundle on the foot of his bed and tore the wrapping off. The fact that he hadn't put the neatly folded underwear in a drawer was reminder that the past couple of days had been a little hectic.

Five minutes later he was working a Windsor knot into a dark blue tie set against a fairly stiff laundry-starched white shirt.

Satisfied with his sartorial efforts, he ran a brush through his short clipped hair and then stepped into a pair of black Wellington boots.

He glanced out the window at the breeze pushing on the juniper trees in the back yard, and pulled a black windbreaker with a modest KFPD logo on the back from a closet hanger.

Badge wallet in the zippered right pocket of the windbreaker, notebook and pen in his shirt pocket, he settled his pistol in the holster on his left hip and was ready to go talk to Tyson James, victim of a vicious beating. Tyson was also the perpetrator of various crimes ranging from petty offenses like shoplifting to major offenses like armed robbery and drug dealing. Why Manfred Giles had tried to kill him was still unknown, and Harmon hoped Tyson James could clear that up.

He poured coffee mixed with a little creamer into a travel cup, shut the coffee maker off and headed through the living room to the front door. On auto pilot now, thinking of the coming interview, he grabbed a KFPD baseball cap from his coat tree and opened the front door just as Christine pulled a Crown Vic in against the curb.

He slid into the passenger seat and snapped the seat belt in place. "Good morning, Officer Downing. No rest for the wicked, right?"

She smiled and pointed to a white bakery sack. "Maple bars for the wicked."

"Ah," he said, "most grateful. All we need now is a Sunday paper and a football game. My Seahawks are playing my 49ers at one o'clock this afternoon."

She signaled a left turn and raised her eyebrows without take her eyes off the road. "Your Seahawks and *your* 49ers? Who do you want to win?"

"Seahawks," he mumbled around a mouthful of maple bar. "They are the underdogs. I root for the 49ers when they play anyone else."

"That certainly clears it up."

She turned right and drove past the same Applebee's where they had met Sergeant Booker the evening before.

With the apprehension and arrest of Manfred Giles, the Klamath Falls Police Department had released the two officers guarding Tyson James and the officer protecting Barbara Caldwell, Mariah's mother.

But the registration desk, the "check in here or die" desk as Harmon thought of it, was staffed by a Sunday volunteer, so once again he produced his badge and his brilliant smile.

The badge worked, but the smile was wasted on the seventy-something volunteer who had become increasingly sour-tempered about the male gender as she aged.

She wrote Tyson's room number on a slip of paper, ignored Mathew's outstretched hand, and gave the note to Christine. "Have a nice day," she said to their retreating backs.

"Well, that was charming," Christine said. "Hmm, I wonder if he's losing his fatal charm?"

Mathew was tempted to say something vulgar, but settled instead for, "Nothing could warm up that old biddy."

"Agreed. Bad marriage, probably."

"No ring," he pointed out.

"Widow," she said. "I'll bet you two bucks."

"No bet."

Tyson James had been moved from the ICU to a room close to the nurse's station. Detective Harmon resigned himself to letting Officer Downing take the lead. She presented her credentials to a small, dark-haired woman wearing a name tag on her white smock. Name tag, smock and stethoscope were like a uniform that said, "Doctor."

Doctor Susan Lee was happy to speak to the police. "Yes," she said, "thanks to new medical procedures, Mr. James will recover. He has a fractured skull, but the brain damage seems minimal. A concussion…a serious concussion, but no long-term effects are anticipated. We were worried about brain swelling, but what swelling there was seems to have subsided."

She pulled a fat five-by-eight envelope from the pocket of her smock. "Here is a set of the photos we took of his injuries.

"He's awake this morning and even managed to feed himself. I know you need to talk to him, but I'm hoping you will keep the interview short and as non-upsetting as possible."

Officer Downing smiled and said, "Thank you, Doctor Lee. We'll do our best to not upset him."

Tyson was wrapped in a blanket and sitting in a chair watching a pre-game TV program when the two officers walked in. He raised his eyebrows in speculation and said, "Cops?"

Downing nodded and both she and Harmon showed him their badges.

Tyson tried to smile, but the stitches in his face, a neat line running from the left corner of his mouth to his ear cost him too much pain. Instead he asked, "How do I look?"

They glanced at each other and Downing shrugged. "You look like hell," Harmon answered. "Have you looked in a mirror?"

"Nope, afraid to."

"You should be," Harmon said. "You have two of the biggest shiners I've ever seen. Your nose is broken, and your head was shaved so the doctors could cover your skull in stitches. Nice neat ones, by the way.

"Now...we have Manfred Giles in jail on some other charges, so maybe you can tell us why he tried to kill you."

He looked from Harmon to Downing and then back to Harmon, weighing the consequences of cooperating with the police. Decision made, he nodded, took a deep breath and started in.

"It was over a problem that's been festering between us for quite a while. He doesn't like anyone telling him what to do, but when he kept talking about what a sweet young thing Mariah was getting to be, I promised him I'd kill him if he so much as touched her.

"And then there was his use of his own product. I swear, it got so he was smoking more weed than he was selling. When he started using meth, I told him our partnership was done. I'll admit to selling that shit, but I don't want partners who use it.

"We got into an argument...again...in his backyard. The next thing I know, I'm here."

Officer Downing asked, "You don't remember him beating on you?"

Tyson shook his head. "No. I remember arguing with that asshole, but after that my mind is a blank."

Detective Harmon said, "Maybe it'll come back to you." He handed his business card to Tyson. "Call me if your memory improves."

Tyson didn't say anything, just laid the card on the lamp stand.

"One more thing," Downing said. "You owe your life to Gordon Tusk. Giles drove you to Tusk's place. When Tusk found out what Giles had done and that you were still alive, he ran Giles off and called 911."

Tyson looked surprised. "Ran Manny off? I wonder how he did that. Manny carries a pistol in his boot."

Harmon and Downing glanced at each other. Tusk had never mentioned a pistol. Harmon nodded and said to Downing, "Lucifer."

"What?" Tyson asked.

"Never mind," Downing said. "You get well. The DA is going to want you to testify at the trial."

Their stop to see Mariah's mom was disheartening. The nurse on duty told them they would need a court order to have access to any information about Barbara Caldwell's health, but she could tell them Barbara was being moved to a nursing facility on Monday morning.

"Why?" Downing asked. "I thought she was getting better."

"Short-term stay or long term?" Harmon asked.

The RN, a tall trim woman who looked to be in her early fifties, frowned and gave them a sad look with her pale blue eyes. She shook her head. "Who knows? Recovery from stroke is as varied as the causes and the people afflicted. She's young. She might recover. But I don't think her stay at the nursing home will be short term."

"And now I've said more than I'm allowed to say as it is." She sighed and said, "I was here when that little girl visited her mom. Saddest day I've had in a long time." She gritted her teeth and nearly shouted. "Damn, damn drugs. Damn those who sell them. And damn those who use them."

9:00 a.m. ~ Lakeview

BUD'S CELL PHONE RANG JUST AS he was pulling on a pair of Wellington boots. He answered with "Bud."

Michelle Trivoli, a smile in her voice, said, "Good morning, Bud. I have a young lady here who would like to ask you something. Okay if I put her on?"

"Sure enough," he said and wondered about what she could possibly want.

"Good morning, Mr. Blair. I…uh…I was wondering if you would like to go to church with me and Michelle. Service starts at ten. They have a lady preacher and I've never seen a lady preacher."

"Wow. I don't think I have either, and I wish I could go with you, but I'm the only officer we have in the south county this morning. So…I have to go to work. How about lunch? I would be delighted to buy you lunch."

"If you can spare an hour for lunch, you can spare an hour for God," she said.

He broke into laughter, the first really good laugh in a long time. He got himself under control and said, "Why you little Jesuit. Trapped me didn't you?"

"So you can go?"
"And so I can. Which church?"
"Presbyterian."

Bud called the dispatcher at the Emergency Services Center. Henry Barnes, nicknamed the Colonel, answered the phone.

"You filling in today, Henry?"

"Yep. They've been short-handed since Nancy left. Haven't filled her job yet."

"I guess I knew that. Anyway, I wanted to let you know I'll be at the Presbyterian from ten until eleven."

"Presbyterian?" Henry asked.

"Yes. Presbyterian."

"As in church, I suppose. You have business there?"

Finally exasperated, Bud asked, "You don't think a sheriff would go to church?"

Henry laughed and said, "Actually, I don't know of any who do."

"Well, this one is going, and you better pray you don't have to call me from ten until eleven because I won't like it."

"'Yassuh, Boss. No calls between ten and eleven this morning. I got it."

Bud, Michelle, and Mariah sat near the back. Bud debated with himself about wearing a weapon in church and finally settled for putting a .25 caliber semi-automatic pea shooter in his jacket pocket.

The service was more intellectual than bombastic, which suited Bud just fine. When he took time to think about it, which wasn't often, he thought of himself as a closet Christian, a cerebral believer. He had never experienced the sudden revelation of a C.S. Lewis, but he nevertheless found a certain magic in the universe and an order that was hard to explain in terms of chance and happenstance.

But his university study of philosophy and theology had never given him any insight beyond an instinct to avoid denominational entanglements. This was his first visit to a church in over ten years... except for weddings and funerals, of course.

He watch Mariah thumb through her Bible, hunting for the reference of the sermon, a frown on her face until she found the right chapter and verse. And then her face relaxed while she mouthed the words of the text.

He glanced at Michelle who winked at him and nodded in Mariah's direction. The glow in her cheeks and the smile in her eyes made Michelle look nearly beautiful. A white blouse and dark slacks set off a figure that Bud had never really noticed or had at least chosen to ignore.

With sudden insight, he thought, *Michelle, you look more like an expectant mother than a police woman.*"

The minister closed with a final prayer and then hurried down the aisle to stand near the front door as parishioners shuffled by and out the door. She shook hands with each person as they left.

"Thank you for coming," she said over and over again, but with an absolute sincerity that kept it from sounding like a badly delivered line in a play.

When she saw Michelle, she said, "It's been a while, but it's so nice to see you. Could you and your friends wait a bit? I have someone I'd like you to meet."

Bud noticed a young couple and a pretty girl about Mariah's age. The girl was sitting in a wheel chair, staring in his direction. As the line of parishioners grew shorter, the man gently rolled the wheelchair down the aisle. He stopped close to the sheriff, and leaned around the wheelchair, holding out his hand.

"I'm Scott Lilly," he said, "and this is my wife Becky and our daughter Amber."

Bud thought, *Ah...the precocious Amber of Amber Alert fame.*

Bud shook hands and then touched Michelle's elbow to get her turned around. "This is Michelle Trivoli, Deputy Trivoli when she isn't in church. And this," he tugged a reluctant Mariah forward, "is Mariah, whom I think you know something about."

Amber looked up at Mariah's stony face and said simply, "I'm sorry."

The minister inched into the little circle, but didn't say anything, just watched Mariah and Amber. With long, shiny, brown hair, slender figures, and clear blue eyes, they could pass for sisters.

When Mariah didn't say anything, Amber tried again. "I didn't know you were hiding from a killer or I wouldn't have told anybody. Honest! But it was so wonderful to think I had actually helped find someone...that...well...I got excited. And I wanted people to know I could actually do something besides ride around in a wheelchair."

Mariah looked at the sad-faced girl sitting in the wheelchair and then startled all of them by kneeling in front of Amber and taking her hand. "I know."

Tears pooling at the corner of her eyes, Amber said, "Thank you. Would you like to see my puppy? He's out in the car."

The adults said nothing until the two girls were out the door. Bud wiped a stray tear from the corner of his eye…the left one. *Always the left one*, he thought. And then he said to the world in general, "Where the hell did this girl come from? How did she turn out so well after all the shit in her life?"

The minister wiped a tear of her own and simply said, "She humbles me."

And then she said, a smile in her voice, "First cussing in my church I've ever approved of. But don't let it happen again."

Michelle agreed to let the Lillys take Mariah to lunch with Amber and the new puppy. As she and Bud walked to their vehicles, Michelle instinctively put an arm around Bud's shoulder and gave him a hug. "You old softy," she said.

6:00 p.m. ~ Guaymas

THE WATCHER WAITED UNTIL THE *NEMO*, a gleaming white marvel of one hundred and twenty feet of luxury, dropped anchor. He drove his rattle bang taxi, an old Taurus to the wharf and handed an envelope to Juan. The thin twelve-year-old-boy dropped into a small pinto-colored dingy, obviously painted with whatever leftover paint the boy scrounged from the boat yards. It was covered in patches of blues, greens, yellows and reds.

The boy rowed out into the harbor and yelled *"Hola!"* until a deck hand leaned over the rail to see what the noise was about.

In clear but accented English, the boy told the deck hand he had a message from Senor Peña, and held up an envelope with a bright read seal.

Captain Kantor and his first officer, Judith Perez, a tall blond who frequently wore a string bikini when in port, *and wears it well*, Kantor always thought privately, were happy to join Senor David Peña and his guests for dinner at the Peña Guide Service *casa*.

That she was most often seen as a bimbo, just simple "arm candy" for the older Captain Kantor, suited Ms. Perez just fine. Intelligence officers can "hide" in one of two ways: be invisible, or be clearly visible…and someone to be merely dismissed…in this case, just a dumb blond.

When she walked onto the covered veranda where they were to eat supper with Peña and his American guests, a soft breeze lifted her long blond hair from the side of her face, and Roger Hildebrand was, maybe for the first time in his life, a little jealous of the older gray-bearded Kantor until Kantor, during introductions told them she was his First Officer, Lieutenant Perez.

As a former SEAL, he understood the business of cover stories. His feelings about First Officer Perez moved from jealousy of her boss to open admiration. He wasn't sure, but he thought the woman in the soft blue slacks and white sleeveless open collared blouse was the most beautiful First Officer Lieutenant he had ever seen. He unconsciously sucked in his gut when he stood to offer his hand.

His reward was a firm handshake and cool appraisal from clear blue eyes. And then she smiled and said, "Are you my SEAL?"

He caught John Bernard grinning at him from across the table.

"I'm not sure what you mean."

"Oh. Well, we can talk about that later."

Dinner over and taste buds dulled at last by spicy food and one or two glasses of a local red wine, Captain Kantor said, "Shall we get down to business?"

Wally nodded at one of the two big waiters standing at what amounted to parade rest in the arched entry to the veranda. It was obvious to all of Peña's guests that the waiters wore side arms under their long tailed white cotton shirts. They were excellent waiters, but no one could miss their true function as armed security.

When Peña noticed Lieutenant Perez watching them during dinner he had smiled and said, "There are a few banditos in Mexico these days. So our life is one of constant vigilance. And I think the outlaws know this, so they leave us alone."

"Have you had any incidents?" she asked.

He shrugged. "No. No. In addition to my small army, I am a very popular man in Guaymas. Many people have jobs because of Peña, so they look out for me and my family. Not a bad arrangement, no?"

"Then why risk it?"

"Oh, that," he said and then laughed. "It is a small thing. I simply hate drugs and drug dealers. I want my son to grow into the fine man he has the potential to be. I don't want some slimy bandito offering him drugs. So…when I can, I do the drug cartels what little mischief I am capable of. So far, they don't know me except as a fisherman."

"And if they find out?"

"Well, then we move back to the States. I have a nice house in the foothills of the Sierra Nevada. Only one road in. Easily guarded. Nice view. Good skiing. Great satellite reception."

"You are a brave man, Señor Peña."

"Not so much that as just disgusted by what the cartels are doing to my country...both of my countries."

The waiter Wally Pidgeon identified in his mind as Guard One carried a flip chart into the room and set it up at the foot of the long table. Guard Two flipped a switch and lights in the ceiling of the open veranda snapped to life.

Wally stood and in his deep gravelly voice said, "This is what I think should happen."

That evening the *Nemo* slipped quietly out of the Guaymas harbor, her wake thin phosphorescent lines on the moonlit Sea of Cortez. Fifty miles south, she would linger off the coast of Cuidad Obregon. Providing there were no boats nearby, the Archer would launch at 0900.

At the Sea of Cortez Guide Service, three people, two men and a tall blond woman wearing a PBS windbreaker, loaded camera equipment in a Jeep Wagoneer and headed for Alamos, a drive of roughly two hours. The medium-sized man with short-cropped dark hair and a three day growth of beard drove. He drove expertly if a little too fast, but then he had to in order to keep up with the taillights of a Crown Vic emblazoned with the logo of the Mexican Army. The Crown Vic led the way with emergency lights flashing, an insistent warning to any vehicles on the highway. The Mexican Army vehicle came compliments of Wally's retired Mexican Army contact. Wally had given his old friend two thousand dollars as a thank you.

And as a bonus, at Cuidad Obregon, after the lead car killed the emergency lights and turned into a gas station parking lot, a second car, this one unmarked but carrying two armed men, pulled in front of the Jeep and led them east through nearly twenty miles of hills to the Hacienda De Los Santos in Alamos, an elegant hotel in the center of the city. Wally had given another two-thousand-dollar thank you for the second escort team.

Posing as a PBS film crew, Roger, John and Judith Perez confirmed their scheduled two-night stay...all routine stuff until Judith produced a genuine PBS Visa card to secure the charges for the room.

Roger raised his eyebrows in question when she turned from the counter. As they followed three valets carrying their luggage, she leaned over to Roger and whispered, "I actually narrated a travel segment for *Globe Trekker*, a piece on the Sonoran Desert in Northern Mexico. So...NCIS has this special arrangement. And truth is often the best cover."

Roger nodded. But he was less focused on what she was saying than he was on the faint hint of some exotic perfume. And exotic wasn't the word floating through his mind. He mentally shrugged and thought, *Stay focused.*

From a lounge beyond the open portico of the hotel entrance, the soft guitar music of a mariachi band carried a clear tenor voice dripping with Spanish pathos into the night.

When the clerk, a neatly dressed young man wearing a white uniform jacket and red trousers, asked them the purpose of their stay, Judith said, "We're shooting a film segment for *Globe Trekker*, a PBS program about the State of Sonora. Our producer wanted us to try and capture the charm of historic Alamos."

"Oh," he said, sounding disappointed. "I thought you were here because of John Cruise."

"John Cruise?" Judith asked.

"*Si.* You know...Mission Impossible?"

She glanced at Roger and John. Roger was having a hard time keeping a straight face. John just shook his head.

"You don't mean Tom Cruise, do you?"

"No, no. John Cruise." But the look on Judith's face told the clerk he had committed some terrible gaff.

Roger rescued the situation by asking, "Do you know of a reliable guide who can help us find our way around? Someone who knows the history of Alamos?"

The clerk brightened and reached under the counter for a brochure. "*Si.*" He unfolded the brochure and proudly displayed a picture of a gleaming white Toyota minivan. "My cousin Henrico. He is a very good guide. He knows all about the history of Alamos. He can show you the bullet marks on the walls of our old jail. Pancho Villa came to break a friend out of our jail, and there was a lot of shooting. Pancho was much disliked in Alamos after that."

Judith gave him a smile. "What is your name?"

He blushed and said, "Philippe."

She slid a twenty-dollar bill across the counter and said, "You have been very helpful, Philippe. If you see John Cruise, I'd appreciate knowing about it. Now...can you arrange to have your cousin here at six tomorrow morning?"

"*Si.* He will be here. *Gracias,* senorita."

Judith rated a small two-room suite, complete with a study desk and a view of the softly lit inner courtyard and swimming pool.

Roger and John made do with smaller rooms, but they couldn't find anything to complain about: red tiled floors; a bedside hand-woven rug; white adobe walls; colorful prints of Sonoran Desert paintings; an open adobe fireplace and a small stack of mesquite wood for a fire. Two windows were set high in the outside wall. Even a tall person would need a chair to see out the window...or in, for that matter. The foot-wide sills gave a sense of how thick the adobe bricks were.

John knocked and Roger shoved his gun bag into the small closet and closed the door. "Who is it?" he asked.

"John."

Roger let him in and then relocked the door. He pointed at the window and said, "What do you think?"

John nodded approval. "The walls might not stop a .50 caliber slug, but they'll stop anything lighter."

"Yep. We just need to make sure we don't get trapped in here."

"Let's do a little recon."

Roger nodded and pulled his gun bag out of the closet. He stuffed Peña's little gift, a small, black .380 caliber pistol into the top of his boot.

He straightened up and said, "Ready." They glanced into the hallway before Roger wedged a light piece of monofilament between the door and the doorjamb, a nearly invisible telltale that would fall if someone opened the door. Not exactly foolproof, but the best they could do under the circumstance. A little extra insurance perhaps.

They knocked on Judith's door and when she answered the door, said, "Taking a walk. Want to come along?"

She shook her head. "I think I'll just call it a night."

DAY FOUR

Day Four

6:00 a.m. ~ Hotel Hacienda De Los Santos

AN OLDER WHITE TOYOTA MINIVAN DROVE slowly past the old Spanish-style church where the early sun brushed the yellow tower with soft pink tones, and then around the palm lined plaza. Henrico pulled to a curbside stop near the entrance of the hotel. Three white-jacketed porters were standing beside a small pile of camera cases and gear bags, waiting to load the van. The three Americans were holding coffee filled plastic travel cups, and sack lunches, compliments of the hotel.

Philippe's cousin Henrico was so impressed by the tall blond woman, the reporter from PBS, that he scarcely noticed the two-man camera and sound crew. Which suited them just fine. Henrico, a medium-sized man in a chauffeur's uniform ran around the front of the van and nearly bowed as he opened the front passenger door for Judith. Roger winked at John as they carefully loaded their gear in the rear of the van.

The porter who carried the hard case for the "camera' looked at John and said, "Very heavy, senor."

John shrugged. "It takes a beating, so it has to be strong."

"And heavy," the porter repeated, eyeballing the case with suspicion.

"Yes. And heavy."

John pushed the back hatch until it locked in place and turned in time to see Roger hand each of the porters a ten dollar bill. Roger tried out his minimal Spanish and said, "*Gracias*."

The suspicious porter eyeballed the Americans without smiling, and then slid the side door closed behind Roger and John. They settled on the bench seat and then looked at each other. John shook his head slightly. "Not good."

Roger nodded and whispered. "A watcher, I think. The question is who does he work for?"

They heard Judith ask Henrico, "Is there some high point where we can shoot some film of the whole town and the valley?"

Henrico nodded and asked. "Do you mind a short walk?"

Judith shook her head and said, "I don't mind walking."

The driver glanced at her trim body and thought, *I'll bet you don't*, but he didn't share his thoughts.

"Okay, then. We'll start with a short drive to the vista. Do you know what you would like to film after that? The church maybe, or the jail Pancho Villa shot up almost a hundred years ago?"

Judith nodded, but added, "I would also like to film the people and some of the old villas. I understand some very famous people own villas in and around Alamos."

Eager to please, Henrico said, "*Si*. I can point some of them out for you."

John leaned forward and spoke over the driver's shoulder. "Any chance we can film the inside of one of those places?"

Henrico shook his head. "There are a few houses in town that are open to tourists, but none of the villas."

John settled back in the seat and said, "Too bad."

The drive into the hills took about twenty minutes. They weren't ever far from town, but the road followed a winding loop of that ended in a dusty cul-de-sac. A thin ribbon of a footpath led to a viewpoint. Roger turned on a hand-held GPS which showed an area map of Alamos and their location.

Henrico helped John and Roger unload cameras and sound equipment. Roger rigged a wireless collar microphone for Judith and fumbled with the job of clipping it in place when a small breeze sent the faint odor of that same exotic perfume to his nose. *Or is that just an over stimulated imagination?* he thought.

John unsnapped the hard case protecting a new, light-weight digital camcorder, found the on switch and put the camera on his shoulder. He was gratified to see the lens make automatic adjustments for focus. Just point and shoot, he concluded.

Roger went through a similar ritual with the high tech recorder and was equally satisfied he could run the thing.

There was an unmarked on/off button on each device. As instructed by a technician from the *Nemo* the evening before, they each pushed the On button, and, except for a one second satellite bounce, were transmitting directly to the *Nemo*, sight and sound. "Be careful what you say," the technician cautioned, "the sound quality is so good you can hear a mouse running through wet grass."

Henrico stowed the hard cases in the rear of the Toyota, then locked the vehicle and followed them to the viewpoint.

Judith motioned Henrico over to stand beside her, and nodded at John and Roger. They really did intend to film a travelogue with a narrative delivered by an attractive blond. With satellite imagery at its current stage of perfection, on-site film was considered extraneous. But you could never tell when it might actually be useful. So it would be cataloged and then archived by some intelligence agency no one had ever heard of.

John hit the On switch and nodded. Judith smiled for the camera, pointed down slope at Alamos and said, "Our wonderful guide Henrico has taken us to a viewpoint overlooking the lovely, historic town of Alamos in the Mexican State of Sonora. The town was established in the late seventeenth century following the discovery of silver.

"Alamos retains its old style Spanish architecture and charm, and has managed to resist the temptation of large-scale commercial development. This gives travelers the sense of stepping back in time, back to a slower-paced period of Mexico's history...when people took time to walk the plaza on cool evenings, listen to mariachi bands, chat with friends, and sip the local wine.

"Henrico told me this viewpoint is seldom used by anyone but local people. It's not on any map, but travelers can get directions and hire a guide at almost any of the wonderful hotels in scenic Alamos. The well-paved road winds around the foothills surrounding Alamos and climbs to this perfect spot for a panoramic view of Alamos and the surrounding hills.

"Henrico, would you point out the prominent structures of Alamos for our PBS viewers?"

Henrico visibly sucked in a gut that was getting away from him and pointed to the town. "You can see the old church on the Plaza. It is the first building in Alamos to catch the morning sun. And of course the white buildings of Alamos. You can also see the large villas on the edge of our city. Those are owned by the wealthy who like the climate of Alamos in the winter."

John pushed the zoom button and the focus of the camera pulled the tower of the plaza church into clear view., Then he panned the city before pulling the focus back to Judith.

He heard Judith ask, "Mexican citizens?"

"*Si*, but some are owned by wealthy Americans who have been coming to Alamos since the mid-1950s. Writers and movie stars mainly."

"Do you know which ones are owned by Mexican citizens?"

"I know about some of them. See the one at the base of our hill, and slightly left of center, the one with the high wall? That is owned by Senor Ortega. He is a very important man. Very wealthy. The one next to it...on the right...was once owned by an actress, someone name Page, maybe. I'm not sure."

The camera pulled the walled compound owned by Ortega into clear focus. John could see the guard towers at each corner and through the lens he thought he could see a man in the shadow of one of the closer towers.

"What does Señor Ortega do?"

"We don't ask."

Judith frowned. "Is it dangerous to know?"

Henrico looked into the camera and said, "No more questions about Señor Ortega. It's time to go. I will take you to a nice B&B that serves an American breakfast."

Judith shrugged for the camera and said, "Señor Ortega seems to be someone to stay away from. But Henrico doesn't want to talk about Señor Ortega, so it's on to breakfast."

They had a brief time together after Henrico stomped back up the path to the minivan.

"Nice," Roger said.

"Yes." John agreed. "Good work, Miss Perez. Ortega's location is confirmed. And it matches the satellite photos. Now for the grand finale."

"Thanks," she said. "Let's go eat before Henrico gets suspicious, and then let's figure out how we are going to ditch him and get back up here by 0900."

"Wouldn't it be nice to take Ortega alive?" John mused. "Think of all the information he could share with us."

"And if elephants could fly," Roger said sarcastically.

8:05 a.m. ~ Lake County Courthouse

JUDGE THOMAS LYNCH ALWAYS ANSWERED HIS own phone calls. He didn't like talking to gatekeepers when he called other offices, so he didn't have one himself. He also detested voice mail and wouldn't pay for the service.

And if the subject of answering services came up, he invariable said, "I'd pay to **not** have people listen to a mechanical voice saying, 'Press one for English,' press two for Spanish,' and then hear it all over again in Spanish, and then press this, press that until you end right back where you started. While I hold office, people can call their county officials and talk to a live person, not a recording saying goofy things like, 'If you know the extension of the person you are calling, enter it now.'"

He picked up his phone on the second ring and said, "Tom Lynch."

The voice of Judge William Prather, Klamath County, boomed into his ear, making Judge Lynch wince and hold the phone away from his head a little. "Good morning, Tom! This is Will Prather calling from Klamath. How y'all doin' this morning?"

"We're just fine, Will. Storm blew out and it warmed enough to melt the snow off the highways. How did it treat you?"

Will chuckled, "There's something about our big Klamath Lake that seems to attract the snow. I think we got more than you did."

"Probably. So...unless you are inviting me to play golf in Palm Springs, which I'd be delighted to do, what's on your mind, Will?"

"I am told, specifically by a Child Welfare caseworker named Emily Gray, that you have in protective custody a runaway child named Mariah Caldwell. Is that right?"

"I guess you could call it protective custody. Because the child was found in Lake County, and because we were told her mother was incapacitated, I appointed Deputy Sheriff Michelle Trivoli as Mariah's temporary guardian. The girl spent last night with Deputy Trivoli. So that's it in a nutshell. You okay with that?"

Will Prather nodded to himself and said, "For now. Emily told me this morning that the mother...let's see...I've got it in a stack here some place...ah, here it is...the mother, Barbara Caldwell, is being moved from the Sky Lakes hospital to a nursing facility. She'll need physical therapy, speech therapy...the whole nine yards before she can take care of herself, let alone a thirteen-year-old girl."

Tom Lynch said, "I see. So we need to find long-term care for the girl, a foster home, or a relative?"

"Emily says her friend in the Klamath Falls Police Department, Officer Christine Downing, ran a computer check and couldn't find any record of grandparents, aunts, or uncles. She even ran it through some kind of genealogy program. *Nada*. Not a one."

"So what do you want from Lake County?"

"A fast track custody hearing...like today, maybe."

"I've got a full calendar, Will, but if your caseworker can get over here today, I'll get our caseworker together with her and maybe we can at least do some longer term planning? What if we just had a conference call about Mariah?"

Prather said, "No. The case worker wants to meet Mariah and talk to Officer Trivoli in person."

Lynch nodded to himself. "I'll shuffle my calendar. Can your caseworker get over here by ten?"

"Sure. We'll have to get someone to drive her over. She says she doesn't do Bly Mountain in the winter." Then Judge Prather said. "Now about that golf game in Palm Springs..."

8:15 a.m. ~ Sea of Cortez Guide Service, Guaymas

GINO MARETTI STOOD BY THE LOW open wall of the second-floor veranda and watched the flat Sea of Cortez and the dozen or so gulls working the shoreline, their quarrelsome cries clear in the morning air. "Love it," he said quietly to himself. "I've got to get in some fishing this year. Catch me a big King salmon out on Puget Sound. Go crabbing. Something, anything on the water."

The faint sound of an outboard skipped across the sea, and Gino listened as the driver ran the throttle against the stop. A black twenty-foot sled climbed up on the step, leveled out and split the surface of the sea, the drone fading away as the boat raced around the point. Half a dozen gulls picked up off the beach and flew after the boat...maybe. You could never tell what gulls were thinking.

Wally walked up beside him and set a white coffee mug on the low wall. "I find I've been missing this," he said, looking out to sea.

Gino nodded, "I can see why. I'm glad I wasn't born here, but if a person has a little money in his pocket, this can be a nice way to live."

Wally nodded and said, "I have news. We just got a call from our team. They've located the Ortega villa. In an hour and fifteen the Archer launches. Thirty minutes after that I make the call to Ortega." He paused, and when Gino didn't say anything, added, "I see you're carrying this morning," pointing to the holstered pistol on Gino's hip. Gino was wearing a blue Mexican style square tailed shirt that covered the pistol. But Wally was an observant, careful man.

"Yeah, I am. I finally got it. I figured out why Special Agent Amanda Spears invited me... ordered me is more accurate... anyway...why she invited me to come along. I'm here to protect your scrawny ass and keep some cartel scumbag from killing you." His tone was almost accusatory.

Wally shook his head. "Don't look at me. I was coming alone until she got involved. Actually I think *she* was going to protect, as you crudely put it, my scrawny ass until someone told her to stay home. She's too well known to the Ortegas."

David Peña, all six feet seven inches of him, walked quietly up and joined them. He took a deep breath of sea scented air and exhaled in satisfaction. "Look at what God made for us. Wonderful is what it is. It's too bad human greed and cold hearts come with it."

Wally smiled and said, "That's to keep people like you and me on our toes, David."

"And gainfully employed," Gino added.

"Cynics. I'm surrounded by cynics. Where are the romantic hearts?" Peña said and then laughed.

"So…" Peña continued, "We're on schedule. All the pieces are in place. The only part I don't like is getting our boys and our girl the hell out of Dodge. You can't outrun cell phones or police radios, and there's only one road out of there."

Wally had worked with Peña too long on undercover assignments to know he would leave anything so obvious uncovered.

"What I'm going to do…or actually what I have done…is have my helicopter on standby in Cuidad Obregon. It should already be on the ground, refueled, and waiting for my signal. It's a twenty-minute hop from Cuidad Obregon to Alamos.

"If necessary, the helicopter will fly to an open hilltop just west of Alamos, a hilltop very close to the highway. If our people can get that far, and if the bad guys aren't too close, we leave the vehicle and fly them out of there. They will be dropped here and we'll all go fishing again, just like we had nothing in the world to worry about."

Gino shook his head. "We're still foreign visitors. If they tumble our team, how do we get them out of the country? This may be Mexico, but even here the police aren't stupid."

David shook his head. "Those details aren't worked out yet. If nothing goes wrong, we freeze up some fish, pack it for transport, ship it home for you, and I fly you back to San Felipe. Then we drive back to the El Centro crossing. Piece of cake."

Wally looked at his old friend, David Peña, and winced. His furrowed brow told Pena and Gino Maretti how much he disliked the plan. "That's so full of holes. If John gets killed, his wife Larae will never forgive me."

"Who are these people with the helicopter?" Gino asked.

"Well…the helicopter is mine. The pilots work for me and are totally loyal."

Wally and Gino just stared at Peña and waited, not saying a word.

"Okay," he said. "We do emergency medical transports, run rescue missions, maintain a medical clinic here and in San Miguel, rescue people who get stranded in the Northern Sonora desert. That kind of thing." He shrugged his shoulders and added, "On the side we do a little surveillance work for some people I can't tell you about."

Wally started to grin and David broke into laughter. "Same scheme as before, *Amigo*. We package information a little differently for each agency, and since they don't talk to each other, we get paid for the same intel several times.

"Besides, I always wanted my own helicopter."

Maretti picked up his coffee cup and took a sip before saying, "And that doesn't bother your conscience."

"No. I put the money to good use. Sometimes the Border Patrol and the DEA get lucky and make a big bust. Sometimes they get lucky because of what I share with them. That puts a little dent in the drug business and a warm glow in my heart. Money is a useful tool if you are mining for information."

Gino nodded, thinking about his snitches in Bremerton. "Yes it is. And some people sell out for very little."

Wally nodded and growled, "Greed and money, my friends. Greed and money."

7:00 a.m. ~ Mirador Overlook, Alamos

HENRICO SULKED AND DROVE TOO FAST for the suspension of the Toyota minivan. When Judith asked him to slow down, he shouted, "When Ortega finds out I took people from the CIA to the vista, he's going to kill me and all of my family. You put me in much risk!"

Judith reached out and touched his arm. "CIA? What are you talking about? We are with PBS," she said in soothing tones, "here to do a simple travel program. It will bring you tourists, keep your hotels full, and keep the guides busy. Let me show you my passport and my permit from Hermosillo to do the film."

She laughed and added, "We're not spies, Henrico. Far from it. Trust me."

Henrico glanced at her and was rewarded with a bright smile, the kind of smile that promised a short trip to paradise.

She patted his arm and said, "Now be a good boy and slow down."

Roger slipped a small Gerber dagger back into the sheath clipped to the inside of his right boot top, and John took a deep breath and settled back into the seat.

Henrico would live to see another day without ever knowing how close he came to losing this one.

"Henrico," Judith said, almost cooing the name, "I understand there is a creek called Cuchujaqui near here that is teeming with all kinds of birds that migrate here each winter. I'd like to shoot some film there. Perhaps you can show it to us this afternoon?"

"*Si*. I can do that." He scootched around in the seat and leaned back, his body language telling the three Americans he was starting to relax, and maybe, just maybe buying their cover story.

An American couple owned the Maria Felix B&B near the plaza. The hostess practically dragged the PBS crew through the house, an open, airy two-story adobe building with shiny tile floors, a brick paved inner courtyard with a small fountain and bougainvillea blanketing a back wall. Two small palm trees offered shade for a stone bench. The only incongruous note was a hot tub in a corner of the walled courtyard.

"It's beautiful," Judith said to the hostess Edith, a lean, fiftyish refugee from the froth and detritus of Los Angeles. "Do you mind if we film the house?"

John had the camera running, panning each room, and Roger had the sound boom extended to catch Edith from L.A. saying, "… the drugs, the crime, and the population pressure was getting so great, we could hardly stand to leave the house. So when we found Alamos on our last vacation, I told Stan we should uproot, sell the L.A. house and start a bed and breakfast here where the traffic is minimal and the winters are simply wonderful.

"The people here have been so kind to us. There is little crime, no drugs and people walk the plaza each evening…just like in the early days. And I was just thrilled when Henrico told us the famous Mexican actress Maria Felix once owned this. Just think of it."

Roger glanced at John and without saying a word conveyed his disgust with Edith. "Airhead," he mouthed.

They heard a male voice say in a skeptical tone, "If it's really true, Edith. You know that Henrico tends to tell people what they want to hear."

They turned and saw a tall, rather gaunt man who looked to be a good ten years older than Edith.

"Stan, this is Judith Perez from PBS. She and her crew are filming a travelogue of Alamos, and they want to film our house. Isn't that wonderful?"

Stan walked over and held out his hand. "Delighted. I came to let you know Isabella has breakfast ready. You hungry?"

They were greeted by Isabella, a small bundle of energy in black slacks and a white blouse who smiled and said good morning in barely understandable English. "This way please." She led them to a room that appeared to be a study and on through an open set of French doors to a tree shaded patio. She pulled a chair back for Judith and seated them at a round hardwood table loaded with well-done spinach soufflés, fresh fruit compote, fresh squeezed orange juice, English muffins, and a coffee urn. Roger and John fell to with the appetites of the damned.

They were on their second cup of Starbucks, made from beans shipped to the Maria Felix B&B via UPS from a shop in San Diego, looking at the film interview on the camera's small monitor with Edith and Stan when Henrico walked in.

"Henrico," Judith said, "Would you like to see what we've filmed so far?"

"*Si.*"

John scrolled back and stopped when Henrico appeared on the screen. "Think of it," she said. "Henrico's Guide Service will be famous. And here comes a scene with your minivan in it."

Henrico grinned from ear to ear, thrilled to think that he, a common man from Alamos would be on American television.

"Now. I've looked at the film, but I'm not satisfied with what we shot this morning at the vista, so I'd like to go back up and shoot it again. Your part will be in the final version, so we don't need to do that again, but I don't think we have done justice to the setting."

She unzipped her day planner and pulled a small FedEx mailer from a side pocket. "I'm anxious for our editor to start working on what we've filmed so far. I think you," she smiled at Henrico, "could drop us off at our hotel and while you mail this we'll run back up to the vista. Okay?"

Henrico looked skeptical, but when she placed a twenty dollar bill on top of the mailer, he said, "Okay."

"And," she turned to Stan and Edith, "maybe we can meet right back here and finish filming your house."

At the Hotel Hacienda De Los Santos, they off-loaded their equipment from the back of Henrico's minivan into the Jeep Wagoneer, and when Henrico's van turned a corner and slipped from sight, they hustled to their rooms, packed their personal gear and loaded the Jeep. They didn't plan on sticking around after the Archer and its two little friends paid a visit to the Ortega villa.

Judith stopped at the front desk and paid cash for three nights, not two. This drew a big smile from the desk clerk.

At eight thirty they were back on the overlook. This time the camera was mounted on a tripod, focused exclusively on the Ortega villa. Roger was slightly down slope from the viewpoint, hunkered in behind a large boulder, staring through the scope of a laser sight designed to "paint" a target for a smart bomb or a guided missile. Through the scope he watched a man in the guard tower on the wall closest to the hill light a cigarette and toss the still burning match into the compound. The casual behavior and body language told Roger the guard was bored, less than totally alert and not really expecting any trouble.

The Americans had earbuds and radios with lapel mikes. Roger and John listened to Judith report to the *Nemo* that the team was in place.

Ten minutes ground slowly by and then John's cell phone buzzed in his jacket pocket. Dennis Moore, John's "temporary" boss, said, "Are you prepared for company?"

"No, Dennis, we're not. There's only one road out of here. Tell me you have some good news."

"I can't do that. I'm wondering if you can see the quads, as in two quads, with two people on each quad, armed with rifles, stirring about in front of the Ortega villa."

John shook his head. "Nope. The house blocks my view."

"I thought that might be the case. I'll watch and see what they're up to."

Roger and Judith listened with interest to John's side of the conversation, and when he said, "Let us know if they head this way," their interest increased tenfold.

Judith's phone buzzed in her pocket and when she answered, she heard Captain Kantor's voice saying, "Judith."

"Yes?"

"Early launch of the Archer. Should be overhead in five minutes. We had some boats moving in on us, so we chose to go early."

"Good. How many arrows does he have?"

"Just two."

She heard Roger say, "Oops. The guards in the towers are all looking our way. I think the quads are coming to check us out."

"We might need some help getting out of here," she said to Kantor.

"Hold," Kantor said. When he came back on line he said, "When the Archer is on station, we can give you a look down via cell phone. ETA…four minutes."

In Guaymas, Walter Pidgeon got ready to call Ortega's private number. He didn't ask his old friend, David Peña how he got the number. And maybe he really didn't want to know. After years of living in Guaymas, Peña had sources none of the intelligence agencies could match.

At ten minutes before the hour, the Archer was overhead and the *Nemo* signaled Peña via scrambled satellite communications it was time.

The operating plan was simple: call Juan Ortega, pose as a rival Reynosa, warn Ortega to stop killing Americans, and have the Archer destroy the largest vehicle in the villa compound with a guided missile. If that started a little war between the Reynosas and the Ortegas, so much the better. Wally picked up a cell phone and dialed the number David had given him.

Through the laser scope, Roger saw the familiar trail of a rocket propelled grenade, an "RPG" in military parlance, headed for the guard tower closest to the vista. "Look at that," he shouted just before the guard tower collapsed spilling the guard into the compound. In the blink of an eye each of the other towers were also demolished.

"What was it?" John asked.

"RPGs, I think. Somebody hit all four towers…almost at the same time. Did you get that on camera?"

"Yeah. I did."

Judith hit a speed dial number and the voice of Kantor was asking, "What the hell is going on?"

"We don't know. Someone attacked Ortega's villa. It looked like they used RPGs to take out the guards." She winced as another explosion lifted the main gate from its hinges. "I'm thinking we need to get out of here."

A second explosion rolled up the hill from the Ortega compound, and the two quads turned and bounced back down the slope. Through the camera lens, John watched the faster of the two, or at least the one driven by a more reckless driver, fly over a small hummock, become briefly airborne, smack a small boulder and pitch pole, scattering passenger, rifles, and driver down the slope.

The engine was still running when the quad came to a dusty stop upside down a good thirty yards beyond the impact site. The passenger and the driver were sprawled, unmoving bundles on the dusty hillside.

The men on the second quad stopped and just stared down the hill. John could see them talking and pointing up hill. The sound of gunfire from the villa seemed to make up their minds. They dropped their rifles on the ground, and with the passenger holding his arms over his head in a sign of surrender, they started working the quad up hill through the boulders, around patches of ocotillo and low growing cactus.

John was on the phone with Dennis Moore who was nearly shouting and wanting to know what the hell was going on. "We didn't do it," John kept repeating into the phone.

The quad spun its wheels climbing the last pitch up to the viewpoint and stopped in front of Roger. The driver killed the engine and raised his hands.

Roger searched his short list of Spanish, pointed down the road and said, "*Vamoose.*" He repeated the word, hoping the two men would understand. Their blank faces told him his Spanish wasn't up to the task. In disgust Roger pointed again and said, "Get the hell out of here!"

Comprehension blossomed on their faces. The rolling concussion of another explosion at the villa galvanized the driver. His hand was shaking as he fumbled with the key to start the engine. The passenger lunged for the rear seat and hung on for life as the quad accelerated and bounced down the thin path toward the parked Jeep and the road back to Alamos.

"What's that?" Roger said pointing down the hill. An armored car looking like something out of *The Dirty Dozen* poked its nose around the corner of the Ortega villa and the steady sound of a heavy machine gun added its voice to the cacophony of rifle fire and muted explosions.

"That's a .50," John said, referring to the hammering of the big machine gun" as he refocused the camera on the armored car.

"Gonna burn it up if they keep shooting like that. Too excited," Roger said.

"You think?" John growled. He kept the camera running and panned back to the villa in time to see five fighters slip out of the small gate in the back wall. Through the lens, John thought he could see two men carrying what looked like RPGs. He watched in fascination as they inched along the wall. A line of dusty puffs pocketed the adobe just over their heads and drove them to the ground where they began returning fire on the attackers. It wasn't focused shooting, just a random spraying of the brush at the base of the hill.

Roger moved over to John and said, "Somebody inside the compound is getting the Ortgas organized. They'll make a fight of it."

John nodded and said, "Too little too late, I think," and watched as one of the Ortega men pinned down at the base of the wall flinched, rolled over and then was still, his face pointed to the sky.

Judith walked over and tapped John's shoulder. "Captain Kantor says we have enough of this on record. We are to pack it in and get back to Guymas."

"Give me a minute," John said as he watched the armored car edge up to the corner of the villa wall. A man dropped from the passenger seat and carefully peered around the corner at the small group of men pinned down by automatic rifle fire. The man motioned the armored car up and hopped back in the passenger seat. The roof-mounted .50 caliber weapon was already firing when the armored car rounded the corner.

It had been a great day for the Reynosa Cartel fighters inside the armored car, a regular turkey shoot, a day of sweet revenge for family and friends killed by the Ortega's during the past five years, but that all changed when the overheated machine gun jammed. The gunner was cursing the machine gun and the driver was trying to shift into reverse when an RPG slammed into the armored car. A cheer broke from the men pinned down by the wall.

The old armored car didn't burn and it didn't explode. It simply died along with the men inside. But rifle fire from the ambushers on the hillside killed all of the Ortega men before they could scramble back to the gate and the safety of the wall.

A small Reynosa assault team rose out of the brush on the hillside, ran to the wall and fanned out, ready to enter the rear gate.

"The party's over, boys," John almost whispered. He took his eye from the camera lens and turned to see Judith and Roger watching the firefight through pocket-size binoculars.

"Yes it is," Roger agreed.

Judith's cell phone buzzed and she let the binoculars hang from the strap around her neck while she answered. "Yes?" She heard Kantor say, "Time to boogey. The Archer will cover your backs."

"Agreed," Judith said and hung up. "Okay, guys. Our PBS assignment has just been cancelled. If we are stopped, we are simply on our way to the police to share our film. Okay?"

Roger slipped the cherished Gerber dagger from his boot, kissed the handle, and tossed it as far as he could into the brush. John and Roger each reluctantly performed a similar ritual with the two handguns. Roger loaded the laser-range finder back into its metal case, John collapsed the legs on the camera tripod, and the Three Amigos trotted along the path to the Jeep.

Down the hill the sound of gunfire had almost ceased, except for the sporadic pop pop of a pistol.

In Guaymas, Wally stared at the phone and listened as an operator explained in Spanish how to leave a callback number. He shook his head, and killed the call.

Gino watched until Wally shrugged and said, "No answer. I wonder what's going on?"

10:00 a.m. ~ Lake County Courthouse

JUDGE TOM LYNCH WAS SITTING AT the table in the small hearing room attached to his office. He was chatting with Michelle and Mariah who were sitting side-by-side across from him. He was interested to hear how Mariah managed to wind up in Lakeview.

He smiled when Mariah said, "...and that darned old cat gave me away."

"I'd say that was fortunate, wouldn't you?" Lynch asked.

Mariah reluctantly nodded, her shiny, dark hair stirring slightly. He noticed with approval the new jeans, Nike tennis shoes, and the new dark blue sweater she wore under her freshly laundered hoody. *Officer Trivoli has been taking good care of this girl*, he thought.

There was knock on the door and Mariah suddenly dug an elbow into Michelle's ribs to get her attention, and Michelle's heart picked up a beat when Mathew Harmon entered the room. He held the door for a tall woman who had to be the caseworker from Klamath County Child Welfare.

If asked right then and there, Michelle couldn't have described the caseworker beyond "tall," but Mariah was focused. She knew the dark-haired woman with the clear ivory complexion and deep green eyes would play a major role in her future.

Judge Lynch rose and reached across the table. "You must be Mrs. Gray."

"Yes. Thank you. This is Detective Harmon," she said and smiled. She held out her hand and said, "And you must be Mariah."

Mariah nodded but didn't say anything. She couldn't help but be wary of this woman. Judge Lynch interrupted her thoughts when he asked, "Detective Harmon? Is something going on I need to know about?"

Mathew Harmon shook his head and looked directly at Mariah. "Not really. Emily said she didn't do Bly Mountain in the winter, and I wanted to see Miss Mariah again, a young lady I really admire. How are you?" He smiled and held out his hand.

Mariah felt her face turning red, in a cynical corner of her mind believing Michelle had more to do with his volunteer drive to Lakeview than she did, but pleased in spite of herself. She held out her small, thin hand and felt him give a light, gentle squeeze. In a small voice she said, "Fine, thank you."

She glanced at Michelle and saw that she wasn't the only one smitten...again...by Mathew Harmon. Michelle wasn't blushing exactly, but a bright spot lit up each cheek bone.

Mathew grinned and nodded to Michelle. "Nice to see you again, Officer Trivoli."

Michelle instinctively held out her hand and was rewarded with a warm, strong hand that held hers a few seconds longer than normal for a handshake.

Emily Gray glanced at the judge with a puzzled frown and Lynch, who was quick to recognize a mutual attraction when he saw it, smiled and winked at her as though they were fellow conspirators. "Well," he said, "have a seat. I have a court recorder standing by to make a record of our meeting. And then we'll report back to Judge Prather in Klamath. Okay?"

Emily Gray nodded and said, "Good." She slid into a chair across from Mariah and Michelle. Harmon chose a chair next to Michelle and was welcomed by the faint scent of soap and shampoo. *I wish I had met you sooner in this life,* he thought. Michelle glanced up at him as though she could read his mind, and it was Mathew's turn to flush a little and to fidget in his chair.

Judge Lynch picked up a phone and said, "Sandy, we're ready."

10:30 a.m. ~ Alamos

HALFWAY TO TOWN THE AMERICANS WERE stopped by two Alamos police vehicles. Two late-model Jeep Liberty 4X4's painted white, each sporting a light rack and emblazoned with black lettering that said *Policia de Alamos* formed an inverted "V" and acted as barrier and rifle rest for the four men in uniform who aimed automatic rifles over the hood of each vehicle.

"Uh, oh," Judith said. "Put on your *Globe Trekker* hats and smile." She hopped out of the car and started a rapid fire conversation in Spanish as she walked toward the blockade. She had succeeded in surprising John and Roger, neither of whom knew Judith Perez was fluent in the native tongue of most Mexicans.

It sounded both questioning and expository to their ears, but when your use of a language is limited to sentences composed of single nouns, it's hard to catch enough words to follow a conversation.

"Quite an operator, isn't she?" John said quietly.

"She certainly is. Think this will work?"

John grinned and said, "It better."

They watched as she produced her PBS identification and another slip of paper with some kind of seal on it. She handed her papers to the tall Mexican dressed in a crisp khaki uniform complete with highly polished Wellington boots and a Sam Brown belt. He was obviously in charge of the detail and obviously agitated. Through the open passenger window John thought he caught the words "Señor Ortega."

Judith shook her head and pointed to the Jeep and said, "Bring the camera."

At a command from the senior officer, two men edged around the police Jeeps and walked down the single dusty track to the American vehicle. With rifle barrels, the men motioned Roger and John out of their rig. They were both expertly patted down by a third man for weapons, and when the man shrugged, Judith said something and the boss nodded.

He spoke in Spanish to the three men and then said in fairly clear English, "You two," pointing at Roger and John, "bring me the camera while my men search the Jeep. There has been a tragedy at the Ortega hacienda, and my friend Henrico says you have been asking questions about Señor Ortega and acting strangely, so...we search. *Comprende?*"

Roger was tempted to try out a "*Si*" but thought better of it and just nodded. John's face was still, a mask of passive acceptance, but inside he was thinking it was a good thing they had tossed their weapons before heading down the hill.

John carried the camera over to where Judith and the Mexican policeman were standing and set the camera on the hood of the police car. He turned it on, and the senior officer watched the whole film, including the scene showing the death of the armored car, and said in disgust, "Reynosa!"

The three men searching the Jeep looked over to their leader in alarm and then back at each other. *Scared,* Roger thought. *The Reynosa Cartel scares the crap out of these guys.*

The leader spat and asked in Spanish if they hand found anything in the Americans' Jeep. The men shook their heads. And then suddenly all was forgiven. The leader smiled and nearly bowed to Judith as he introduced himself as Ramon Aguilera, chief of police for the city of Alamos. "I hope you understand why we had to question you, *senorita*," he said to Judith. "And I hope you won't air the attack you filmed. Maybe only the part where you interview Henrico? On your *Globe Trekker* program, as a courtesy to the citizens of Alamos?"

Judith framed her answer carefully, thinking that their lives might depend on a correct answer. "We have been treated with great kindness and great respect by the people of Alamos, and we have no wish to shame your people and your city. You have my word that nothing about the battle will ever see a PBS broadcast."

"Amen," John said quietly.

"You may have our disc, Senor Aguilera, as our guarantee," Judith said. "We plan to visit again later in the year and finish our film of your lovely city, and I want to spend some time filming Cuchujaqui creek when we come back."

With a perfectly straight face, John hit the eject button and caught the silver disc as it slid from the side of the camera. He looked a question at Judith, and she said, "Please give Señor Aguilera the disc."

Getting into the act, Roger said, "You sure?"

"Yes."

They were in the hills west of Alamos headed for Cuidad Obregon before Roger said from the back seat, "A massacre, wasn't it?"

Judith turned from the passenger seat to look directly in his eyes. Her eyes were steely and her mouth grim when she said, "I can't feel sorry for anyone who brings that poison into my country."

Roger felt defensive and said, "I was only commenting on the battle."

John snorted. "Hell, if people didn't buy it and use it, they wouldn't bother to smuggle it in."

Judith turned to look out the windshield. Roger barely heard her when she mused, "Are we working on the wrong end of the problem?"

11:00 a.m. ~ Lake County Courthouse

MARIAH WAS FURIOUS WITH EMILY GRAY for suggesting she be moved to a foster home in Klamath County. "I won't leave Michelle," she kept saying.

"But you will be in the same school with your friends, and you will be close to your mother," Emily said reasonably. "Don't you want to see your mom?"

"Michelle will take me to see her, won't you, Michelle?"

Just as frightened as Mariah of being separated, Michelle said quickly, "Absolutely."

Emily was shaking her head when Michelle asked, "What if I lived in Klamath Falls? Couldn't I be her foster mother? She'll be in the same school and close to her mother."

Emily hesitated and said, "I suppose, but the fact remains that for now you live in Lakeview."

Michelle surprised herself as well as the Judge and Mathew Harmon, when she blurted out, "I'm moving to Klamath Falls in two weeks. Can I have two weeks to get us a house and get settled?"

"Wow," Emily said in admiration, "you really do care. Okay, then. Mariah will be in a temporary foster shelter until you have a place of your own. Agreed?"

Both Michelle and Mariah blurted, "No!"

"I mean," Michelle added more reasonably, "Mariah feels safe with me. We are friends, and I think she's had enough loss. She should stay with me."

Judge Lynch said softly, "What about school?"

"I'll home school Mariah until we get moved. I want this child to stay with me!"

"What will you do for a living?" Emily asked.

"I have enough savings for six months, and I'll get a part time job with the KFPD while I go to school. I have a degree in criminology, but I want a second degree in social work. That's where my heart lies."

"I'll run if you take me away from Michelle," Mariah warned sternly.

And suddenly Emily Gray was laughing and both Judge Lynch and Mathew Harmon joined in.

Mariah and Michelle were both a little embarrassed, but secretly proud of each other.

Michelle wrapped an arm around Mariah and whispered, "If you run, I'll shoot you."

"No you won't."

"Will, too."

"Won't."

"Will."

And then they were both smiling with relief as they recognized they had won this round.

Mathew Harmon looked at Michelle and said, "Could I have a minute?"

Michelle arched her eyebrows and said cautiously, "I guess so."

"A private minute."

"Oh."

In the hallway, he said, "I don't know how to put this, but I know someone who needs a house sitter for a few months...maybe as long as a year. The place is a small farm just outside the city limits of Klamath Falls. It's a nice house, maybe a bit large for two people, but it sits on forty acres of irrigated ground. The owner grows a little alfalfa. There's a small orchard, an indoor horse arena, horse barns, and a bass pond. I know you could live there rent free just for taking care of the house and keeping an eye on things."

He paused and asked, "Want to see it? I have a picture in my phone."

He pulled up a picture of a farm house, one of those newer "old fashioned" houses, two tall stories with a big covered porch that ran around three sides of the house, a bright yellow house with white trim. Nothing in the picture showed any neglect.

"Nice. Seems like a lot of house for free."

"You have to pay the utilities, your own phone and your own TV," he said.

She set her jaw and said, "I can tell you right now I like the idea, but I don't set irrigation pipe and I don't ride horses."

He laughed as the tension went out of the conversation. "Oh... not a problem. A hired hand tends the horses and does the little bit of farming the place needs. He even does the yard. What the owner wants is someone to be there and sort of keep the bad guys warned the place isn't empty."

"Before I accept, I have one more question. What school district is it in?"

"You'll like this. It's in the Henley Junior High School district. Same school she is absent from right now."

Michelle held out her hand and said, "Deal. When do I meet the owner?"

He looked embarrassed and said, "I was thinking about saying I was the agent for the owner, but I don't think I'd better start lying... not to a cop and a trained investigator like you. I...uh...I happen to own it, but everything I said is true. I don't live there. I inherited it from my grandfather, but I already own a condominium in town and I live on my boat in the summer time. I like horses, but I'd rather sail than ride."

She stiffened and said, "I can pay my own way. I don't accept charity."

"It's not charity. It's the same deal I made with the last house sitter, a college student who graduated and moved away. I really am looking for a sitter. Here," he said and pulled a newspaper ad out of his wallet. When she had read it and looked up at him, he added, "Please help me out," and tried hard not to grin.

A grin of her own, which she tried unsuccessfully to keep at bay, tugged at the corner of her mouth, and in a sudden rush of warmth she stepped close and gave him a fierce hug. "Thank you," she whispered in his ear.

His return hug was nearly as aggressive, but a hard yank on his sleeve stopped him short of downright lechery. "What?" he growled, looking down at Mariah.

"This is not the place for that," she answered in a stage whisper. And all three of them laughed.

"Guess what?" Michelle said, and then continued before Mariah could guess. "We have a place to live...a really nice place to live. Mathew is going to let us house sit for him...on a ranch just outside of town. And you can keep going to the same school. Isn't that wonderful? Show her, Mathew. Show her the picture."

He had always thought he was immune to feminine wiles, but the use of his given name by Michelle ripped the cover of his defenses. That kernel of affection for Officer Michelle Trivoli stirring deep in Detective Mathew Harmon's soul sprouted and took root, and he knew he was falling in love with this woman. And he was suddenly afraid of losing someone for the first time in his adult life.

Their euphoria was dampened, but only a little when the judge cautioned that Michelle's designation as a guardian and foster parent was temporary and hinged on the recovery of Mariah's mother or Emily Gray's search for a suitable relative.

Michelle had nodded and said, "I understand," but without a lot of enthusiasm at that prospect.

11:30 a.m. ~ Lake County Sheriff's Office

BUD'S RESPONSE TO MICHELLE'S RESIGNATION WAS less that enthusiastic. But she was so excited she failed to notice when she gave him a hug and said, "Thanks for being a great boss and terrific mentor." And then went on excitedly about moving to Klamath Falls to be Mariah's foster mother, and going back to school to get a degree in social work, and having a terrific place to live and what a great person Detective Harmon was. She only slipped and called him Mathew one time while she was describing the farm she and Mariah were going to live on.

She ran down finally and when she saw the hard line of his jaw, she said, "Oh, Bud. I'm so sorry, but I think I've been leaning in this direction ever since the Casey affair. I have to do this. And I have to live in Klamath County to be Mariah's foster mom."

He swallowed his disappointment, not really knowing why he was disappointed instead of being happy for her, and said, "My loss. I guess I'm not ready to see you leave for greener pastures." He gave her a wry smile and added, "Go with my blessings. You take care of Miss Mariah and I'll forgive the rest. Two weeks, huh? Guess I'll have to bring Lonnie on as a permanent deputy now."

"Good for you, Bud. And good for Lonnie."

He sat at his desk after she left and pondered his grief at her departure. His musing was interrupted by Karen Highsmith who knocked and then brought in a steaming cup of fresh coffee.

"Sad, isn't it, Bud?"

"Yep. And I'm not sure why it should be. She's doing the right thing and we'll mush along after she is gone. We always do."

Karen shook her head and said, "We women understand these things. Want me to guess at why it makes you sad?"

"No, I don't."

"Well, I think it reminds you of Nancy, and I think you feel like the women in your life are always leaving you. First your mother dies much too young. Then your first wife Linda divorces you. Nancy breaks your engagement and leaves. And now Michelle resigns."

"Michelle works…make that worked…for me. Makes it a different relationship."

Karen sniffed and said, "Still a lot of losses for one man to carry."

He looked at her and then snorted. "Oh, horseshit, Karen. I'm just wondering how I'm going to run this department until I can get two new deputies on board. Right now, I'm wondering how Larae, Lonnie Beltram, and I can police this huge county until Roger and Sonny get back. I can tell you this much, budget or no budget we're going to hire a clerk, and we're going hire another deputy. So you get busy and make the jail pay its own way. You hear?"

She grinned and said, "That's the sheriff we all know and love. The fighter, not the pouter."

"I wasn't pouting."

With a wave of her hand, she turned her back on him walked out the door. "Believe what you want," she said as she walked down the short hallway.

6:30 p.m. ~ Guaymas, Sonora Mexico

DAVID PEÑA, WALTER PIDGEON, AND GINO Maretti were seeing the film of the raid on the Ortega hacienda for the first time on a huge flat screen David had installed to watch his beloved San Diego Chargers. Judith had brought a copy of the disc from the *Nemo*, anchored once again in gleaming white splendor in Guymas harbor. Unknown to the Mexican authorities, the disc Judith had given them was merely a copy of the digital record transmitted to the *Nemo* by John's camera and the camera onboard the UAV.

It was still just as fascinating to Roger, John, and Captain Kantor as if they were seeing it for the first time. In vivid color, the disc brought the horrendous carnage up close and personal on the big screen. The microphone was everything the tech on the *Nemo* had promised. The explosions and the sound of the machine gun and rifle fire echoed through Peña's big den.

He finally hit the mute and then stopped the film. "Enough," he said in disgust. "You know what this means, don't you?"

"War between the Reynosas and Ortegas," Wally growled.

"That's what we wanted, wasn't it?" Gino said.

"Yep," Roger said. "But war is still an ugly business."

"Fortunately, we didn't do a thing to start it. Clean hands," John added, "but cold hearts." He looked wistful when he added, "I really wish we could have interrogated those two who surrendered at the overlook. Might have learned something useful."

Pena's cell phone rang and he frowned when he saw who the call was from. "Peña," he answered.

"This is Diego Garcia, Senor Peña. I have a message for your American friends. Tell them to go home and leave Mexico to Mexicans. What's the old American saying? We kill our own snakes? That's not right. Maybe you know the word?"

In spite of himself, David smiled and said, "I think you want the word 'scotch'. As in 'scotch our own snakes.'"

"*Gracias.* That's it. What I want to tell your American friends is that we Reynosas believe the killing of Americans is bad for business. That was the reason we had to deal with the Ortegas. Their only answer was to kill people. So...we think maybe they won't do that anymore." Garcia paused and then added, "And tell that sheriff in Oregon, no one in our business will be coming after him or any of his friends. We Reynosas declare a truce."

"You think that will make him lay off the drug traffic?"

"No. Of course not. He's a man of principle...and very good at surviving, I think. No. We'll leave him and his county alone."

"I'll let him know."

"And Senor Peña, another thing. You should really stick to your philanthropic endeavors and keep you nose out of our business. You have a lovely wife and a handsome boy. Both of them need you, so we'll let bygones be bygones. You stick to fishing and your mercy missions. Understand?"

David didn't answer until he was listening to dead air.

They all watched without saying anything, sensing that something sinister had just happened.

David took a deep breath and looked at the phone and then at his companions. Finally he said, "I have just been offered my life in exchange for a truce with the Reynosa Cartel." And then he related the conversation almost verbatim because he had that kind of memory.

Wally was the first to say, "I'm sorry, my old friend, to have put you and your family at risk."

Pena waved the apology away and said, "Nothing to be sorry about. But I do have a mole in my organization, don't I? So…until I find out who that is, and I will, I'm shutting down any anti-drug activity. I'm not sure I believe they will leave your sheriff alone, but…" he shrugged, "…who knows. We can only tell him and see what develops."

Epilogue

GREEN-UP PAID ITS WELCOME SPRING VISIT to the high desert. Brown hillsides gave birth to Spartan flowers and patches of green cheat grass. The Lombardi poplars and the cottonwoods and willows budded out. Northbound squadrons of migrating Canada geese, snow geese, ducks, and marsh birds dropped in on the lakes of Warner Valley, some to stay and others to rest before beating their way to Canada and on to the Arctic.

A young biologist working her internship at the Summer Lake Wildlife Refuge spotted a wading Western Avocet and noted the time and place on her log book. A great blue heron ignored the moving shadow created by several thousand snow geese that drifted over the marsh and settled with a flash of black-tipped white wings in the muddy flat beyond the main dike, an emphatic reminder of the perpetual change of seasons.

In Christmas Valley, the alfalfa sprouted in John and Larae's fields, and twenty calves were ready for the auction. Larae was fairly bursting out of her maternity smock. And Deputy Roger Hildebrand looked forward to playing uncle to a newborn. Wally bragged to anyone and everyone who paid a visit to the Christmas Valley Lodge that he was going to be godfather to the new baby.

Neither John nor Larae were willing to share the sex of the baby with anyone else, but Wally kept buying blue sleepers, blue blankets, tiny blue socks, and blue baby bottles. Larae was amused, but she thought maybe it was a case of overkill when he pulled a pair of tiny denim overalls from a Fred Meyer sack

Billie told anyone and everyone who stopped by the Christmas Valley Lodge that Wally thought he could influence things in favor of a boy child. "And maybe he can," she always concluded with a smile.

In spite of a sharp spring breeze, Dell BeBe and Bud, bundled up in warm jackets and baseball caps, motored across Dog Lake to anchor Bud's boat in against a weed bed. Molly was curled up on a pad of carpet in the bow of the boat soaking up the sunshine. Bud noted the gray in her muzzle and felt a momentary pang of regret that his buddy was getting old.

Bud and BB watched their rod tips with casual interest and listened to the rip, rip sound of a powersaw echoing across the water as a builder trimmed and fitted the pieces of BB's new log house. The walls were nearly up and roof trusses were scheduled for delivery in a couple of days.

True to his word, Dell BeBe retired from the Portland Police Bureau after a stormy career that spanned nearly three decades, countless Bureau Chief's, numerous suspensions, scathing newspaper attacks, and hundreds of arrests. He told Bud the hangover from his retirement party lasted three days and he couldn't remember much beyond the speeches of his fellow officers, most of whom were plastered before they got there.

His contractor had broken ground next door to Bud's cabin at Dog Lake a month earlier. The log house would dwarf Bud's modest cabin, but then it was going to be BB's primary residence. "Wait until you have four or five months of snow out here, and then we'll see," Bud warned him.

BB only snorted and said, "Country living ain't for the faint of heart."

"Ain't for the faint," Bud mocked gently. "Next thing you know you'll be doing rap in the Indian Village." In truth Bud was happy to have BB for a neighbor. As sheriff, he was long on acquaintances and damned short on friends. The people he felt closest to worked for him, so true friendship was held at arm's length.

BB pointed to Bud's rod tip and said, "I think you're getting a bite."

Bud nodded. "You could be right." But he made no move to pick up the pole or set the hook.

"Got a letter from Gino last week," Bud said.

BB waited and finally said, "And?"

"He retired from his job in Bremerton and he and his lady friend, Ruby, are starting a detective agency. He's going to be a PI."

"I thought he said he didn't want to get hooked up with her," BB observed.

Bud chuckled and said, "I guess he changed his mind. Sent me a picture of her. She's a very pretty lady. So maybe that had something to do with it."

Lonnie Beltram was happy in his permanent job as a Lake County Deputy Sheriff. And Gordon Tusk's sister, Beatrice Tusk, had been hired by Bud as a probationary deputy. She was cute, she was smart, she was quick to laugh, and all five-feet-five inches of her were as tough as old leather. Along with half the other bachelors in Lake County, Lonnie thought he might be in love. But he knew, or thought he knew Bud wouldn't approve of intimacy between partners.

Sonny Sixkiller's success at ferreting out the arsonist trying to burn down the Deschutes National Forest, or at least one of the arsonists in Central Oregon, made it easy for the new Deschutes County Sheriff to offer him a job as the Undersheriff for Deschutes County. Bud had taken the news of Sonny's departure without the same angst he felt when Michelle left. The only thing Bud asked was, "What about you and Carol Conner?"

Sonny shook his head, and said in disgust, "I can't see how it would work. I mean, how does a cop talk to his wife if she owns a newspaper?"

Bud nodded. He understood and wondered again how he and Asa Connor, owner of the *Lakeview Times*, had ever gotten to be friends.

Bud held out his hand and they shook. "Congratulations, Sonny. You've been a good friend and a good cop." He gave Sonny a wry smile and said, "I'll miss you…I think."

Sonny didn't say anything, but he nearly crushed Bud's hand with the intensity of the moment.

Special Agent Spears was welcomed back into the NCIS fold in Silver Dale, Washington, given a merit citation and a small increase in pay. She became so immersed in her job that finding time for a visit to Lakeview and Bud Blair just wasn't possible. "Not right now," she said to herself. "But later for sure."

In Guaymas, David Peña laid a trail of false information for the one person he thought might be spying for the Reynosas, Guard Two in Wally's system. When the Reynosas acted on the information, Peña and Guard One quietly, in the middle of the night subdued the traitor, taped his mouth shut and encased him in miles of Saran Wrap. It was past midnight when Maria Tia's brother backed a dump truck into the driveway of a known Reynosa stronghold, raised the bed and dumped the traitor out on the ground. Not one of Peña's foremen ever admitted to knowing why Guard Two was gone. And none of Peña's sources could ever tell him what happened to the man after he was discovered in the Reynosas' driveway.

Gordon Tusk had asked Sergeant Booker to meet him at Applebee's. Booker was surprised when Tusk asked him for help to become a policeman. "The word on the street is you work to salvage drunks. And I know alcoholics who stay clean can have their records expunged," Tusk argued. "Why not me? I did twenty-seven months of rehab in prison."

Booker shook his head and then smiled and said, "The police in Chiloquin tell me you have turned a new leaf. That's in your favor, and you helped us with the Giles business. Tell you what. I know an attorney who works this kind of case. What if I put you in touch?"

Mariah was learning to ride the horses Harmon kept on the small ranch. And she was in the school choir thanks to a surprisingly clear, strong soprano voice. She was friends with Stacey again. Mathew Harmon had returned the photos he had taken from her room that first traumatic night, and he and Michelle were spending more and more time together. Mariah approved.

Michelle took Mariah each week to visit Mariah's mom. Barbara gave signs she recognized Mariah now, but if she was making progress toward full recovery, it wasn't apparent to either Michelle or Mariah.

From prison, Manfred Giles was appealing his conviction, and preparing to sue the Klamath Falls City Police Department for making it impossible for him to experience the joys of fatherhood.

In Yakima, Nancy Sixkiller picked up the phone and dialed Bud's personal cell number. She had rehearsed her speech, but it all went out the window when Bud answered. She was suddenly close to crying. She choked back her tears, and all she could say was, "Bud, I hope you don't hang up on me. I wouldn't blame you if you did, but I've had a lot of time to think about it. I want to come home. Mama is living with Verna now. She doesn't need me. But I need you."

There was long silence at the other end of the line. Then Nancy could hear Bud take a deep breath.

"Nancy," he said…

~

Acknowledgments

THANKS, AS ALWAYS, TO VI, MY companion, patient critic and loving wife. This one was outside my comfort zone, but Vi kept me focused and encouraged. Her years of social work gave me a solid source for authentic background and "fact checking."

Special thanks to long-time friend Peter Flowers for being my "off-site" safe storage and an early reviewer of *Mariah's Song*.

Eva Long, editor of my four previous books, gets better and better at suggesting important changes without causing discouragement. Thanks, Eva.

Thanks to daughter Jennifer Watson for a good job of reviewing and proofreading the book.

And finally, thanks to book readers everywhere. You make the effort worthwhile.

About the Author

ROD COLLINS has done a little of everything: teacher, newspaper editor, logger, truck driver, soda jerk, construction worker, wildland firefighter, fire lookout, aerial observer, and business consultant.

More important, he is a devoted husband, father, and grandfather. And, like Louis L'amour, he has walked the land his characters walk.

Mariah's Song is fourth in the Sheriff Bud Blair crime-adventure series set in the high desert of Eastern Oregon: *Spider Silk, Stone Fly,* and *Bloodstone,* and *Not Before Midnight.*

Rod is also the author of the award-winning business reference guide: *What Do I Do When I Get There? A New Manager's Guidebook.*

Bitter's Run and *Abiqua* are Rod's novel set in the post-Civil War era. You can visit Rod and learn more about his works at **brightworkspress.com.**

www.ingramcontent.com/pod-product-compliance
Lightning Source LLC
LaVergne TN
LVHW041703070526
838199LV00045B/1182